I WILL FOUND YOU

A NOVEL

JULIA SALVADOR

ALTERNATE ENDING

Curious about a different ending? All my readers are in for a treat! Just flip to the link at the end of the book for an exclusive alternate ending. Happy reading!

PART I

Angel or demon?

"The life of the dead is placed in the memory of the living."

— Marcus tullius Cicero

1

———

Where are you?

That question's stuck, lingering in my head, always shadowing my thoughts. I'm terrified I'll breathe my last without ever knowing your whereabouts.

I know death's coming. It's just a matter of when. Here, in this dank, suffocating basement, the hope of seeing you again offers a flicker of comfort. I want to believe we'll meet again somewhere beyond this life.

I can't predict when he'll return, but one thing is certain: pain awaits me. Just the thought sends shivers down my spine. I've witnessed his cruelty toward the other women he's abducted—both before and after you. None have been spared. Now it's my turn.

I try hard to shove these horrific thoughts aside, distracting myself with memories of you, sis.

Our last conversation is now a blurry memory, weighed down by my grief and drenched in my tears. Rapid, blurred images flicker in my mind, like skimming through a photo album too fast.

Your voice—when did I last hear it? Why is it fading

away? I'd trade anything to remember that moment, to find you just as you were before you disappeared. You know I love you, right? I might not have said it enough, might have ignored all those times you showed you cared. I short-changed our phone calls. Left your messages on read, always prioritizing something else. I might have come off as unappreciative. But deep down, I wanted to make you proud. You were my guide, my hero. My anchor in stormy seas. You, the forgiving big sister.

Me, the resentful little one. Now, it's been a year and five days since we last spoke.

Confession: I've been logging into your Facebook. I knew it'd get under your skin. You despised when I pried, but I kept at it, hoping it might somehow bring you back. But you never returned.

The not knowing is eating me alive. Sometimes I accept that you're gone, maybe abandoned in some thick, dark woods. But at times, a glimmer of hope flickers within me. What if, by some miracle, you're still out there? I'm still here, even though it feels like my clock's ticking down.

The anxiety's rolling back in.

There was another woman here. Even with the blind-fold, I knew from her unrelenting, nerve-wracking sobs. They resonated in my very core. I wanted to yell at her, tell her to shut it. I would've if I wasn't gagged. You know me. Then he took her away. Now, the silence where her sobs once echoed, feels like a gaping void, and I miss the sound.

How long since they left? She won't return, but *he* will. He's coming back for me.

Wait! A sound pierces the silence, yanking me back to the here and now. I hold my breath. I know that sound—keys unlocking the door.

He's back.

2

———

"You've arrived.
Your destination is on your right."

Despite the wipers' desperate attempts, visibility was a joke. No house in sight.

He killed the engine. Drawing a deep breath, he swung the door open and bolted up the driveway, rain assaulting him from all angles, soaking him through in seconds. Squinting against the deluge, he reached the front door, his refuge just a key-turn away. But the key refused to cooperate, resisting his attempts to turn it in the lock.

"Damn it!"

Thunder grumbled somewhere far off. Wrestling the stubborn key out, he squinted at the three remaining keys, hoping against hope the next one would work. With trembling hands and a silent prayer, he selected another key and tried again. This time, the lock yielded, and he stumbled inside, grateful to escape the storm's fury.

He flicked the light switch and was greeted by the partial illumination of the hallway—a bulb was out. *That would have to wait*, he mused, trudging forward. He could barely keep upright, let alone deal with household chores. Every ounce of him screamed for rest, but passing out before he hit the bedroom seemed a distinct possibility. The sofa in the living room? Now, that looked like a more doable option.

But something was wrong. He shuffled into the room, a shiver crawling up his spine. Everything was as it should be and yet... not. Maybe it was the pounding headache that hadn't let up—one more mystery in a day that seemed full of them.

He needed aspirin.

His eyes flicked to the kitchen to his left, where a window framed a garden view. The aspirin was there... mixed in with utensils, or was it with the canned goods? He ransacked every drawer and cabinet, discovering the bottle amid the chaos. He felt like an alien in his own home, and it bewildered him. A used glass sat in the sink. Too beat to search for a clean one, he rinsed it, filled it with tap water, and grimaced at the potent chlorine taste as he gulped it down. In his haste, the aspirin bottle toppled, scattering pills across the counter and floor. Bending to collect them before the cat could pounce, he swept up every single one, including those that had rolled under appliances. As he straightened, his head smacked into an open drawer. Pain rocketed through his skull, a cry tearing through the silent house. He gingerly touched the throbbing spot, then inspected his fingers, a wave of dizziness washing over him as he closed his eyes, taking a steadying breath. When he opened them again, the kitchen seemed to sway before stabilizing. Something wet slid down his cheek—blood.

Trying to keep the room from spinning, he took a moment, hand pressed to the bleeding wound. Once the world steadied, he made his way toward the bathroom, leaving a gruesome trail on the walls.

He surveyed the damage in the mirror. A nasty bump was forming, but it was the dried blood smeared across his face that caught his attention. Tracing it to its source, he found a stitched-up laceration. At least he wouldn't need more stitches.

While rifling through the medicine cabinet, it struck him just how well-prepared he seemed to be for medical emergencies. The aspirin would have to wait—too risky with a head injury. Sleep, too, was off the table, despite his body's loud protests.

He slumped onto the couch, flipping on the TV with a vacant stare. A cheerful weather reporter prattled on about the upcoming rainy days. He rested his head against the cushion, eyelids heavy but determined to stay open. He felt like something out of a fairy tale—Goldilocks, maybe, if Goldilocks were on the run from... something. On any other occasion, he might've laughed it off. But today was different; something bad had happened. He could feel it in his bones —this was not just another day.

3

————

He'd dozed off! Given his head injury, it might've been a deadly mistake. That realization struck him the instant he woke up. His next thought? Figuring out the source of the noise that had jolted him awake.

He sprang up, swung the front door open, but there was nobody in sight. Could it have been someone at the door, or had he imagined it?

Just as this thought crossed his mind, a lightning bolt tore through the sky. Startled, he retreated, slamming the door closed. Then, in an instant, the house plunged into darkness. "Great!"

Groping along the wall, his hand missed the switch, finding instead the handle to the basement door. Standing at the top of the staircase, he felt as though he were peering into an abyss. Thankfully, there was a flashlight right on the wall, there for emergencies like this. He clicked it on, the beam slicing through the darkness and landing on the old wooden stairs leading deeper into the house. He had to venture down and check—the fuse box was somewhere there.

However, halfway down, he stopped dead in his tracks, a childish fear gripping him. He half-expected to find some creature from his nightmares lurking in the shadows below. And then he noticed it—the faint scent of perfume mingling with the mustiness of the basement air. It was delicate, sweet, unmistakably feminine. Along with the fragrance came a sound, soft but undeniable. Was it a whisper? He strained his ears. No, it was a moan.

"Hello? Is anyone down there?"

This time, there was no doubt about it—he wasn't alone. He hurried down the rest of the stairs, gripping the flashlight tight, prepared to use it as a weapon if necessary.

Upon reaching the bottom, he paused. There, in a corner, trying to escape the beam of his flashlight, was a figure. A woman, lying on a pile of blankets on the cold basement floor.

4

———

Zoe felt his presence just inches away, his breath steady and close. He had never been this near before. The unexpected warmth of his hands grazing her cheek made her pull away.

"Easy," he whispered.

His voice gave her chills. He'd never spoken to her before.

"Let me get that off," he said, his fingers loosening the fabric.

Once again, she felt his touch glide along her nape and through her hair as he worked to remove her blindfold. Zoe blinked into the dimness, raising her bound wrists to shield her eyes from the flashlight's glow.

"What happened?" he asked, removing her gag.

She turned her head, avoiding the harsh flashlight beam.

"Who did this to you?" Receiving no response, he tugged her toward him. "Answer me."

Wincing in pain, Zoe looked away.

"Are you hurt? Let me see." As he began unbuttoning her blouse, the fabric slipped away, exposing her shoulder.

She flinched under his touch.

"Sorry," he muttered, a flicker of concern in his eyes. "I didn't mean to... I'm just trying to help."

Zoe closed her eyes as he pretended to examine her. She wanted to scream.

"You're bruised, but nothing's broken or out of place," he assessed.

"How would you know?"

He furrowed his brow, puzzled.

"I just do."

Now that her eyes were adjusting, Zoe saw him. The man who had haunted her thoughts for months. Profilers had pegged him as a white male, aged between thirty and forty, capable of earning his victims' trust. And they weren't wrong. Despite his scruffy beard and messy hair, he was attractive. A scar graced his right eyebrow, softening his gaze. He seemed lost, innocent, resembling the bad boys that often triggered a woman's maternal instinct. But his stormy, ocean-blue eyes revealed the turmoil within.

"Where's my sister?" she blurted.

"Your sister?"

"Gabriela Rossi. You took her, didn't you? Last Halloween."

After months spent trying to decipher him, with thoughts of him consuming her days and nights, she had fallen into the routine of speaking to him aloud, much like a child would with an imaginary friend. And now, there he was, seated on the floor. His eyes were shut, head lowered, resembling a little boy who'd been caught red-handed in some mischief.

"You killed her," she pressed.

He locked eyes with her, his expression unreadable. *Get a grip, Zoe,* she urged herself. *Stay quiet, or he'll hurt you.* But she couldn't help herself, drawn in by his very presence. Something about seeing him up close made him seem less like the monster she'd pictured in her mind. Her heart pounded with a mix of fear and adrenaline.

"You killed her and dumped her body, just like the others."

"The others?"

"Have you forgotten Klaudia Nochbauer and Laura Messing?" Zoe's voice was sharp, every word edged with accusation.

He gave her a blank stare.

"And Selma Lorenzen? Does she mean anything to you?" she continued, pressing him further.

Zoe tried to gauge his reaction, but those names seemed to bounce right off him. To him, these women were just objects for his twisted desires.

"I know nothing about them or your sister."

"Really? And that woman from before? You don't know her either?"

He raked his fingers through his hair, looking genuinely lost.

"She was chained up, just like me."

Zoe gestured toward the blankets, pausing as she recalled the stifled, desperate pleas of her fellow captive.

"You took her away to kill her," she concluded.

"It wasn't me. You're just talking nonsense."

Zoe wasn't buying his lies.

"You took her to some off-the-grid spot, away from the hustle and bustle. Some uncharted place like old ruins or a falling-apart building. Maybe an old house or a barn."

His eyes widened in realization.

"A run-down barn," he whispered. "How the hell did you know?"

Zoe leaned back against the cold, damp wall, taking a deep breath to steady herself.

"That's where they found your victims. Klaudia in some old cabin in Italy, Laura in a barn in Germany, and Selma out in a Belgian forest. Just like what happened to my sister. You did this to her, you—"

"Stop!"

Zoe watched him head toward the stairs. But just as he began to take the first few steps, he turned back around.

"It doesn't make sense," he mumbled. "All I recall is an old barn in the middle of nowhere, with the wind slamming a door before the rain started. I must have passed out. I found myself on the ground, ran to the car with keys ready in the ignition." He mimicked each motion as he recounted the story. "I started the car, and the GPS asked for a destination. I replied *home*, and it led me here."

"This isn't your home."

"What?"

"You don't bring your victims *home*. You're a wanderer, a predator. So, since we're not at my place or yours, this must belong to the woman you snatched earlier."

"I didn't do any of what you're saying. You've got the wrong person."

"Then enlighten me. Who are you?"

He seemed stunned by the question.

"I... I don't know."

Zoe had had enough of this game. He was going to kill her either way.

"You know what? Let me tell you what you are. A monster. An utter psycho! You pick your victims randomly, facing them head-on, never even bothering to hide your face. They don't see it coming. They walk straight into the traps you've laid out. And by the time they figure out who they're up against, it's way too late. The terror you put in their eyes? You thrive on it. It gives you a rush, a sense of power you can't get anywhere else. You drag them to godforsaken places where their screams go unheard. And it's only after they're gone that—"

"Shut up!" he yelled, muffling her with his hand.

So there you are, she thought, heart pounding. *Showing your true self.* He raised his hand, and Zoe braced herself, thinking he'd hurt her. But all she felt was a gentle touch on her face.

"You've got it all wrong," he whispered. "And I'll prove it to you."

She watched him leave. The stairs groaned under his footsteps, followed by the slam of the door. And then, silence. Relief flooded her as she realized she was still breathing.

5

———————

After shutting the basement door, he paused, suddenly feeling as if he had stepped straight into a nightmare. He found himself teetering on the edge between reality and fantasy, trapped in a surreal blend of the two.

The sunlit living room was real, as were the birds chirping outside. But the woman in the basement? Had he imagined her? Maybe if he went back down, she'd be gone. But just a few steps into the descent, her presence was palpable again. He retreated, needing time to think.

Should he call the police? And say what? That he woke up disoriented in the middle of nowhere with no memory of who he was? They'd never believe him.

As he looked around, taking in the furniture, trinkets, and bookshelves, he was struck by a growing sense of alienation. Everything seemed oddly familiar, yet he was certain he had never lived here. The woman in the basement had been right about that. His eyes then drifted to the floor, landing on a handbag that looked as if it had been hastily searched through. Curiosity piqued, he knelt down for a closer look, discovering a gun inside marked "Property of the State," complete with a serial number. Was this a police weapon? Picking it up, he felt its unfamiliar weight in his hands. Definitely not his.

He emptied the bag, spilling its contents onto the coffee table. Amidst the everyday items, he found keys, medication, and a wallet. Ignoring the money, he looked at the ID. The woman in the photo, though with longer hair, was unmistakably the woman in the basement—Zoe Rossi. Born July 19, 1992, in Marseille and now residing in Paris. *Even more beautiful in person,* he thought, looking at the portrait. A weird feeling of *déjà vu* hit him. Where had he seen her before? No matter how hard he tried, he just couldn't put the pieces of his memory back together. He sighed. Since the past was slipping away, he needed to focus on the here and now.

As he scanned the room, he noticed bills and prescriptions scattered on a table—all addressed to a Marianne Deconti. He muttered the name to himself, and in an instant, an image popped into his head: a blonde, probably in her early thirties, with a pixie cut. A rush of feelings hit him hard. Clutching his head, he staggered over to the sofa. No matter how much he tried to shake it off, her face stayed with him. Where did he know her from? Was she his girl-friend? *No,* he thought. She wasn't his type. Maybe just a friend or a colleague? And why did he have her keys? Had Mari given him a spare? *Mari...* that's what the guys called her. Yeah, that felt right; they were close. There must have been moments when they hung out, snapping selfies together. He just needed one picture of them, maybe toasting with their glasses, to confirm it. But finding none, his search turned to something else—a computer, perhaps. There had to be one around here somewhere.

Venturing into the bedroom, his eyes quickly landed on

a laptop resting on the bed. After a brief hesitation, he lifted the lid, bringing the machine to life and revealing a Facebook page titled 'Find Gabriela'. He paused, his gaze drawn to the images of the two women on the screen. The sisters bore a resemblance, yet it was clear Zoe was the younger of the two.

Shifting his focus, he started to read her most recent post. In it, Zoe Rossi announced her departure for Bordeaux, a city not far from the haunting Landes forest in southwestern France. It was here that a fourth victim of the Reaper had recently been discovered. She suggested there might be a match with Gabriela's description. Her message was a mix of dread and hope. She wanted to see for herself if it was her missing sister.

The post had been shared eighteen times and garnered thirty-two comments, most of which were messages of support. He began to read one, then two...

Feeling a tightening in his chest, he stood up to open the window. As rain continued to fall, the crisp air carried the heavy scent of wet grass. This familiar aroma soothed the chaotic pounding in his chest. Eyes closed, he thought of the Reaper. *Me?* He shook his head. It couldn't be, but he had to check. He moved back in front of the screen, typing *Reaper Landes forest* into the search engine. He tensed, expecting his face to appear on the screen any second, but a headline about an elusive killer, nicknamed *The Reaper* by the author, surfaced as the top result.

The article took an unexpected turn right from the start. Instead of diving into details about the killer, it zeroed in on the victims. Highlighted were a 28-year-old realtor from Germany, a 32-year-old horse riding instructor from France, and a 25-year-old hairstylist from Denmark. What made it all the more chilling? Each one was kidnapped from one country, only to be discovered in another.

He pondered on their names: Klaudia, Laura, Selma. But none rang a bell.

Weeks later, the bodies were found in remote spots. Soon after, Europol, the EU's police force, stepped in. They brought together experts from every country hit by this wave of crime. While the autopsy details remained under wraps, certain clues suggested a single, lone killer. One horrifying detail stood out: every single victim had lost their head, and those heads were nowhere to be found.

They had photos of the victims, pulled from family albums and ID cards, to go along with the reports. As he carefully looked at each face, hoping not to recognize anyone, a wave of nausea overcame him.

Before he knew it, he was bent over the toilet, sick to his stomach.

6

———

Anthony Lavera let out a groan, shifting himself to the edge of the bed while keeping his eyes shut. He swung an arm out, clumsily searching for his phone on the nightstand, desperate to put an end to its relentless buzzing.

"Yeah?" His voice came out gravelly and thick.

Normally, he'd glance at the caller ID, but right now, even cracking an eyelid felt like a marathon.

"Is this Mr. Lavera?"

The voice grated on his nerves, nasal and sharp.

"Keep it down, will you?" Anthony muttered.

He sat up, grimacing. It felt like a marching band was playing inside his skull. The guy on the other end kept yammering, but all Anthony could think of was the aspirin in his bag.

"You there?"

Still dazed, Anthony lumbered toward the bathroom. The stench of puke hit him, and his stomach revolted again.

"Sir, are you okay?"

The phone slipped from his hand, crashing onto the

floor. He barely made it to the toilet in time, emptying his stomach once more. Afterward, he slumped against the wall, drained. Realizing the caller was still on the line, he picked up the phone with a scowl.

"Who are you, and why are you calling me so early?"

A pause.

"It's half-past two, sir. PM."

Anthony pulled the phone back, staring at the screen. Sure enough, 2:32 PM.

The voice on the other end took a moment before asking, "I need to confirm. Are you Mr. Anthony Lavera residing at 15 Harbor Lane, Marseille?"

The question jolted him upright, panic coursing through him.

"Who's asking? Are you a cop?"

"Yes. Detective Gauthrie from Landes PD."

Thoughts raced. The Landes? That vast, pine-covered region down southwest?

"We've got a gray Toyota Yaris from Avis out here. Says it was rented in your name."

Anthony sprinted to the window with a view of the hotel's parking lot and quickly pulled back the curtains. Blinding sunlight struck his eyes, making him flinch as if he were a vampire caught in daybreak.

"Sir?"

"Just hold on a sec!"

Squinting, he approached the window again. The hotel lot was deserted. No Toyota. Spinning around, he noticed his jacket near the door and rummaged through its pockets. No car keys. *Shit!*

"Zoe must've taken it," he murmured, struggling to keep his cool.

"Your wife?"

Anthony's fingers brushed the ring on his finger.

"No. Sister-in-law."

"When's the last time you spoke to her?"

His gaze swept across the room, taking in the sight of Zoe's improvised bed on the couch, surrounded by scattered takeout containers. There, too, was her whiskey, left untouched.

"Mr. Lavera?"

The officer's voice seemed distant, muffled by the throbbing in Anthony's ears. Zoe didn't drink, and he knew it. But he hated drinking alone, so he poured her a glass, anyway. He'd lost count of how many he'd downed. But it still wasn't enough to drown out the memory of their fight from the night before. He'd definitely crossed lines you shouldn't cross with your sister-in-law. But what haunted him wasn't what he did. It was what he might have said. If only he could remember what that was.

"Last night," he managed to reply. "Is she okay? Was there a crash?"

Another pause.

"Just stay put, okay? We're sending someone. Where are you?"

"At a hotel, near the airport."

He rattled off the hotel's address.

"All right. We'll be there in half an hour. Can you get a photo of your sister-in-law? And if you can, grab one of her garments. For our K9 unit to pick up her scent. And while you're at it, grab her toothbrush too."

Anthony felt a lump in his throat.

"Toothbrush?"

"For DNA testing."

Stunned, Anthony ended the call. Zoe was in trouble, and it was on him. Thirty minutes. He took a quick, cold shower, threw on clothes, and almost overlooked Zoe's things in the bathroom. Slipping on his jacket, he realized the car keys weren't the only thing gone. His gun was missing, too.

7

———

Zoe watched him come down the stairs, her back pressed against the damp wall. As he approached, she realized just how tall he was—she had to tilt her head back to meet his gaze, those piercing blue eyes in which many had lost themselves. In his hands, he carried a tray. She flinched when he knelt down next to her, her head making a dull sound against the cinder block wall. After setting the tray on the floor, he sat cross-legged, bringing them face to face. Now, they were on the same level, eye to eye.

"Don't scream," he warned as he removed her gag.

She coughed, wiping away saliva with the back of her sleeve.

"No one would hear me anyway," she shot back.

He let out a sigh. "Here, have some water."

He held the glass to her lips, and Zoe eagerly took a sip. She hadn't had anything to drink since waking up in this basement hours ago. But she gulped it down too quickly, causing her to choke and erupt into violent coughs.

"Easy there," he murmured, steadying her with his arms. His hands patted between her shoulder blades. "You okay?"

His voice was a soft whisper, his warm breath brushing her cheek, causing her to tense.

"I'd be better if I weren't tied up."

They were close, too close.

"I can't do that yet. Not until I'm sure you trust me."

"But I do!"

He shook his head. "No, you don't. You're still scared."

"You don't scare me," she spat. "You disgust me."

Her words hung in the air. A heavy silence settled between them. He turned away, his expression unreadable. Zoe knew she was treading on dangerous ground. Should she act the compliant captive? Or should she resist, ready to battle for her life? Which strategy would save her?

Guess I'll find out soon enough, she thought, bracing herself as he reached for something on the tray. Her heart raced, expecting to see a knife. But instead, he held up a cloth filled with ice and carefully placed it on her injured shoulder, a momentary relief from the sharp sting. Just as she was trying to make sense of the gesture, he produced a box of pills.

"Found these in your bag," he said casually, popping out two pills and dropping them into his hand. "I figured you might need them."

Zoe's eyes darted to the orange tablets she'd been taking for the past month. Only her neurologist knew about them. If word got out, her dance career would be over—no company would want a dancer at risk of having a seizure onstage.

"These yours?" he asked, holding the pills out to her.

She bit her lip, caught off guard.

"Don't lie. You know it's risky to stop taking them. Your doctor must've warned you."

With a reluctant nod, she opened her mouth, allowing

him to place the first pill on her tongue. It went down easily with a sip of water. The second pill, however, caught in her throat, and she had to take another sip. She barely had time to catch her breath before he spoke again.

"Look, we're both in deep here. Believe me, I didn't kidnap you. You have to trust me."

Zoe studied his face, for any hint of deceit or malevolence. She was certain he was playing her—this was all just another scene in a role-playing game where he pulled the strings.

"Did you regain your memory?" she questioned.

"No."

She detected a flicker of hesitation.

"So why should I trust you?"

"Well, for starters, I don't have the slightest desire to kill you."

"Comforting."

His lips twitched upward, a hint of amusement.

"It's the truth. If I were this guy, this Reaper you keep mentioning, I'd feel the urge, wouldn't I?"

"I don't fit the victim profile," she said, hearing the words come out almost on their own.

"That's not true. And deep down, you know it. You're just trying to test me."

She glared at him, unable to help herself.

"I've seen pictures of the murdered women. On the Internet," he added, eager to clear up any misunderstanding. "They don't look alike. Klaudia Nochbauer was a blonde with blue eyes. Laura Messing was a redhead with green eyes. Both were divorced. Then there's Selma Lorenzen, brown hair and brown eyes, like you. But she was single, whereas you..."

His eyes dropped to the wedding band on her finger as he took her hand.

"...you're married."

She snapped her hand back, causing the cloth filled with ice to fall to the floor. He picked it up and placed it back on her shoulder.

"Have you been married long?" he inquired.

"I'm not—"

She stopped herself short. *Shut up! Don't tell him anything!* If he believed the ring was really hers, maybe she stood a chance.

"That's none of your concern."

"You're right. I apologize. I didn't mean to pry."

His gaze lowered, and he let out a sigh.

"What about this Reaper? Do you think he's married?"

"The police haven't ruled that out. People like him? They just try to fit in, act like everyone else. It's how they stay hidden."

He flashed that smile again.

"*People like him*, you said? So, you think there's a chance I might be innocent?"

Zoe didn't even catch the subtle implication of her own words earlier. She'd need to be sharper if she didn't want him getting the upper hand.

"Mind if I get another glass of water?" she asked.

"Of course."

She sipped slowly this time.

"You hungry?" he asked, setting the empty glass aside.

She hesitated before replying.

"I'd rather have a cigarette."

"You know those things are a one-way ticket, right?"

"At this point, does it really change anything?"

"Because you think I'm going to kill you?"

"No. Because I have a brain tumor," she said, the confession tasting strange as she voiced it.

"Are you serious?"

Accepting that fact had been hard for her. When the doctor broke the news, it felt surreal. This sort of thing is supposed to happen to other people, not her. Zoe sighed, looking away. This conversation was spiraling into the bizarre.

He studied her for a moment, the weight of her words settling between them. "Anyway, you should eat something."

He broke off a piece of the sandwich and held it to her mouth, like coaxing a toddler to eat. Zoe's cheeks burned with humiliation, especially as her stomach betrayed her with a telltale growl. She turned her face, defiant.

"What did you put in it? Sleeping pills? Poison?"

"No, that was in the water you drank. Just kidding," he added right away, noticing her horrified look. "It's just a sandwich, promise."

She watched him take a bite, and her nose picked up the scent of tuna mixed with mayo. She hadn't had a meal since before her abduction.

"See? Still alive. And just to clear things up, you're safe with me. But you need to eat. I need your assistance, and you're no good to me, all weak and famished."

"For what?"

He undid the ties on her ankles, helping her stand up.

"We're going to find out who I am."

8

Zoe emerged from the basement like a specter rising from its grave.

Expecting bright light, she instinctively lifted her arms. But it was unnecessary; every curtain was closed, bathing the house in a soft darkness. She looked around. The room had a clear feminine touch.

"Whose place is this?"

"Marianne Deconti," he replied.

The woman who had shared her cell before he took her came to mind.

"I knew her," he added.

Zoe shivered.

"How do you figure?" she pressed.

"Just a hunch. That's it," he responded.

"A hunch?"

"I know, it's not enough. There should be evidence."

Zoe glanced around. The living room was as chaotic as if it had been burglarized, though valuable items were still scattered on the floor. Clearly, he had conducted a meticulous search earlier.

"Fine. I'll help you," she conceded.

While she still didn't believe his amnesia story, she needed to buy time. That was her chosen strategy. As long as she let him believe he wielded power over her, she was safe. Or so she had read in one of those countless books about serial killers. It was time to put theory into practice.

"It would be easier if my hands were free," she added, convinced he would decline.

He approached, examined her wrists bound together by thick layers of heavy-duty tape, and sought an end to pull.

"How should I go about it?" he queried.

"There might be a box cutter somewhere. Probably part of the murder kit."

"A what?"

"A murder kit. You know, the kind serial killers have. Chains, pliers, tape, blindfolds…"

He rolled his eyes.

"Come on, I have a better idea."

He dragged her into the kitchen. Like the living room, Zoe was struck by the mess. Drawers were strewn all over the floor, contents scattered everywhere. He shuffled through the utensils with his shoe. She watched as he hesitated, eyeing a pair of dull scissors and a paring knife, before settling on the knife.

"Come closer. Put your hands here."

As he held her wrists on the countertop, she looked away. The tape was so tight that it seemed impossible he could cut it without also cutting her flesh.

"Ready?"

She nodded.

"Okay, here goes. Don't move!"

Zoe watched him with a mixture of apprehension and

curiosity. She couldn't be sure, but it looked like he was just as worried about hurting her.

After a few careful tries, he managed to cut through the tape without hurting her, and Zoe felt her wrists free at last. For a fleeting moment, she considered escaping. She could shove him and make it to the front door in a few strides. But if it was locked, he would catch her.

"Don't even think about it," he said, as if reading her thoughts.

He was pointing a gun straight at her. Zoe recognized the Sig Sauer she'd borrowed from Anthony.

"I won't hesitate to use it, believe me. I don't want to, but if you try anything…"

The last time she saw someone handle a gun with such hesitation, she was watching herself in the living room mirror during Anthony's crash course on firearms. Except this time, the safety was off.

She raised her hands in surrender. Despite his unsteady grip, she didn't dare test him. Even if he'd never shot before, it didn't mean he couldn't hit her—beginner's luck was a real thing, after all.

They returned to the dining room. Despite the mess around, Zoe took a moment to notice the room's elegant and cozy ambiance. Subtle touches hinted at a woman living alone: pastel wall colors, delicate curtains, a crystal vase, and vibrant candleholders caught her attention. She took a few steps, aware of the Sig Sauer tracking her every move.

"Did you check the secretary?" she asked, turning around.

He was perched on one of the couch's armrests, casually pointing the gun at her.

"Yeah. Just bills and paperwork," he replied.

"Do you mind if I double check?"

He shrugged.

"You're the search expert."

She froze. *Search expert?* Where had he gotten that idea? Then it clicked—Anthony's service weapon! He must think she's a cop. Her mind raced. Should she let him continue believing the misconception? Or should she correct him? She wasn't a cop but a dancer on hiatus at the Paris Opera. On second thought, being mistaken for a cop might be to her advantage.

"Zoe?"

"Sorry, yeah. It's just... technically, we shouldn't be going through people's stuff without gloves or a warrant. You know, for fingerprints and legal reasons and all."

He quirked an eyebrow. "Well, since I've already touched everything, the glove thing is kind of pointless. And the warrant... well."

Busted! Damn those crime shows!

"Uh, yeah, true. But you get the idea."

She went through the items in the large drawer, finding a mix of envelopes and papers. Mostly bills, just like he said, but there were also some old prescriptions.

"She was prescribed Paroxetine," Zoe read aloud.

"That's for depression," he remarked. "But it can also help with some obsessive-compulsive issues."

"You sound like a doctor."

He shrugged.

"Maybe I am one."

She replaced the prescription and picked up an unopened envelope. Inside was a pay stub. The employer's address was on the top right.

"She worked at Pasteur Hospital," she said.

She read the address again. 30 Voie Romaine, Nice. Zip: 06000. *Nice?* That was over five hundred miles from the

Landes forest, she thought, struggling to hide her discomfort. Had she traveled eight hours without any memory of it? Had he drugged her?

"Maybe I work there too. That would explain why I know a bit about dislocations and medications."

For the first time, Zoe began to harbor doubts. Had she misjudged him? Was Marianne Deconti a colleague, a friend?

"We could go to the hospital, see if anyone recognizes you," she suggested.

Moments later, she found herself in the trunk of a car. Bound and gagged, just like Marianne Deconti had been mere hours earlier.

9

———

The police helicopter hovered above, a hawk searching for prey. Below, in the dense Landes Forest Reserve, an abandoned Toyota sat on a forest path. The door was wide open, headlights blazing. Near the car, technicians found a scattering of cigarette butts and traces of blood inside. It was human blood, Type O positive. Now, they needed a DNA match to confirm if it belonged to Zoe Rossi.

In the back of a squad car, Anthony strained to listen to Detective Gauthrie.

"You recognize this?" Gauthrie asked, holding up a clear plastic bag.

Anthony took it with both hands. This had to be a nightmare. That was the only explanation.

"It's Zoe's phone."

He attempted to turn it on through the bag.

"We've checked. The battery's dead," Gauthrie cut in.

He extended his hand, signaling for Anthony to return the device.

"So, why was your sister-in-law almost a hundred miles from your hotel?"

"I... I don't know."

"She was meeting someone?"

"What?"

"We found another car's tracks. An SUV. We're still figuring it out, but we've got a tire print."

Anthony was lost. None of this made any sense. Unless...

"Look, Lavera, I'm gonna shoot straight—the outlook's grim. We think your sister-in-law got jumped, maybe even hurt."

Or worse, thought Anthony, but didn't dare say it aloud.

"We're searching the surrounding area for now."

"Do you think Zoe might still be in the forest?"

"Her phone was found about ten yards from the road, so it's plausible she went there. The question is, did she go willingly?"

The dense, secluded forest was the logical place to search—it provided a refuge from prying eyes.

"Did she say anything to you?" Gauthrie pressed.

Anthony shook his head, still struggling to accept what he was seeing. His eyes moved from the technicians collecting evidence, to the silent forest, to a group of teenagers nearby. They were smoking, waiting to leave.

"They're the ones who tipped us off," Gauthrie explained. "This place is usually quiet, more so during this season."

Anthony had no trouble believing that. The narrow road wound through the dense forest. Not a spot most would choose for leisure.

"Truth is," Gauthrie continued, "without the media circus, she could've been here for days before anyone noticed."

"Media circus?"

"Yeah, well! Crime scenes draw crowds. Maybe that's

also what brought your sister-in-law out here? What do you think?"

A shiver ran through Anthony.

"This is where you found the Reaper's fourth victim, isn't it?"

The officer didn't take his eyes off him.

"Lavera, why don't you spill it? What are you holding back?"

Anthony sighed.

"The fourth victim... it might be my wife, Gabriela."

10

———

"In four hundred yards, turn right."

He was hunched over the windshield, squinting at the approaching cluster of buildings at the boulevard's end. His GPS-guided trip through Nice hadn't jogged any memories until now. Something had changed; he was certain he had been here before. The Pasteur Hospital, located on the city's outskirts, was less than twenty minutes from Marianne Deconti's home. This is where they had first met. It had to be.

His mind was foggy, grasping at hazy impressions rather than clear recollections.

"You've reached your destination."

The blinker's steady rythm filled the car, sounding like a ticking bomb. His grip on the wheel tightened as he drew closer to the parking lot, his mind wrestling with indecision. Just then, a loud honk from the car behind shattered the moment, urging him to make a choice. The other driver, clearly losing patience, wanted him to hurry up. On impulse, he hit the gas. The car's tires screeched as he sped down the road, leaving the city behind. He ignored the honks and surprised faces of people on the street, even running a red light. Watching the hospital get smaller in his rearview mirror, he finally let out a breath and pulled over, as if finishing a wild escape.

Every bone in his body screamed to leave Nice behind for good, but where would he go? As he sat there, contemplating, his eyes landed on an elderly woman sitting across the street, waiting for her bus. He offered a tentative smile, but she averted her eyes. What was his next move? Turning back could draw unwanted attention, but he needed answers. He had to understand who he was, and that meant returning to the hospital, even if it made him look suspicious.

He glanced back as the bus, carrying the elderly woman, rolled away. A pang of paranoia hit him; he half-expected someone to have noticed his odd behavior. But the bus melded into traffic, taking his trepidation with it as it disappeared. He reignited the engine.

Ignoring the GPS, he sought a more secluded spot near the hospital. He found one across the Paillon River, hidden between warehouses by the train tracks. Out of sight, he popped the trunk. Inside, Zoe Rossi was bundled up, cushioned against the hard floor. Her eyes, however, held no gratitude. "We're close to the hospital," he informed her. "I'll proceed on foot. Won't be long." Despite the adhesive securing her wrists and ankles, she wriggled. He checked the tightness of her bindings and the gag stifling her words —though he could still make out the muffled curses. "I'd conserve your energy if I were you. Nobody's around." He paused. "I'm sorry about this." And with that, he closed the trunk.

He surveyed his surroundings. Mountains loomed over the unfamiliar city, enclosing it on all sides. Nearby, a freight train crawled along its tracks. Even though the hospital was out of sight, he estimated a brisk, straight walk would get him there in ten minutes. Ten minutes to clarity.

As he passed a funeral home, his pace slowed. His heartbeat seemed out of sync with his proximity to the hospital; the closer he got, the more forcefully his heart pounded in his chest, urging him to turn and run. But not today.

Moments later, he stood frozen in front of the hospital's main doors, unable to take another step. How should he tackle this? Walk up to the front desk and ask if anyone recognized him? That might land him in the psych ward. Maybe linger in the lobby, hoping for a familiar face? But that could take all day, and raise eyebrows, potentially leading to a mental health check or even an arrest.

He was deep in thought and didn't notice the automatic doors opening. Two men in white coats stood talking, not paying any attention to him. Yet, something about them felt unsettling. As he watched, their coats began to seep a bright red, as if freshly stained with blood. A metallic scent, chillingly familiar, wafted to him. Was it blood he smelled? The sensation overwhelmed him, and soon everything around— the trees, the sky, the whole hospital—was bathed in a deep crimson haze. This ominous tide pressed closer, threatening to engulf him.

11

Trapped in the car's trunk, Zoe found her knees pressed to her chest, her wrists bound tightly behind her.

She couldn't escape the overpowering scent of gasoline and burnt rubber. It pervaded the air, assaulting her nostrils, stifling each breath she attempted to take. She tried to draw a deep breath through her mouth, hoping it might lessen the discomfort, but the gag hindered her.

In the pitch-black trunk, all Zoe could hear were her own shallow breaths. He had been right; he'd warned her to pace her breathing. The way he shut that trunk, it felt like he was sealing a coffin. Right away, her mind flooded with disturbing images: discarded bodies, skeletal remains. Corpses discovered in car trunks—whether left abandoned at the bases of cliffs, hidden beneath forest canopies, submerged in lakes, or parked in plain sight in a busy shopping center parking lot. While she believed her kidnapper had a more intricate plan for her, she couldn't dismiss the graphic crime reports she'd heard on the news. Would he even return? The harrowing thought persisted. What if the police found her like this, her decaying body betraying her presence? Panic consumed her. Like a trapped animal, she fought with the last of her strength, but it was a losing battle. And when she tried to scream, Zoe choked on her own spit.

Her thoughts blurred, likely from lack of oxygen. Breathing became laborious, and the pounding of her heart felt torturous. But this felt different from when she'd been out of breath backstage at the Opera, striving to stay silent so as not to disturb the dancers taking her place. The ballet dancer's cardinal rule: conceal the pain and never let the audience witness your distress. She'd mastered it.

Desperate to remain conscious, she willed herself to relax. Her heartbeat slowed, and her breathing steadied. But this respite was temporary; another surge of terror loomed.

In search of comfort, she tried to recall childhood lullabies. But memories of her father's harsh voice, reproaching her mother every night, consumed her. She remembered his dark blue police uniform, the resonance of his boots in their apartment, how his gun pulled down his leather belt, and the gleaming badges that had once made him seem like a heroic knight in her naïve eyes. He was a commendable cop but a terrible husband. His presence haunted her until she left for Nanterre at eleven, the home of the Paris Opera ballet school. The auditions were rigorous. Zoe had a single shot. It wasn't until her elder sister, Gabriela, encouraged her that she considered dancing as a career. Gabriela, her guiding light, had once dreamt of dancing but was denied the chance. She coached Zoe, showing her that dance was not just a career, but a lifeline. "If you make it, you'll attend a boarding school. Away from all this," she'd told her. The prospect of escaping their turbulent life was all the motivation Zoe needed. She trained for the audition for a full year, even forgoing her cherished Nutella sandwiches and sweets to lose weight. She barely made the cut, but Gabriela, optimistic as ever, observed that it simply meant there was more room for growth. Those years at the school were both her hardest and most fulfilling. When times were tough, while others reached out to their parents, Zoe always turned to Gabriela. Forever cheery, always there. After her parents' separation, Zoe was sure of her destiny on the Opera stage.

"One day, I'll be a prima ballerina," she had vowed to Gabriela. But now, none of that seemed to matter. She was faced with the stark reality that she could die in this dark, confined space. Would Gabriela be waiting for her, bathed in light at the end of a celestial tunnel? Would she be wearing the jogging outfit from the day she disappeared? What would she say to her?

At a loss for words, Zoe began to hum, reminiscent of when she was eight, her small fingers intertwined with her sister's, both of them hidden beneath a blanket as the raised voices of their parents escalated in the next room. It wasn't a recognizable song, but the gentle rhythm of her voice, even muffled by the gag, brought comfort. It reminded her of a cat purring to soothe its anxieties. What worries could a cat possibly have, anyway?

Her mind continued to wander, losing all sense of time until a series of sounds snapped her back to reality: the creak of a car door, the rumble of an engine coming to life, and the crunch of gravel beneath tires. The monster was back.

There was no joy in this realization, no cause for celebration. But in this perverse twist on a fairy tale, she felt an unexpected surge of relief, perhaps even a fleeting moment of gratitude. She was no longer alone. He had come back.

12

———

His hands, smeared with blood, rested on the steering wheel —a haunting illusion he couldn't escape. How he had managed to return to the car was a blur. Looking back, he saw the entire ordeal as a grotesque error. He should've trusted his instincts. The urgency now was to flee, to create as much distance between himself and this nightmare as he could. Nice had transformed into something eerie, almost extraterrestrial, bathed in a suffocating red glow reminiscent of Mars.

As he sped toward the mountains, the city receded steadily in his rearview mirror. Soon, a solitary concrete barrier was his only companion along the mountain road. He took a deep breath. The sky transitioned from an ominous red to a heavy, rain-laden gray. That's when it hit him—he'd been on this road before, going the other way, the time he mixed up Mari's place with his own.

He turned off the GPS. No more mistakes this time. He knew exactly where he was heading.

13

———

The car roared down the straightaways and slowed down around each bend. The winding mountain road seemed endless.

Zoe's stomach churned with dread, her mind racing with dark thoughts. Was she being taken to her own crime scene? The idea took root, and she couldn't shake it. She was about to become the latest in a series of victims. With her face pressed into a cushion, all she could hear was her own labored breathing. Panic welled up, threatening to overwhelm her as saliva pooled at the back of her throat. *Please someone, help me!* Those were the words she would have screamed if the duct tape hadn't sealed her lips, muffling her cries. Her body shook with uncontrollable shivers until the car halted.

The trunk flew open, and squinting into the fading sky, she saw him. Her kidnapper. His face was inscrutable as he leaned in, peeling off the tape with surprising gentleness.

"Are you okay?" he asked, his voice calm.

Zoe remained silent, her mind racing.

He set to work on her bindings. "I'll free your legs first. Just—try nothing."

Once she was on her feet, the mountains unfolded around them, their beauty almost surreal. For a moment, she forgot the ominous purpose of their journey.

"Where are we?"

He shrugged. "Not sure."

He gestured to a steep path that disappeared into thick foliage. "We should get moving. Night's falling."

Relief flowed through Zoe's sore muscles as she began to move, but the moment was fleeting. The cold press of a gun against her back snapped her back to the grim reality. To her astonishment, he seemed just as tense.

They walked in silence, the gravel crunching beneath their feet, punctuating their heavy breaths.

"How much farther?" Zoe gasped.

He pointed to a distant crumbling shack. As Zoe followed his gaze, she felt a shiver run down her back.

As they drew closer, the stone building appeared on the verge of collapse, as if a single gust of wind could bring it down.

Zoe watched her captor as he crouched to run his fingers over the grass, laying his hand flat as though feeling for the pulse of the earth. His tousled blonde hair, caught in the wind, shone like golden wheat in the sunlight. When he looked up and met her gaze, her heart pounded—not from exertion, but fear. If he was truly the Reaper, Marianne Deconti's body would be nearby.

He seemed to sense her thoughts and stood, his eyes scanning the area before settling on an old barn.

"Remembering anything else?" Zoe asked, her voice barely above a whisper.

He shook his head, moving toward the shack.

The moment he vanished inside, Zoe held her breath. Part of her wished the unstable building would collapse on him. But when he reemerged seconds later, white as a ghost and retching, she realized this situation was far from what she expected. *Run! Get out of here!* A voice screamed in her head, but her body wouldn't respond. She was frozen, watching him in horrified fascination. When he finally looked up, his eyes were filled with tears.

"It's Marianne, isn't it?" Zoe asked, her voice filled with desperation. "Just say it!"

He hesitated, his expression tortured. "I... It's not that simple."

"What do you mean?"

"There's someone in there, but... the face..."

His voice trailed off, leaving an eerie silence. Zoe's mind raced. *None of this means anything*, she tried to convince herself, refusing to believe his reaction was genuine. Killers like him felt nothing, maybe except for the thrill of their dark fantasies. This had to be an act—a twisted game designed just for her. He was trying to plant seeds of doubt in her mind.

"Let me see," she demanded, her voice steady.

He looked at her, shock written across his face. "Are you sure?"

She nodded, determination burning in her eyes. "I need to."

He hesitated, glancing back at the shack with uncertainty in his eyes. "You think it's your sister?"

"There's one way to find out."

14

The old wooden door creaked as it swung back and forth in the wind, almost as though it were extending an eerie invitation.

Zoe felt her heart pound in her chest. Birds that had been perched on the remaining roof beams suddenly took flight, their wings creating a soft, whirring sound as they disappeared into the sky. A solitary feather drifted down, twirling gracefully and sketching patterns in the air before settling on the ground near a woman's prone body. She lay on her back, partially exposed, her skirt rucked up around her waist. Her face was obscured by several layers of plastic wrap, and around her, the ground bore the marks of her final, desperate struggle for life; her hands had clenched fistfuls of earth amidst her convulsions.

Cautiously, Zoe approached.

"It wasn't me," a voice said suddenly from behind her. "You have to believe me. I'd never do something like this."

She spun around to face him. His vibrant blue eyes were now cloudy and distant. "Just because you don't remember doesn't mean you didn't do it," she retorted.

He sighted. "Is it your sister?"

Zoe turned back and edged closer to the lifeless body. "No," she said after a moment, her voice a blend of sadness and relief. "Gabriela has a birthmark on her left thigh."

He reached out to touch her shoulder, and though she tensed, she did not pull away.

As raindrops began to seep through the damaged roof overhead, Zoe realized that crucial evidence might soon be obliterated. "Hand me that tarp," she said, motioning with her bound hands.

Working together, they covered the body and hurried to the car. The engine roared to life, and Zoe found herself watching from the back seat as he navigated the muddy path around the barn. Then, he stopped the car.

"I need a minute," he said, leaving the engine idling. The windshield wipers kept a steady rhythm, sweeping away the rain. Darkness enveloped them. Finally, he broke the silence. "We wait."

"For what?" she asked, her voice filled with confusion.

"You mean, for *who*—for *him*. The man who did this to Marianne. He wasn't finished with her."

Puzzled, Zoe sought for more information. "What was he trying to do?"

"He wanted to move her. The newspapers reported he never leaves the head at the scene, right?"

"Yeah, so why'd he leave her?" she pressed, searching his face for clues.

He smirked, a glint in his eyes. "Something—or someone—interrupted him."

"Oh, and that *someone* would be you?"

He nodded. "I think I surprised him. That's probably why I've got this bump." He gingerly touched a wound on his head.

Zoe tried to piece it together, though his story didn't quite add up. She felt drawn to believe him, but questions buzzed in her head. What was he doing at a secluded crime scene to begin with? And if he really did step in, why didn't the killer silence him too? Her gut told her to be careful. Yet, she had revised her judgment on one thing: she believed him now when he said he couldn't remember who he was.

15

———————

"Want some coffee? I've just brewed a fresh pot," Detective Gauthrie offered, "Or maybe some tea?"

Anthony shook his head. "No, I'm good." He popped a mint into his mouth, attempting to dispel the sour taste of bile lingering there.

Gauthrie looked at Anthony for a bit, then went back to his computer. "So, Miss Rossi flew from Paris to Marseille just to see you?"

"That's right," Anthony said. "She heard about another Reaper victim and got on the next plane to tell me. We both hurried to Bordeaux, hoping it wasn't Gabriela."

As Gauthrie typed, he asked, "Why do you think the body we found could be your wife?"

Anthony took a deep breath. "Gabriela disappeared around this time last year."

"The same way the others did?" Gauthrie wanted to know.

Anthony nodded, his throat tightening. "Yes." He sank back into his chair, a wave of grief washing over him. Thankfully, Gauthrie chose not to probe further. "When she heard the news, Zoe was convinced it was Gabriela. We immediately boarded the first flight to Bordeaux, and..."

"And then?" Gauthrie prompted, his tone gentle.

Tears welled up in Anthony's eyes as he whispered, "I can't lose her too..."

After a brief pause, Gauthrie pressed, "What I don't understand is why you didn't head straight to the morgue to identify the body?"

"That was our initial plan. We were supposed to go together today." Anthony's voice was filled with regret.

"So, why did your sister-in-law go to the crime scene so early, especially when the body wasn't there anymore?"

"In the morning?" Anthony asked, a hint of surprise in his tone.

"Yes. The motel's cameras caught Miss Rossi leaving around six. Why'd she rush to the scene? Why not wait for you?"

Anthony let out a deep sigh, sensing there was no point in hiding anything. Gauthrie had already pieced much of it together. "We had a fight," he said, voice tinged with regret. "I drank a bit too much. The stress of facing the morgue... we're talking about identifying my wife's body here, damn it!"

"Your wife, yes. Yet, with all the hotel rooms in Bordeaux, you both ended up in the same one?"

Anthony's jaw clenched, his patience wearing thin. He had come seeking answers, not to be subjected to a barrage of questions.

"All the hotels were booked. We left in a rush, no reservations. It was late. We had more pressing matters to attend to. Are you satisfied now, or are we going to continue this back-and-forth?"

"I'm just trying to understand what your sister-in-law was thinking," Gauthrie explained.

Anthony looked away, his mind racing. "I think she was just freaked out."

"You think?"

"Zoe... she doesn't really express her feelings."

Gauthrie leaned back in his chair, digesting the information. Anthony felt the gravity of the situation settling in. He should have been there for Zoe; she was completely alone. He had messed up, and now she was gone. Yet, one thing didn't quite make sense: why had she gone to an empty crime scene?

"What does your sister-in-law do for a living?"

"She's a dancer."

"A dancer? Like your wife?"

"No, Gabriela taught Zumba. Zoe does ballet at the Opera. Why do you ask?"

Gauthrie shrugged. "Just curious. So, she came all the way from Paris to Marseille just to see you?"

"That's right. She showed up out of the blue, wanting me to go with her to Bordeaux."

"And she was the one who told you about the body?"

Anthony paused, shifting on the chair. "Yes," he replied. "Why do you ask?"

"When did she tell you?"

"Yesterday afternoon. I was rushing to pack before our flight. Why? What's happening?"

Gauthrie maintained a stoic expression. "The news about the body wasn't released until last night, on the eight o'clock news."

The room fell silent.

"Maybe she found out online? You know, through social media?" Anthony suggested.

"Possibly... But considering the location, apart from the man who discovered the body, who else would've known?"

"It only takes one person to start a rumor online."

"That's quite a stretch. The man who found the body—a retired science teacher and avid birdwatcher—was shaken up. Even if he did tell someone and it got online, I can't see how she would've found out so quickly."

The two men locked eyes.

Anthony paused. "Zoe's started a Facebook page," he said. "And she has a Twitter account, too. She's been looking for clues about Gabriela."

"You think someone tipped her off?"

Anthony nodded.

"We should check her profiles, see if anything looks out of place."

Moments later, Anthony watched, his face ashen, as Gauthrie made a call to the Bordeaux forensics lab.

16

———

Zoe struggled to keep her eyes open. The relentless rain hammering against the car had kept her alert until now, but fatigue began to overtake her. Leaning her face against the chilly window, she squinted into the inky void outside. Everywhere she looked, the night seemed absolute. No hint of light reached out for miles—no car beams, no street-lights, no glow from house windows. Neither stars nor moon pierced the stormy sky. Even the mountain had vanished, swallowed by the enveloping darkness.

Zoe's mind circled back to Marianne Deconti, lying just a stone's throw away—Marianne, who no longer felt fear, hunger, or the pull of sleep...

"Are you cold?"

Zoe jerked to attention, her thoughts scattering.

"Uh, no. I'm okay."

"Liar. I can hear you shivering."

Fabric rustled and seat springs creaked as he shifted from the driver's seat to join her in the back.

"It'll get colder," he whispered, drawing near.

His arms enfolded her, pulling her close.

"Just relax, Zoe," he whispered against her cheek. "Let go."

Eyes closed, she held back tears. But then she realized he couldn't see them anyway. For the first time since her abduction, she thought of Anthony. Was he out there, frantic with worry? He'd become the brother she never had, a pillar during her toughest times. Their relationship hadn't always been smooth. When she first met him through Gabriela, she had reservations. Even after he and Gabriela wed, Zoe was wary—he'd taken her sister away. Because of him, Gabriela stayed in Marseille instead of joining her in Paris. But after Gabriela vanished, Anthony and Zoe found comfort in each other. Why had he complicated everything? That night at the hotel had forever changed things between them. Anthony, fueled by alcohol, had blurred the boundaries between brother-in-law and his wife's sister. He'd overstepped, and the weight of that mistake will linger between them forever. After that fateful night, she'd decided to remove him from her life. Now? She'd give anything to see him just once more. She imagined him talking to the media, portraying her as an emerging star in the dance world. Her picture would be everywhere; colleagues and friends would paint her as a woman consumed by her ambitions, often neglecting her personal life. Few close friends, no significant other, and a distant family. Zoe felt a sting of regret for the young woman who had forgotten to truly cherish life.

Escape felt unreachable. She knew what her captor was capable of—his warmth was deceiving, sending shivers down her spine. She focused on his rhythmic breathing. It lulled her, easing her anxiety, and her eyes grew heavy. *Just five minutes*, she told herself.

When she next awoke, morning dew clung to the windows, and sunlight broke through the clouds. She sat up, realizing she was alone. *The barn*, she thought, shivering. He must be with Marianne.

Without hesitation, she checked the car doors and noticed the keys in the ignition. But with her hands tied, driving was off the table. She scanned the surroundings. The road beckoned. If she started now, she could put distance between them. He wouldn't know which way she'd gone.

A hawk's piercing cry above reminded her of of the death that lurked nearby.

Zoe hesitated, glancing at the trail to the barn. Instinct urged her to flee, but doubt tethered her in place. What if he spoke the truth? What if he was innocent? She had to find out.

Heart pounding, she stealthily approached the barn, peering through a gap in the stones. It felt like glimpsing into the abyss of Hell itself.

17

Kneeling beside the body, he grappled with the fragments of his past.

Multiple layers of plastic wrap concealed the dead woman's face. To jog his memory, he needed to see her clearly. With care, he cradled her head, peeling away the plastic. As the last layer lifted, a soft sound akin to an exhale emerged—perhaps Marianne's last breath—trapped beneath the suffocating mask.

Up close, her skin bore a haunting purple hue. Her features were contorted, eyes bloodshot with burst vessels. Two thumb-shaped bruises, each an inch or so long, marked the base of her neck, sending an icy shiver down his spine. The undeniable evidence of strangulation.

"Did I do this?" The question escaped his lips, his voice quivering.

His fingers traced her bruised throat, finding a disturbing fit within the indents. And as he came into contact with the decomposing epidermis, images invaded his mind. They intertwined with the present, blurring lines of reality.

There she was, Marianne Deconti, alive and panic-stricken on the ground. As he attempted to restrain her, she lashed out. One forceful slap subdued her, but not for long. She retaliated, her nails digging deep into his forearms, causing him to release his grip.

The flashback faded, replaced by the harrowing sight of Marianne's inert form. He rolled up his sleeves, the crescent-shaped scars from her nails undeniable. Overwhelmed, he crumpled next to the woman he may have ended.

Under the bright daylight, he examined his hands, moving them as if gearing up to play a piano piece. Even with all the evidence against him, a part of him couldn't accept that he was a killer.

A piercing scream shattered his introspection. For a fleeting moment, he wondered if it was another twisted memory. But no, it was real, and it was coming from outside.

"Zoe!"

18

Anthony waited all night for a call that never came. Dawn broke, and still, silence. It wasn't until the morning fully settled in that Detective Gauthrie reached out. Anthony had been promised an update about Zoe. When he found out Europol was involved, a meeting was set at the Bordeaux Forensic Medicine Institute.

Walking in, a man with white hair and casual attire approached him. "Mr. Lavera," he began, extending his hand, "I'm Inspector Dorsey. I'm on your sister-in-law's case."

Anthony recognized the name instantly. Dorsey was the lead of the Europol investigation team set to catch the Reaper. He'd worked on some major cases, like that of Laura Messing. She was an English teacher who vanished from her house in Normandy. They later found her body in a forest in Germany.

Dorsey motioned to a nearby room. "Come with me."

Once inside the sparsely furnished office, Anthony, driven by his anxiety, asked, "What's our next move?"

Dorsey observed him, noting his evident distress. "I

understand your concern, Mr. Lavera. Sit down, and I'll fill you in."

Anthony took a deep breath, trying to calm himself. "It's not by sitting on our ass in a chair that—"

Dorsey raised a hand, signaling for Anthony to pause.

"We have a K-9 unit and a helicopter combing the forest as we speak. If Zoe is out there, we'll locate her."

Yet Anthony detected a hint of doubt in Dorsey's voice. "And her phone? Any leads?"

"Just a moment, Mr. Lavera. Based on what you've shared, you and Zoe came here from Marseille, fearing your wife was the Reaper's fourth victim," Dorsey stated.

Anthony felt a jolt of anxiety. "Is that why I'm here? You want me to identify her, don't you?"

"Yes. The coroner is prepared. Are you?"

Anthony stood up fast. He looked determined. "Let's go."

Anthony sensed Dorsey's stare on him, that intense scrutiny typical of police officers—always observing, always deducing, regardless of whether you're a suspect or a victim.

"You're aware of the condition in which we found her?" the medical examiner inquired.

Anthony knew. Zoe had immersed herself in the case, uncovering every detail about the victims and the alleged murderer. Each victim had been decapitated. As such, he was sure the body before him would be missing its head.

"Are you ready?"

Bracing himself for the undeniable stench of decay, Anthony gave a nod.

The coroner unzipped the body bag like a surgeon making a precise cut.

Taking a deep breath, Anthony stepped closer to the

table. "That's not her," he murmured, his voice distant and almost ethereal.

The coroner raised an eyebrow. "Are you sure? You barely looked."

But Dorsey gestured for the examiner not to insist.

19

———

Zoe bolted, her body pitched forward like a sprinter leaning into the home stretch. She breathed steady, resisting the urge to look back. A minute into her sprint, she could hear his breaths—harsh and uneven—closing in behind her.

"Zoe!"

She felt her heart skip. He was catching up. She would soon be within his firing range. Oddly, she felt a wash of relief. This quick end seemed kinder than the slow, tortured deaths she'd read about, the horrific ends met by the other women.

"Zoe!"

His voice was right beside her, making her heart skip again. Then, like a butterfly caught mid-flight, she was on the ground with him on top of her. They struggled for a moment, gasping for breath.

"Stop!"

They froze, locked in a standoff. Zoe on her back, him above, pinning her down with his weight. She couldn't move, but felt his grip loosening. Their eyes met.

"I remember," he whispered. "I was over her like this, trying to—"

"Strangle her?"

He rolled off, laying next to Zoe in the wet grass.

"I didn't kill her. There has to be another explanation."

She turned her head slightly to study his face as he stared up at the sky.

"Like what?"

"I don't know. Maybe I was helping her. And she hit me, thinking I was *him*."

Zoe sighed, unimpressed.

"You ever think about why he didn't come back last night?" she shot back. "Simple. He didn't have to; he was already there."

Their eyes locked again, electric with tension.

"You're right. If I am the Reaper, I've walked right into your theory, haven't I?"

She couldn't shake the theory from the behavior analysis team: the killer was driven by necrophilic urges. That made sense of the hidden heads—he intended to come back for unspeakable acts possible only in death. Flashes of the barn scene came rushing back to her, of him caressing the corpse with a disturbing tenderness.

Despite everything, she looked at him, at his strong jawline and intense eyes, and thought he was somewhat attractive. A handsome monster, like a carnivorous plant, using its vibrant hues to lure in its next victim.

"I know how it looks," he said.

"And I know what I just saw."

"You *think* you know. But I didn't touch her. Not like you think. I just wanted to see her face. To remember. I wish you believed me."

“Why?”

He looked at her, puzzled.

“What does it matter whether I believe you or not?” she said. “It doesn’t change the fact that you’re not letting me go.”

He stood up, dusting off his jeans.

“If I let you go, my face will be splashed across every newspaper and every TV screen,” he responded. “I’ll be in cuffs before I even figure out who I truly am. Am I wrong?”

She met his gaze, her eyes filled with a mix of fear and defiance, but she said nothing.

After a tense pause, he extended his hand to help her up. “We need to go.”

“No.”

“What?”

“I’m not going with you.”

“Zoe—”

“I’m not afraid of you.”

He smiled, amused.

“Well, that’s reassuring!”

“I mean it.”

“So do I. But do serial killers make jokes?” he quipped with a half-smile.

“You’re the only one laughing.”

“Shame. I thought it might convince you I’m not the Reaper.”

“Nothing will convince me.”

She looked around, frustration flashing in her eyes.

“We’re in the middle of nowhere, and you want me to believe you just happened upon a murder? Why would anyone be out here?”

“That’s what I’m trying to figure out. I may not remember, but I still feel," he said quietly, looking at the barn nearby. "I was here for a reason."

"And that is?"

"I was searching for something. Still don't know what, but I'll find it."

20

Inspector Dorsey slumped down behind his desk, a weary expression on his face.

"Need a drink or something?" he asked. "There's a vending machine right outside. Feel free to grab some snacks as well, if you're up for it."

Anthony shook his head and lowered himself into a chair.

Dorsey leaned forward, locking eyes with him. "I don't mean to push, but how can you be so certain it's not your wife?"

"Gabriela had a birthmark on the upper part of her left thigh," he replied. "Plus, she never had an appendectomy."

Inspector Dorsey nodded, his expression unreadable.

"You mentioned she disappeared after her morning run..."

Anthony squirmed in his chair. Dorsey was on a hunt for answers.

"I was still asleep when she left," he began, his voice distant, as though he was reciting from a script meant for someone else. "When I woke up, she hadn't returned. I tried calling her cell, but she had left it at home. It wasn't the first time she'd done that, so I wasn't worried at first. I just went to work as usual."

"At the narcotics unit," Dorsey interjected, a hint of something more in his eyes.

"Right. It was a calm morning, so I caught up on some paperwork—preliminary reports and such."

Dorsey showed a brief flash of camaraderie, familiar with the monotony.

"Around nine o'clock, I received a call from the gym owner where Gabriela worked. She hadn't shown up for her first class and was absent for the next as well. I tried calling home, but there was no answer. A colleague accompanied me back, but by then, it was clear Gabriela had never returned from her run."

Dorsey leaned back, his brow furrowed in contemplation.

"How did your sister-in-law make the connection between Gabriela's disappearance and the Reaper?"

"A newspaper article mentioned the killer would send a package to the victim's family, usually including a piece of their jewelry."

Dorsey snapped to attention.

"Did that happen to you? Did you receive something?"

"Yes, Gabriela's wedding ring. At first, I thought it was her way of sending me a message," Anthony admitted, his voice catching slightly.

"Did you keep the envelope?"

"There was no point. I believed she was ending our relationship, severing ties with me."

"That didn't seem odd to you? She could've just asked for a divorce."

"True, but Gabriela never was one for simplicity."

Dorsey couldn't quite hide his disappointment.

"So, when did this package arrive?"

"A month after she disappeared."

"And that was it?"

"What do you mean?"

"Did you receive anything else? Any letters, or perhaps a postcard?"

Anthony's body tensed.

"The media didn't mention that," he said, his voice quivering. "Did that happen to the other victims?"

"Answer my question first."

"Nothing else arrived, just the ring. Unless..."

"Yes?"

"I moved not long after that."

"You moved?"

Anthony, his eyes misting with pain, looked down.

"Yes. We had just bought a house together," he began slowly. "Our relationship had been strained, and I thought... I thought a new place might signify a fresh start for both of us. I believed that if we changed our surroundings, our relationship might improve."

"And where is this new house located?"

"In the seventh district of Marseille," Anthony responded, a touch of defensiveness in his voice.

Dorsey leaned back, thinking. "The seventh district? Isn't that place pricey?"

Anthony bristled, irritated, but he restrained himself. He knew that making enemies would not aid in his search for Zoe.

"It was a good deal," he stated. "It all happened quickly. The owners, a British couple, were eager to sell. Gabriela was thrilled, so we signed the pre-contract, gave our notice, and paid the deposit for the movers."

"And then she disappeared."

Anthony sighed, his face showing a mix of sorrow and frustration.

"I could have backed out of the whole thing, but truth be told, I was more than ready to leave our old place behind."

"Because of the memories," Dorsey surmised.

He stared at the ceiling, trying to rearrange his thoughts.

"And you didn't update your address for the mail?"

"I did. But there's always the possibility that some of it got lost along the way."

"We believe the killer sends everything all at once. You should have received both the package and the postcard within a day or two of each other, under normal circumstances," Dorsey stated, skepticism evident in his voice.

"Is that significant?"

He slammed his hand onto the desk. "Of course it is! If you had received that postcard, it would've been clear that Gabriela was a victim of the Reaper. I would've been on the case much earlier, and your sister-in-law might not have fallen into the trap that was set for her. Now, we're scrambling to piece everything together!"

"A trap?"

The inspector swiveled in his chair, reaching for a file on his desk.

"Someone messaged her on Facebook the day she disappeared."

He handed Anthony a printed sheet. On it, a man named Frank claimed to have information about the serial killer.

I was walking my dog and taking pictures in the woods. I have a passion for photography. I was focusing on a fox when I heard footsteps. Assuming it was another animal, I continued. But then I noticed a man and a woman. They were close, arm in arm. Her attire struck me as odd; she was in running gear, even though there are no trails nearby. I didn't think much of it until later, when the news reported the discovery of the fourth victim in that very forest. That's when it hit me; the woman I saw must've been her. I scoured the pictures I took that day. Most are blurry, but in one, you can somewhat make out the man. I've stayed away from the police due to my history with poaching—just the idea of setting foot in a police station terrifies me. But if these pictures can help catch the guy who took your sister, they're yours.

The message also included details for a meeting, along with GPS coordinates—the exact location where Zoe's rental Ford Focus was discovered.

Dorsey slid a stack of printed sheets across the desk, each filled with various photos. One depicted a man in his sixties, with white hair and stubble, smiling next to a Labrador. The remaining images were various nature scenes.

"This is all a sham," Inspector Dorsey declared. "The name used is from a B-list horror movie actor, and the photo of the man? We found it on a stock photo website."

"And these?" Anthony said, pointing to the landscape photos.

"Some might be stock photos, but others seem real," Dorsey replied, marking them with his pen. "This one," he tapped a picture, "looks like it's from the Sonian Forest in

Belgium. And this one might be the Gran Paradiso National Park in Italy." He took a moment, then said, "You could almost see where the last two victims were buried with these. But we never told the public those spots."

"So, you're saying the person Zoe was supposed to meet..."

"...is the killer, the one Europol has been chasing for months. But we've made progress. We traced the IP address from the message. It pinpointed a location in Nice. The name associated with it? Marianne Deconti, a nurse there."

Anthony's eyes widened, taken aback.

"Nice? As in the French Riviera?"

Dorsey nodded. "Yes, Nice. As in that glamorous city on the Mediterranean coast of France."

"Have you reached out to this Marianne Deconti?" Anthony asked.

"Yes, but no response so far. Her hospital says she's on leave until tomorrow. I'm heading there in an hour. You're welcome to join if you'd like."

21

———

Zoe felt trapped in a nightmare. The car bumped and slid on the muddy road, with her tied up in the back seat. She listened to the GPS give directions. After a risky drive down the mountain, they reached the main road. Now, they were on their way to Marseille on the A8, a major motorway in the south of France.

Her captor had already taken a significant risk by not hiding her in the trunk, but choosing to take the highway? That was outright reckless. Zoe had been missing for a full day; law enforcement across the country should be searching for her. He had to be aware of that. Perhaps he bet that no one was searching for him or Marianne Deconti's car, which wouldn't be missed until the nurse failed to show up for her hospital shift the next day. Or maybe he was too consumed in his desperate search for identity to care. Regardless of his thought process, he diligently followed the GPS, taking them ever further from the barn.

Feeling dizzy, Zoe curled up under the blanket, the familiar scent of Marianne's jasmine laundry detergent surrounding her. Poor Marianne... Zoe tried to block out the horror by thinking of her small Paris studio, just a few Metro stops away from the Opera. That small, noisy apartment was her first home in the city. She'd planned to move out once she earned more, but her dance classes and performances always got in the way. Even though it was cramped, she loved its view of the Eiffel Tower when leaning out from the balcony.

The thought that she might never see her home again shook her. She wouldn't be complaining about her upstairs neighbors' late-night activities or politely accepting meals from Ms. Song, her friendly korean neighbor. She wouldn't have any more arguments with the mailman.

Tears welled up. She clenched her lids tightly, a single tear escaping. Then, surrendering like an animal resigned to its fate, she drifted off to sleep.

"We'll run out of gas soon," a voice pierced through her slumber.

Zoe jolted awake, his words resonating in the confined space of the car.

"We're close to Valence," he added, his voice steady.

Valence? The city, located in southeastern France, was hours away from Nice and the French Riviera. Zoe found it hard to believe she had slept that long, but the aches spreading through her body, stiff from hours in the same position, seemed to confirm it.

"I need the bathroom," she murmured, rubbing her eyes to dispel the sleep.

He didn't respond, but moments later, the car slowed to a stop.

"We're good. Coast is clear," he said, helping her into a sitting position in the back seat.

Zoe found herself at a sparse rest stop, featuring

concrete picnic tables and less-than-inviting public restrooms.

"No tricks," he warned as he untied her.

He helped her out of the car, and a stiff wind hit her. Dead leaves swirled around, and trees rustled above. She shivered, her thin blouse no match for the chill.

"Here, take my jacket."

"Th-thanks," she stammered, her teeth chattering.

As they walked to the restrooms, Zoe was unsurprised when he followed her into the women's side, checking each stall before gesturing to one.

She tensed when he kept the door ajar. "I'm not undressing in front of you."

"I won't look," he assured.

"That's not the point," she retorted.

He sighed, resigned. "Fine. But don't lock it. You've got five minutes, then I'm coming in, ready or not."

With the door closed behind her, Zoe undid her jeans and squatted, trying her best to ignore the unpleasant smell wafting up from the drain.

"You done in there?" his voice cut through her concentration.

She jumped, frustration in her voice. "Just give me a minute."

"It's because I'm here?" he questioned.

She rolled her eyes. "You think?"

"All right, fine. I'll wait outside. But no funny business."

Zoe tried to relax. Between the cold and the stress, her bladder muscles seemed paralyzed. Suddenly, she heard the sound of running water, as if someone had turned on a tap. And then, as if by magic, she was finally able to relieve herself.

When she emerged from the restroom, she couldn't help but meet his gaze.

"Feel better?" he asked, a hint of a smirk on his face.

"Yes, thanks. The faucet trick was smart."

"Good. Let's get moving."

"What about you?"

"I'll use the restroom at the gas station. Need to fill up and grab some food, anyway."

He glanced around, making sure no other cars had arrived during their stop.

"All right, let's go."

He unlocked the car doors. "Turn around. Hands behind your back."

Zoe felt the rope tighten around her wrists once more. When she turned back, he was opening the trunk.

"You can't be serious," she exclaimed. "I told you I won't try anything."

"I know. But I can't risk someone spotting you and getting curious. I'll leave your legs free, but remember: one wrong move, and it'll be more than just you getting hurt."

"Do I have a choice?"

The question was rhetorical; she knew she didn't. Resigned, she climbed back into the trunk as he pulled out a roll of duct tape.

"I'm sorry," he apologized, placing a strip over her mouth. "But I can't take any chances."

The drive to the gas station took all of ten minutes. The car eventually came to a halt.

Gasoline fumes sneaked into the trunk where Zoe lay. The hum of the pump, dispensing fuel, followed by the gas cap being secured again, filtered through to her. The car door opened and slammed shut; footsteps walked away, waning. Silence ensued, but was short-lived. Muffled voices reached Zoe—a mother and daughter, deep in an argument, oblivious to the abducted woman mere feet away.

Zoe could've tried to get their attention, but she held back. His threat, uttered before the trunk was slammed shut, echoed in her mind. If she tried to escape or sought attention again, people would die. Whether he was bluffing, she couldn't be sure. So, Zoe stayed put, curled under a blanket, while the pair continued to argue about a party the teenager was adamant to attend.

"You're too young," the mother said, trying to reason with her. *"Besides, you have school tomorrow."*

"But I'm sixteen!" the daughter shot back, defiance clear in her voice. *"All my friends are going. I can skip gym."*

Their voices faded into the distance, likely continuing their heated exchange in the car on the way home. After a short while, the sound of footsteps approached again. He was back.

The car started and, as Zoe shut her eyes, hoping to drift into an unconscious state, it became evident they were stopping again. When she emerged from the trunk this time, a new scene was before her: endless fields of harvested crops, sporadically interrupted by distant mountainous shapes, like icebergs in a sea of dry grass. Not a house in sight.

"So, is this where you're planning on doing it?" she asked.

"Doing what?"

"Killing me."

He sighed.

"I borrowed fifty euros from you. Enough for gas and a little food. And this."

He rummaged through a plastic bag with the gas station's logo, pulling out a t-shirt.

"Didn't know your favorite color, so I got white, size small. But let's eat first."

Setting the shirt aside, he reached back into the bag.

"Tuna mayo or chicken salad?" he asked, sandwiches in hand.

"I don't care, as long as it's edible."

He peeled the plastic cover, breaking the sandwich into pieces.

"Come here."

Despite her distaste, the smell of the grilled chicken made Zoe's mouth water.

"I'd prefer if you untie me," she said, sitting up, clinging to a semblance of dignity. "I'm too old to be fed like a baby."

He tilted his head—a gesture she recognized as his expression of indecision.

"Not yet. Maybe later."

"Then keep your damn sandwich!"

"Stop acting like a child and eat!"

He tried to feed her again, but she turned her head, refusing.

"You look pale; I assure you, some sugar will do you good."

Now he was pretending to care about her well-being, tempting her with sweetness, or in this case, a preservative-laden sandwich. But she wasn't having it. That's when he threw her off balance once again.

"All right, Zoe. You win."

Before she could process the turn of events, he spun her around. Zoe tensed, shutting her eyes. Was he going to punish her for her defiance?

"Are you left-handed or right-handed?"

She opened her eyes.

"What?"

"From the way you wear your watch, I take it you're right-handed?"

He retrieved a pair of scissors from a backpack on the passenger seat—the same backpack that held the rope, tape, and God knows what else—and gestured for her to extend her wrists.

To Zoe's disbelief, he was finally setting her free. But as she was about to thank him, he took her hand and began wrapping tape around their wrists, binding them together. His left to her right.

"This way, if you get the urge to bolt, you'll have to drag me with you."

With that, he placed the sandwich in her free hand.

"Eat."

Resigned, Zoe took a bite. So, this was what the coroner would find in her stomach: half-digested pieces of a chicken sandwich, coffee, and a chocolate bar. At least it wasn't the worst last meal.

"You didn't answer me earlier," she said, mouth full.

He looked puzzled.

"About what? Oh, whether I plan to kill you here? Sorry, but I still don't want to."

"When, then?"

He stopped eating to look at her.

"You're in a hurry to die?"

"I want to know how much time I have left."

"I see. Well, quit smoking, keep taking your meds, and you might live long enough to tell this story to your grandkids."

Zoe wasn't in the mood for jokes.

"Is that what you tell all your victims? Give them false

hope? And they believe you, of course! They have to! I get that, but I won't—"

Before she could protest or even grasp what was happening, he pressed his lips to hers, leaving her breathless. A car zoomed past them, its horn blaring, as he pulled her into an embrace.

"Why did you do that?" she demanded, shoving him away.

"I don't know... I panicked."

"What?"

"Yeah... I heard the car coming. I didn't want anyone thinking we were fighting or something."

"Fighting? You've kidnapped me. You—"

He silenced her with a finger on her lips.

"I'm sorry, okay?"

She shook her head, adamant. "Don't ever do that again."

He backed away, leaving Zoe to wrestle with the pounding in her chest that seemed to be screaming a warning she was determined to ignore. She turned, not wanting him to see the chaos in her eyes. Thankfully, he seemed oblivious to her internal struggle and shifted the topic.

"I picked up a road atlas at the gas station," he said, his voice casual.

Zoe looked at him, skeptical. "Why? You have a GPS in the car."

"GPS is great if you know where you're headed. I don't. Thought I'd look at the atlas, see if any town names rang a bell."

"Did it help?"

"No, but it gave me another idea."

He opened the atlas, flipping through the pages. "We are here," he showed, his finger hovering just above Valence.

Zoe leaned in to get a better look, but he had already turned the page. "Marianne is there, at the barn, just an hour's drive from her house," he pointed out.

Hunched over the map, he marked the two locations with a 'X'. Drawing a line to connect them, he met Zoe's eyes. "Where did they find the other victims?"

Zoe swallowed hard. "You're going back to those places?"

"I'm not sure yet. Maybe it'll help me remember."

With her free hand, she flipped through the atlas. "Klaudia was found in northern Italy, here," she said, pressing her finger to the glossy paper near the Franco-Italian border.

"Gran Paradiso National Park," he read aloud, as if savoring each word.

"Ring any bells?"

"No."

Still, he marked the spot. "And where did she live?"

"Munich."

"Munich," he echoed, making another mark on the map. The two X's were roughly four hundred miles apart—a solid seven-hour drive.

They repeated the process for Selma Lorenzen, last seen in Amsterdam and later found in Belgium's Sonian Forest, and for Laura Lassiter, an English woman living in Normandy, found dead in Germany's Black Forest.

"And the fourth victim?"

"They found her body this week in the Landes Forest Reserve," Zoe offered.

"The Landes..." he murmured, flipping through the atlas pages. When he found the right spot, his finger paused on the page, hovering over the vast expanse of pines in the southwest of France.

Zoe took a deep breath, feeling the weight of the moment. "But I don't know her name or where she lived. That's why I went to Bordeaux."

Setting the atlas aside, he looked at her. "Did you think it was your sister?"

"Why not? Gabriela was kidnapped in Marseille, which is just a seven-hour drive from the Landes Forest."

He returned his attention to the map. "True. But all the other victims were taken in one country and killed in another. Klaudia from Germany to Italy, Laura from France to Germany, Selma from the Netherlands to Belgium."

"I know all that. But it's still possible. And if you..." She hesitated, her eyes searching his for a moment before she corrected herself. "I mean, if the Reaper hadn't taken me, I would've gone to the forensic institute in Bordeaux to see the body."

"It wasn't your sister," he stated after a pause.

"How can you be so sure?" she demanded, then caught herself. If anyone knew where her sister was, it was him.

"The woman in the Landes Forest was Inez Monteya, kidnapped four months ago in Malaga."

Her throat tightened as she watched him mark the two new locations.

"Now that you remember, tell me. Where is my sister? Please, just take me to her. I just want to see her one last time. After that, you can do whatever you want with me."

"I don't know where she is. And you're wrong. My memory hasn't come back."

"Then how did you know about Inez Monteya?"

"At the gas station, the manager had the TV on. They

were talking about the latest victim and about you. You're all over the news," he added after a moment's pause.

"I see. So, you're planning to get rid of me soon."

He shook his head, looking away. "Yeah, you're annoying. But that doesn't mean I have to kill you."

Zoe watched, her breath caught in her throat as he immersed himself back into the atlas, flipping through the pages until he reached the ones marked with crosses. Like an artist critically assessing his finished piece, he paused to scrutinize each mark, his expression unreadable.

What did he see in those lines and colors? Was it the chaotic blend of greens, browns, and blues depicting forests, mountains, and waters? Or was it the grisly scenes of his victims' final moments that played in his mind? Klaudia's body being buried, Selma's gruesome decapitation, Laura and Gabriela's final breaths. Zoe couldn't erase those images from her mind; they were etched into her memory forever. Soon, she realized, she would be one of them, her body subjected to the analysts' scrutiny. And then it hit her: he wasn't pondering over his past deeds. He was planning her demise, deciding on the perfect spot to dispose of her body. Her thoughts were abruptly interrupted as he pointed to a spot on the map. "Wolves Forest, in Normandy," she read aloud, her voice laden with the weight of realization.

"Does that name ring a bell?"

She shook her head. "And you?" she asked after a beat.

"I feel like what I'm searching for is there, in that forest. Once I discover it, I'll know who I am."

"What are you hoping to find?"

"I don't know. We'll see when we get there."

He closed the atlas and cut the tape binding their wrists. "Turn around, please."

She expected to be restrained again, but found herself

left alone in the back seat as he climbed into the driver's seat. He set the GPS to take him to Wolves Forest in Normandy, choosing to avoid major roads. Travel time: 10h 19m.

"It's a long drive," he remarked, glancing back at her. "I don't want to put you in the trunk for the rest of it, even though maybe I should."

"Thank you," Zoe murmured.

She was sincere; he had given her hope. He could have lied, telling her that she wasn't newsworthy. She would have believed him. After all, who had ever cared about her before?

Lying on the backseat, she found herself turning his words over in her mind. Everyone was searching for her. It was good news, but relief was elusive. *Enough*, she silently commanded herself, summoning her inner strength. She was going to make it through this. The 'how' was still unclear, but she knew she would.

22

Zoe's eyes flew open, every sense alert. The car's humming engine shifted from a soothing lull to a disturbing stutter. Tires crunched on gravel, and the car swerved, halting. In the thick dark, only the headlights shone bright.

"We're out of gas," he announced, his voice tinged with resignation. "Looks like we're stuck here till morning."

Zoe's voice remained steady despite the cold unease crawling up her spine. "I've been lying like this for hours," she said. With her legs drawn up and hands bound in the back, she pleaded, "Can you let me out just to stretch? My legs are cramping."

The confines of the car seemed to close in on her, pushing her to the verge of losing her composure.

"Fine," he relented.

He assisted her out of the car and sliced through the tape binding her wrists.

She took a deep inhale, savoring the sudden rush of relief. It had been an eternity since she last moved freely. Keeping her emotions in check had drained her. He, too, looked exhausted from the relentless eight-hour drive, punctuated by only a few stops.

"I need to walk around a bit," she murmured, moving before he could respond.

A metallic click made her flinch. She knew that if she turned around, she'd see the gun pointed in her direction.

"Don't stray too far," he warned.

She stepped forward, her shadow stretching from the headlights. Fields spread out around them, fading into the dark. They were stuck between Clermont-Ferrand and Blois, a city known for its historic castles in central France. The cold air made her shiver, and she moved to keep warm.

Then, his voice broke the silence. "Where are you going?"

She hadn't realized he was following until he was right on her heels.

"It's colder than I thought," he remarked, draping a blanket around her shoulders. "We need to find shelter soon, or we'll freeze out here."

As they prepared to climb back into the car, the sound of another engine caught their attention. An old truck approached, its window descending with a creaky sound.

"Y'all need any help?" asked the driver, a man appearing to be in his sixties.

Zoe's gaze landed on the hunting rifle lying on the passenger seat. She wasn't the only one who spotted it—her kidnapper did too, shooting her a warning glance. Knowing that any sudden move could be dangerous, she remained silent, but her captor jumped in with a response.

"We got lost," he explained. "My wife and I were trying to find a hotel, but we've had no luck."

The man in the truck looked puzzled. "A hotel? Out

here? You've got to be joking. There's nothing like that around these parts."

"Our issue right now is that we're running low on gas."

"Well, shoot! Why don't y'all come over to my place? It's better than any hotel, I guarantee!" As he spoke, he shifted the rifle from the passenger seat, making room for them. "You folks got any luggage?"

Zoe felt the grip of her kidnapper tighten around her. She wondered what they would say to explain their lack of luggage.

"Stupid question, I know! Of course, you do!" the driver chuckled, oblivious to her discomfort. "Unfortunately, my truck's packed to the brim; not a space left. But don't you worry, my place has everything you'll need."

With no backseat available, Zoe and the man who held their fates in his grasp were forced to squeeze together in the front. He pulled her close—so close she could feel his heart racing. Strange... Men like him were believed to be void of emotions, except perhaps the thrill of killing. Yet the man gripping her now radiated fear.

"I'm Roger!" their host announced, grinning. "Roger Pasteur. Like the guy with penicillin."

There was a pause, filled with awkwardness, and Zoe realized it was their cue to introduce themselves.

"I'm Zoe," she snapped.

She then turned to her captor, prompting him to introduce himself.

"Johan," he said, before adding, "And for the record, it was Alexander Fleming who discovered penicillin."

Roger chuckled, embarrassed. "Well! Have I been getting it wrong all these years?" He laughed again, but this time it turned into a cough.

"What about that Louis Pasteur guy?" he asked, still

coughing.

Zoe tried to recall what she had learned in school.

"He was pivotal in developing vaccines," Johan interjected. "Back in the 1880s, he saved a boy from rabies with the first-ever vaccine. It was revolutionary."

Roger squinted, tilting his head. "You a doctor or something?"

Johan paused, searching for the right words. The silence lingered.

"You folks from the Coast?" Roger inquired.

Both Zoe and Johan gave him puzzled looks.

"The Coast?" Johan echoed.

"Yeah, the '06 area? That's the Côte d'Azur, the French Riviera, right?"

Zoe felt her captor's fingers tighten around her waist. Roger must have noticed something on their license plate.

Roger squinted a bit. "But you don't got that Southern twang. You sure you're really from there?"

Johan grinned. "That's right. I'm from Normandy."

Zoe's mind was racing. Was he telling the truth? And if he was, did that mean he was starting to piece things together?

"Normandy? Oh, I was there for an agricultural expo some time ago. Which part you from?"

Realizing she needed to change the subject, Zoe thought quickly. Any other time, this would be just casual chit-chat. But not today.

"We're from the northern coast," she interjected. "We're heading there for my in-laws' big anniversary celebration. We're on a rare break, so we decided to road trip, stopping wherever we fancy. We veered off course because I've always dreamed of seeing the Loire Valley castles. You've been there, haven't you?"

"Oh, the castles? Heck yeah! My wife dragged me to visit every single one of them."

"Do you have a favorite?"

Roger adjusted his cap, taking a moment to think. "For specifics, you'd have to ask my wife. But there are some local farms around here. If you buy from them, you might find something unique for your in-laws. Drop my name, and they might even give you a discount."

"That sounds great. What do they sell?"

Zoe smoothly changed the subject. Now it was Roger's turn to talk, filling the gaps in conversation. The driver, always up for a chat, pointed out landmarks, sharing snippets of history and local lore.

Suddenly, the truck bumped over a rough patch. Johan pulled Zoe closer to steady her. Below them, the vehicle groaned, sounding like an old creaky porch swing.

"The farm's just up ahead on the right," Roger announced, flipping on his blinker, more out of habit than necessity, given they were the only ones on the road.

A "For Sale" sign stood on the property, advertising eight hundred acres of soy and corn. Roger and his wife felt they had aged out of farming and were planning to move closer to their daughter, Aurelie, by the next planting season.

Lights from a house twinkled in the distance, and a woman, wrapped in a cardigan, stood waiting, her expression a mixture of curiosity and caution.

"Give me just a moment," Roger said with a warm smile, "She's probably wondering who's coming over at this hour."

Zoe and her captor watched as Roger spoke with his wife. After a few words, she gestured for them to come inside.

"Come on in! It's chilly out here," she called, wrapping Zoe in a warm, comforting embrace.

23

"Marianne Deconti lived in a townhouse on a quiet hill in the suburbs of Nice.

Anthony watched Dorsey park the car, shattering the silence.

"Wait here," Dorsey instructed, heading toward the house.

As he disappeared from view, curiosity got the better of Anthony, and he got out of the car. Nearing the entrance, he caught sight of Dorsey at the doorstep, gun in hand. Anthony's heart raced. "What's happening?"

Dorsey shot him a warning glance, gesturing for him to stay back. But Anthony was not one to just stand by. Seeing the front door slightly ajar, he moved quickly inside, barely noticing Dorsey's protests. "Zoe!" He called out as he raced down the hallway. The living room was empty. "Zoe?" The kitchen looked like a whirlwind had hit it. Panic surged within him, thoughts racing.

"Dammit, Lavera! You trying to get shot? Get out!"

"We need to find her! Maybe she's in a bedroom?"

"Let me handle this. Go back to the car and call for backup."

Dorsey pressed on, and Anthony hesitated, briefly regretting his lack of a firearm. It didn't take long before Dorsey was back, looking grim. He holstered his weapon, frustration evident in his eyes. "I told you to head to the car."

Anthony pointed urgently. "What about that door? Did you check there?"

Dorsey's gaze landed on a hidden door disguised as part of the wall. It looked like it could be a closet, but when opened, a staircase leading down to the basement came into view, dimly lit by a single light bulb. The light still being on suggested someone had recently been there. Fear tightened its grip on Anthony.

"Don't worry, I've got this," Dorsey said, sensing Anthony's resolve. "I'll take the lead." Gun at the ready, Dorsey made his way down. "It's clear!"

Anthony's descent was rushed, nearly tripping in his haste. The scene was haunting: Rolled-up blankets, an empty food tray. This was where Zoe had been. Her perfume still clung to the air.

"We're too late," he murmured, guilt weighing him down.

Dorsey called him over. "Hey, Lavera! Look at this."

Together, they examined an earring caught in a blanket.

"That's Zoe's!"

"Are you certain?"

"No doubt. So, what now?"

Dorsey took a moment before answering. "I'm calling for backup. We need a crime scene team here. We also need to speak with the neighbors."

Anthony felt the weight of helplessness. "So, we just... wait?"

Dorsey sighed. "It's our best option."

24

———

Chantal Pasteur had retreated to the kitchen, leaving her husband to entertain their guests. Throwing more logs onto the fire, Roger beckoned, "Come on over. Get warm."

Zoe and her captor inched closer to the fireplace. His grip on her was firm, akin to that of a husband's protective hold on his wife. Despite this, Zoe sensed his tension; he was poised for action, ready to draw the gun she had seen concealed at the back of his jeans, under his shirt, its handle within easy reach should he need it. The thought of snatching it crossed her mind, but her attention was drawn to the photographs adorning the mantel.

They captured the key moments of Aurelie's life, the only daughter of their hosts. There was baby Aurelie, snug in Roger's embrace at the hospital, taking her first steps as a toddler, proudly showing off a gap-toothed smile at eight, and as a teenager, her complexion marred by acne. The most recent photo featured a glowing Aurelie in her wedding gown, standing beside her husband. In Zoe's mind, the next picture was easy to imagine: Roger, cradling a baby once more, but this time, his granddaughter. The cycle would come full circle. Unless, of course, they all met their end tonight. And that's why she chose to keep a low profile. At least for now...

Johan looked down at the dog that had bumped into him. "What's his name?"

"Frisbie," answered the farmer with a chuckle.

Zoe eyed the dog, which seemed to revel in Johan's gentle petting. The *Beware of Dog* sign at the entrance had prepared her for a menacing, drooling monster. But to her surprise, a senior spaniel had peeked out. Then slowly withdrew back indoors.

"He might not look it, but he's twelve," Roger added, proud.

Satisfied with the attention he had received, Frisbie sauntered back to his bed by the fire.

"Man, we're gonna miss him when he's gone, huh, buddy?" Roger mused aloud.

The spaniel, raising an eyebrow, snorted and closed his eyes—the epitome of an old man disturbed from his slumber.

From the kitchen, Chantal's voice permeated the air. "We're out of hot water!"

"I got it!" Roger called back, his voice echoing through the house.

Then, turning back to his guests with a more composed demeanor, he added, "I'll just fix the water heater. That way, if anyone wants a shower later, there'll be plenty of hot water."

Zoe and her fake husband were alone in the living room. The space was packed with old family furniture, making the room feel cramped. All around, various trinkets and hunting prizes jockeyed for position. In the midst of this nostalgic clutter, a flat-screen TV looked conspicuously out of place. Her captor noticed it, too. Their eyes locked, and Zoe could tell he was pondering the same questions she was. Had the homeowners been watching the news?

Suddenly, the sound of dishes shattering snapped them out of their thoughts. Chantal Pasteur was clearly uncomfortable with them being there, though maybe not for the reasons they suspected.

On the kitchen's linoleum floor, pieces of a broken porcelain plate were scattered everywhere.

"I'm such a klutz!" she exclaimed, her voice laced with frustration.

Intent on being the consummate hostess, Chantal had opted to use her best dishes, reserved solely for the most special of occasions. Zoe made a move to assist with the cleanup, but Johan was quicker on the draw.

Her mind raced—she was confident she could snatch it away before he could react. She began to free her hands, taking a deep breath as she prepared to make her move. *One, two...*

"What the hell was that?!" Roger's voice boomed as he stormed into the kitchen, causing Zoe to back up in shock until she was cornered against the countertop, her face pale.

"Roger, seriously? Why the yelling?" Chantal exclaimed, as yet another plate slipped from her grasp. "Look at this mess now!"

Meanwhile, Johan remained calm, his gaze locked onto a small drop of blood pooling in his palm.

"Are you hurt?" Chantal shift her attention to him, her tone accusing as she added, "This is your fault, Roger."

"Oops, my bad," Roger mumbled, his voice low.

"Don't just stand there! Fetch the first-aid kit!"

Zoe locked eyes with Chantal, sensing the silent expectation that she act the part of the perfect wife. To her reluctance, she complied.

"Let me see, *honey*," she said to the man who could rival the devil himself.

He appeared pale. Was he unnerved by the sight of blood, or was he just putting on a show? Did he catch on when she attempted to grab his gun?

"It's nothing, Zoe," he assured her, though his tone carried a hint of uncertainty.

She flashed him a brief smile and guided him to the sink. While she rinsed his hand with cold water, she maintained eye contact with him. Once the bleeding began to subside, he studied the cut, looking at it, detached, as if it wasn't his own, carefully examining its depth.

"Got everything here!" Roger announced, reentering the room with a box filled to the brim with first-aid supplies.

With a straight face, Johan looked over the box. "Got a needle and thread?"

The farmers exchanged puzzled glances.

"Just kidding, Roger. A bandage is all I need."

Chantal's eyes widened, her hand at her chest. "You had us there!"

Roger chuckled. "For a second, I thought you were gonna stitch yourself up. Like in that Stallone film… Rocky!"

"That's Rambo, not Rocky," Chantal corrected him.

"No, I'm pretty sure it's Rocky. He sews his wound, pushing the needle through like this," Roger illustrated.

"You're mixing them up."

"You sure?"

"Yep. Right, everyone?"

Talk turned to other movies as they settled for dinner. Zoe observed Johan as he assisted Chantal with the dishes.

His charm was infectious, and it was clear their hosts were smitten.

"It's been an age since we've entertained guests," Chantal mused, placing a steaming pot at the center of the table. The room was permeated with the tantalizing scent of freshly baked bread and hearty stew. "Just a humble meal," she added.

"It smells divine," Zoe remarked, attempting to sound casual despite her genuine appreciation.

Johan leaned forward, allowing the aroma to envelop him. "This brings back memories of a dish my mother used to prepare. I'm eager to taste it."

A smile lit up Chantal's face as she guided everyone to the table.

Zoe allowed Johan to pour her a drink, playing the part of a doting husband. She wasn't fooled, aware of his manipulative tactics, but played along for the sake of Aurelie's parents, hoping their act was convincing. As they sat side by side, their attention shifted to Roger. The seasoned farmer had a wealth of stories to share. Like a veteran recalling past battles, he started with a tale of how he broke his hip, falling off a ladder, and then smoothly transitioned to another story about a finger injury.

Chantal, familiar with these tales, stood up to clear away an empty dish heading to the kitchen. Returning with a selection of cheeses, she asked, "So, how did you two cross paths?"

Roger stayed quiet, just as interested in the response.

Just as Zoe was about to craft a lie, Johan's hand tightened around hers. "I was entranced by a sketch of her," he began, his tone soft.

Chantal and Roger exchanged glances, their intrigue piqued.

"We share a mutual friend," Zoe interjected. "An artist. He once asked me to model, and the sketch stayed in his studio."

"It was just a basic pencil sketch," Johan said, locking eyes with Zoe. "Nothing detailed."

Zoe raised an eyebrow, trying to keep track—less was more when making things up. But she went with it.

"Like many artists, he..."

"Albert," Johan supplied.

"Yes, Albert. He started with that draft. I have the finished piece, but he kept the initial sketch in his studio. That's where you saw it, isn't it?"

Lost in thought, Johan responded, "I was captivated. The woman in the drawing lingered in my mind." His gaze scrutinized her, as if superimposing her face onto the fictional drawing. "You styled your hair differently," he remarked.

Before Zoe could interject, Johan's fingers deftly undid her hair tie, allowing her locks to cascade.

"It was more like this..."

He swept away the unruly strands of hair, as if trying to align the portrait with its subject. Their eyes locked once more, and Zoe could tell he wasn't faking it. If he was, he deserved an Oscar.

Noticing their hosts were still paying attention, she wrapped up her story.

"And Robert... I mean, Albert, introduced us at one of his art openings. And just like that! We reconnected, fell head over heels, and..."

"You two tied the knot," Chantal deduced, her eyes fixed on her wedding band.

Seizing the chance to divert attention, Zoe inquired, "What about your daughter, Aurelie? How long has she been wed?"

Chantal fell for it, just like Zoe had hoped.

"Can you get the photo album?" she asked her husband, who saw it as the perfect opportunity to duck into the restroom.

Wanting to keep Chantal occupied, Zoe dived into questions about her daughter, Aurelie. Where did she study? Was she happy with her job? Had she thought about having kids? To Zoe, the questions seemed endless. Not that Aurelie's life was fascinating, but discussing it was an excellent diversion. The deeper they got into the conversation, the less Chantal would snoop around. By the time dinner was almost over, Zoe thought they had avoided any trouble. But she hadn't considered just how curious Chantal could be.

"Have you two thought about starting a family?"

Zoe and Johan were caught off guard, struggling to find words.

"Um..."

Their shared silence spoke volumes, but luckily, Roger was quick to step in and defuse the tension.

"Ease up on the interrogation, Chantal! They're our guests."

Roger motioned toward them, suggesting a change of scenery. "Come with me. I'll show you to your rooms."

25

Aurelie's room was at the end of the top hallway. It was big, with a new queen-sized bed, ready for when their daughter and son-in-law visited. But a slight musty smell showed they didn't come often.

Roger opened a closet door to reveal neatly stacked fresh towels and linens on one shelf, with Aurelie's old garments on another. She had left them behind when she moved to the city.

"Pick what you like," he offered, nodding toward the clothes. "She won't mind at all."

Zoe felt a momentary surge of relief. Noticing the sizes, she realized Aurelie was petite, just like her, which meant the outfits would fit perfectly. It was one less concern. Just then, Chantal walked in, carrying a pile of men's wear.

"These are too big for you," she said to Johan, "but they're clean."

As Chantal's gaze lingered, Zoe pretended to be captivated by a blouse.

"Come on, let's give them some space," Roger said, gently nudging his wife toward the door.

The moment the door clicked shut, Zoe let the hanger fall from her grasp. "I think I'm gonna be sick," she muttered, her strength fading as she slumped onto the bed.

Johan remained silent. She never thought she'd feel so relieved to be alone with him. The worst was behind them. By dawn, they would be miles away, leaving the unsuspecting couple safe and sound. Yet unease gnawed at Zoe. She had noticed Chantal's scrutinizing gaze throughout the evening. With her face potentially plastered all over the news, she couldn't help but think that Roger's wife must have spotted the striking similarity between her and the young woman everyone was searching for. Now, the big question was whether Johan—or whatever his name really was—had noticed, too. And as Zoe pondered this, she couldn't shake the feeling that 'Johan' sounded too specific to be made up. Maybe he was closer to recalling who he really was than she realized.

"Stay put," said the man who had been occupying her thoughts.

"Where are you going?" she whispered.

He moved down the hall without a word, prompting Zoe to follow.

"What's going on?" she whispered, catching up to him at the stairs.

He turned, placing a finger to his lips for silence. Below, Roger and Chantal's voices floated up, intermingling with the soft clatter of dishes. Zoe and Johan strained to listen, but there was no mention of the police, no connection made between Zoe and the missing woman. Just mundane chatter about furnace repairs and giving their daughter a call.

· · ·

"I prefer to sleep on the left side of the bed. Is that okay with you?" Johan said as they reentered the room. He locked the door, pocketing the key afterward.

Zoe sat on the edge of the bed, her gaze fixed on him as he set the gun on the nightstand. Their eyes met, and as if second-guessing himself, he tucked the gun back into his jeans. He waited until she reclined.

"God, it feels good to be in an actual bed again," he remarked, sinking into the sheets. As he settled, the bed shifted, drawing them closer.

When their arms brushed, Zoe stiffened in surprise.

"We've got a long drive ahead of us tomorrow, don't we?" Johan said, attempting to lighten the atmosphere and redirect their focus.

Zoe's thoughts raced. How was he planning to pay for gas? They were still a good three hours away from the Wolves Forest. He must have some sort of plan. Perhaps he was considering using Roger's truck tomorrow, after ensuring Roger and his wife wouldn't interfere. Or...

"You need to relax," he said, cutting through her thoughts.

She flinched. "What's in that forest?" she pressed.

"You've already asked."

"I know, but did our dinner conversation jog any memories for you?"

"Why would it? Oh... Because of the portrait?"

Zoe didn't believe the portrait was real. "No. You made that up."

"How can you be so certain?"

She rolled her eyes. "If I'd sat for a portrait, especially with someone named Albert, I would've remembered."

He seemed to mull it over. "Perhaps it was based on a photograph."

"So, you truly think you saw a drawing of me?"

He paused for a moment before responding. "Maybe not, but Chantal and Roger seemed convinced. That's all that matters." He took her hand, much like Chantal had at dinner. "That's quite the ring," he observed. "From Anthony?"

Fear tingled down Zoe's spine. "How do you know about him?"

"You talk in your sleep."

"I do?"

"You also snore a little, you know."

She stared at him, shocked. "Really?"

"Yeah. Anthony never told you?"

She felt a surge of panic and her thoughts spun. What else did he know about her life? "You've been spying on me! Have you? How long have you been planning to kidnap me?"

He placed a hand over her mouth, his ear turned toward the door, listening intently to ensure their hosts remained unsuspecting.

"Being honest here," he whispered, "you said his name several times in the car, when we spent the night by the barn."

Her eyes widened in realization, thinking back to her moment of vulnerability.

"If I remove my hand, will you promise not to scream?" he asked, his voice soft but steady.

She hesitated, then gave a small nod.

"Do you trust me?" he asked again, wanting to be certain.

Another nod.

He eased his hand away, giving her space as she swiftly wiped at her lips. His gaze lingered, and then he spoke, a hint of curiosity in his tone. "You keep fidgeting with it," he remarked, nodding toward the ring she was twirling.

"You make me uneasy," she admitted.

He sighed, his gaze shifting toward the nightstand. "Your husband's a cop, right? And that gun belongs to him. But you're a dancer. I saw something about it at the gas station."

"Just because I'm a dancer doesn't mean I can't use a gun."

Johan smirked. "Did Anthony teach you?"

Zoe remained silent, her heartbeat loud in her ears.

"Do you have kids?"

She blinked, taken aback. "Why?"

"I'm just curious. You didn't answer when Chantal asked at dinner," he pointed out, his gaze intent on her.

She had pondered the idea of children in the past, but it had been far from her mind lately. "No... not yet."

"Is it because of your career... or the tumor?"

She stiffened at his question. How much did people know about her condition?

"You brought it up before," he pointed out, noting her surprised expression. "Did you forget?"

"I was joking," she snapped, her voice sharper than she intended.

He looked at her, his gaze unyielding. "Brain tumors can cause seizures. Hence, the medication I found in your bag."

"Believe whatever you want."

"How long have you known?"

She attempted to steer the conversation away, but something in his eyes made her pause. Was that genuine concern she saw? "Why the act? Why pretend to care?"

"I'm not pretending. But if you don't want to talk about it, that's fine."

"It's been three months. Are you satisfied now?"

"What happened?"

She sighed, the weight of the memories pressing on her. "I had an accident during a ballet performance. I was the lead. My partner made a mistake, and I fell hard. They found the tumor in the ER. A low-grade glioma."

He offered a small, reassuring smile. "That's not cancer."

"No, but they've advised surgery. If I go through with it, I might never dance again."

He frowned, his expression contemplative. "Would it really be the end of the world?"

She looked at him as if he were from another planet, which, in a sense, was true. A swirl of emotions, from frustration to sadness, churned within her. What could he possibly know of the countless hours of training she put her body through, the pain, the tears, and the fierce competition with the other dancers in the company? Each of them, like her, dreamed of their shining moment in the spotlight, and the very thought of pausing even for a few months felt like an insurmountable setback. With a heavy sigh, she finally uttered, "You can't understand."

"Try me."

She took a moment to gather her thoughts. "Being on stage changes everything for me. The hurt and sadness just vanish. I get totally lost in the music, the dance, and the bond with the audience. It lifts me up. I can't live without it."

"It sounds like an addiction."

"This is my life," she said, pausing for a moment. "You think I'm crazy, right?"

He watched her intently. "You're full of passion," he said. "But is a dream worth your life?"

"I didn't say I'd never have the surgery. It's just that I believe it's too soon to end my career. I feel perfectly fine, so why shouldn't I dance as long as I don't show symptoms, at least until the usual retirement age for dancers?"

He looked taken aback. "You talk of retirement as if it's just around the corner."

She smiled. "Most dancers retire at forty-two. That gives me," she paused, calculating, "around fifteen more years to chase my dream."

"And if you don't make it?"

She fell silent. The idea of failure had no place in her plans.

"Tumors like yours... they're unpredictable."

His voice held a note of certainty, but she noticed a flicker of discomfort in his eyes as he spoke. He seemed more informed than the average person.

"Anyway, you should be hearing this from a specialist, not from me."

She exhaled. "For your information, I've got an appointment with a top neurosurgeon. They say he's the best in the field."

"And? What did he say?"

"I haven't seen him yet. My appointment got rescheduled last week."

"What about Anthony? What does he think?"

Her expression changed slightly. "I have told no one else. Anthony doesn't know."

"But he's your husband. Shouldn't he be the first to know?"

"Anthony... He's my brother-in-law."

Johan leaned in. "So you're not married?"

Drawing a deep breath, she replied, "This ring belonged to Gabriela."

"Why are you wearing your sister's wedding ring?"

She looked down, tracing the band with her finger. "You haven't connected the dots?"

He shifted in his seat. "I'm not seeing how I fit into this. Unless..." He paused, realization dawning, "it ties back to her disappearance?"

She nodded. "Each family received a unique keepsake. One got a pair of earrings. Another received a necklace. And the third, a bracelet."

"And your keepsake was this ring."

"It was sent to Anthony," she whispered, "a month after Gabby disappeared."

"I'm so sorry," he said, genuine sympathy in his voice.

She looked at him, taken aback. His genuine reaction momentarily made her doubt her initial assessment of him. "The postcards were the cruelest part. Each one was crafted in the victim's hand, bearing messages like 'I love you' and hinting at their locations."

"And your sister?"

Her eyes glistened, and she shook her head. "We only received the ring."

She studied the wedding band on her slender finger, noticing how out of place it looked.

"May I?" he asked gently.

She paused for a moment, then gave him her hand. "It's beautiful," he noted," but seems tight."

His touch made her flinch. "Numb?" he inquired.

"It seems so."

"The ring is restricting circulation. You should take it off."

She remembered her failed attempt to remove it earlier but didn't voice it.

"Let me help."

In the bathroom, he carefully applied soap to her finger. "This might be uncomfortable," he warned.

Their eyes locked. The compassion in his gaze was unsettling.

She nodded in agreement. The ring resisted for a moment before sliding off, making her wince.

"Are you okay?"

She merely nodded, examining her swollen finger.

He rinsed the ring and wiped it dry before handing it back to her. Zoe looked at the ring resting in the palm of her hand. Tears were streaming down her cheeks.

"Zoe..."

She brushed the tears away. "It's nothing," she murmured, diverting her gaze.

His fingers touched her face with unexpected gentleness. They felt too soft for someone accustomed to manual labor. She couldn't help but question her previous assumptions about him. Maybe the police were wrong, or maybe he wasn't the monster she'd believed him to be. She hoped for the latter. No man, not even her father, had treated her this way before. His touch sent shivers through her, a warmth enveloping her, comforting yet overwhelming.

"I want to kiss you."

She felt rooted to the spot as the words hung in the air. When he drew her close and their lips met, she found her resistance fading. She should have pulled away, fought him off, but she responded in kind, allowing his hand to slip beneath her shirt. But the image of Marianne Deconti flashed in her mind. She imagined those very hands strangling the nurse, and the sheer terror Marianne must have felt in her last moments.

"You're trembling," he observed, breaking their embrace.

It was more than a tremble; her entire body quaked. He

guided her to the bedroom, laying her down and covering her with a blanket.

"I'll be right back," he promised.

Zoe's heart raced.

"Don't hurt them," she whispered.

A flicker of pain crossed his eyes."I would never."

He left, leaving the door ajar. She feared for the old couple, and she had to act fast. Gathering her strength, she got up and tiptoed across the room. Instead of going downstairs, she stopped at the top of the staircase. She strained her ears, listening. No shouting. No gunshots. Just Chantal and Johan's voices, low and indistinct, from somewhere below.

Just as Zoe contemplated turning back, a spark of inspiration hit her. She ought to leave a clue. But first, she had to find something to write with.

When he came back, Zoe was lying in bed, breathing evenly, pretending to be calm. Hidden inside a novel on the nightstand was her hurried note. The book, "The Princess of Clèves", was an old school read left by Chantal and Roger's daughter. It was one of those books people keep for memories. Zoe had read it too. A tragic love story. She hoped this book might be her savior now.

Johan entered with a glass of water and a pill. "Here, drink this," he urged.

"What is it?" Zoe asked, her voice edged with suspicion.

"For your benefit," he assured her, his tone calm.

She looked doubtful, but he continued, "It's just a muscle relaxant. I don't want you to suffer any spasms. Your regular medication is in the car, but this will help for now. If you have doubts, ask Chantal. She provided it."

Zoe gave a slight shake of her head, clearly wanting to avoid further interactions with the other occupants of the house. Taking a deep breath, she swallowed the pill with a few sips of water.

"There you go," he said, setting the glass back on the nightstand.

His fingers brushed the edge of the book hiding her note. A jolt of panic raced through her. Did he see it? As he began to lift the book, her heart threatened to leap out of her chest. Desperate for a distraction, the first name that came to her mind spilled out, "Who's Camille?"

He shifted his gaze from the book to her.

"You've been mumbling names in your sleep too," she said, trying to keep her voice steady.

He paused, contemplating her words. "I don't know," he finally replied, his tone guarded.

She felt he was hiding something, but he was back to focusing on his book.

"I need to freshen up," she announced, hoping to buy herself some time.

His eyes locked onto hers, his focus sharp. "All right," he responded, holding her gaze for a moment longer than necessary. "Chantal mentioned the hot water is back on."

As she moved toward the bathroom, anxiety churned in her stomach. Would he sift through the book in her absence? She could feel the intensity of his gaze, and just as she was about to shut the bathroom door, his voice broke the silence.

"Just leave it cracked a bit. I promise I won't look."

"You're already looking," she retorted, her fingers trembling slightly as she began to undress.

There was something in his gaze—an intensity, a desire—an emotion she didn't expect from someone who despise women and revel in control and manipulation.

"Sorry." He looked away, but she caught the brief, lingering glance he stole before shifting his focus.

Zoe waited. He had moved out of her direct line of sight, but she hadn't heard the bedroom door open or close. He was still there. Nearby.

"You're a beautiful woman," his voice broke the silence. "Sorry if I made you uneasy."

She heard the distinct sound of the bathroom door closing, seemingly to offer her some semblance of privacy.

Her heart still raced as she stepped into the warm embrace of the shower. She'd yearned for this moment—a brief respite—yet found it unexpectedly challenging to lather the soap over her skin. "Hurry," she whispered, urging herself. As she tried to rinse off, an inexplicable lethargy overcame her movements. When the soap slipped from her grasp, she nearly lost her footing in her attempt to catch it. In her rush to dress, she put her t-shirt on inside out.

As she stepped out of the bathroom, hair still damp, she spotted him reclined on the bed. Against her better judgment, her eyes darted to the nightstand. The book was closed, but she wasn't certain he hadn't looked inside. Doing her best to appear nonchalant, she joined him as he pushed to make room for her. All Zoe wanted was to open that book to check if the note was intact. If only she had a moment alone in the room.

"Are you not going to shower?" she asked, trying to sound casual.

"Later." His gaze remained fixed on her, as though he expected something.

Suppressing a yawn, Zoe felt an unexpected surge of drowsiness, perhaps from the red wine Roger had offered them. Or could it be...

"What did you do to me?" she asked.

"Shh… Just relax. You need to rest."

He stroked her hair, in a manner one might use to calm a child. "Don't fight it, Zoe. It'll all be over soon."

She clung to consciousness a little longer, as the face of her captor faded into the dimness.

26

Zoe had just closed her eyes for a bit, her steady breathing indicating she was deep in sleep.

He lay down beside her, propped on an elbow, seizing the moment to observe her. For the first time, he could gaze at her uninterrupted, without her instinctively pulling away in fear.

He studied every feature of her face, inhaling her unique scent. His hand hovered above her, casting wavering shadows before gently brushing her forehead. His fingers glided down, tracing the outline of her nose and lingering on her lips, appreciating every tiny imperfection.

The portrait was real, not a figment of his imagination. He'd seen a detailed sketch of Zoe once before—an exact replica, down to the finest details, including the small chickenpox scar on her forehead. Yet, he couldn't recall when or where he'd stumbled upon it, nor could he remember the artist. But the emotions that had surged within him upon first seeing that drawing were now amplified by her tangible presence, making him feel as if this was all meant to be.

He covered her with a blanket and stood up. Grabbing

the clothes Chantal had provided, he made his way to the bathroom, leaving the door slightly open to keep an ear out for Sleeping Beauty.

As he wiped away the fog on the mirror, his reflection stared back at him. The scruff of his unshaved beard was soon hidden beneath a layer of shaving cream. Starting at his left cheek, he angled his face, guiding the razor with precision. However, on the third pass, the blade slipped, nicking his chin.

"Who the hell are you?" he whispered, staring at his bloody reflection.

The cut wasn't deep, but it bled profusely. The sight of the blood pooling in the sink triggered an unsettling sense of *déjà vu*, as if he had experienced this before. His head spun, and a wave of dizziness washed over him. Clutching the counter, he closed his eyes for a moment. Fragments of old memories, blurred and disjointed, rushed back to him. The nausea overwhelmed him, forcing his eyes open. The room appeared to spin around him. He took slow, deep breaths, willing his surroundings to stabilize. Gradually, everything came back into focus. He rummaged through the drawers, finding makeup remover pads to stem the bleeding. Turning on the tap, he watched the blood mix with the water, the sink slowly filling with a pale pink swirl. After a moment, he reached down and shut off the tap. The pipes groaned in response.

Zoe remained unconscious, her features softened in sleep. Without her usual guarded expression, she seemed younger, almost peaceful.

He slid back under the covers beside her, wishing he could surrender to sleep as she had. Yet, tasks awaited his attention. Given their life on the farm, he assumed Chantal and Roger probably wrapped up their days early. The hush that filled their home seemed to back up his guess.

He decided to bide his time, playing it safe before exploring the silent house. For now, he turned off the lights.

In the stillness of the room, he listened to Zoe's steady breathing. Earlier, she had asked, *"Who's Camille?"*

"Camille," he whispered into the darkness.

Suddenly, everything was bathed in a deep red.

27

When Zoe blinked her eyes open, Johan stood there, shirtless, gazing out the window as the first hints of dawn touched the fields.

A tattoo of massive wings sprawled across his back, extending from one shoulder blade to the other and spilling down his arms. When he moved, it appeared as though he might take flight, reminiscent of a creature from an ancient legend.

"Sleep well?" he asked, glancing her way.

Intricate tattoos of snakes adorned both his arms, their gaze seeming to fixate on her, almost daring her. With each muscle movement, they appeared to come to life.

He noticed her staring. "Everything all right?"

As he approached her, the illusion of the snakes tightening their coils around his arms grew more pronounced. When he reached out, she thought one might lash out at her. Their details captivated her: the glistening scales, the flick of a tongue, and the fangs ready to strike, poised to deliver venom. It struck her then—the sensation she felt was eerily similar.

She pulled back the sheet to inspect herself, prompting a chuckle from Johan.

"You drugged me?" she accused.

His face darkened. "Would you have preferred I tied you down?"

Attempting to get up, dizziness overwhelmed her. She steadied herself on him, noting the fresh scent of a recent shower. The thought crossed her mind he might have waited for the drug to work before cleaning up.

"You were intense last night," he remarked.

She braced herself, thinking he'd mention their kiss, but he sidestepped the topic.

"You needed the rest," he continued. "So did I."

Zoe's gaze landed on a chair, spotting clothes she recognized as those Chantal brought over. She then noticed the book on the nightstand, its cover turned face down. Did she leave it like that? Her memory was hazy.

"Your tattoos are incredible," she commented, hoping to lighten the mood. "They have a story, right?"

He shrugged, the wings on his back appearing to flutter. "Not sure. I wasn't even aware I had them."

As he began buttoning an oversized shirt, she found herself fascinated by his dexterous fingers.

"It must have taken a while," she observed. "Did it hurt?"

"If it did, I'm glad I don't remember. What about yours?"

She felt her cheeks warm up as she realized he'd noticed her small butterfly tattoo. It had been a painful yet memorable experience for her.

"Once was more than enough," she admitted.

He gave a nod, making it seem like he got the picture.

His oversized shirt draped over his jeans, conveniently hiding the gun he always carried. "When I check out my tattoos," he said after a beat, "I can't help but wonder if they're Albert's work—the same guy who did your portrait."

Zoe kept silent. She was curious about the alleged drawing, but she figured he was trying to mess with her head. He probably wanted to confuse her and make her feel safe, just like a snake does before it strikes. She didn't want to ask him about it and play into his game. What if there was no portrait, no mystery to crack, no truths waiting in the shadows? For all she knew, he was leading her into the woods with something much darker in mind. Her best hope was that Chantal or Roger would see her message.

As she dressed, she glanced at the book, eager for a chance to see if her note was still hidden. But she couldn't risk getting caught. Seizing a moment when he wasn't looking, she slid it under the pillow. She counted on Chantal's curiosity to drive her to look.

"We should get moving," she said.

On the first floor, the smell of breakfast filled the air: the familiar scent of coffee and toast. Tears welled up in Zoe's eyes.

"You okay, honey?" the elderly woman asked, her sharp eyes catching the emotion.

Zoe managed a weak smile. "It's just... Lately, even the smallest things make me tear up."

"You think you could be pregnant?"

Zoe and Johan exchanged a quick glance.

Chantal, noticing the moment, gave Zoe a comforting pat. "When I was pregnant with Aurelie, I cried all the time. Remember that, Roger?"

Roger rolled his eyes. "I hear you just fine, dear. No need to raise your voice."

Chantal and Roger, early birds, had finished their breakfast. The morning sun was barely up, but Zoe was eager to hit the road. Every minute they lingered put the farmers in danger.

Spreading out a map on the table, Roger showed their spot near Blois in the Loir-et-Cher region, nestled within the central part of France. "The nearest gas station is about six miles from here."

As Zoe helped Chantal with the dishes, she became lost in her thoughts. Even as Johan seemed focused on the map, she felt his watchful eyes on them. "Thanks for everything, Chantal."

Chantal waved it off. "It's no trouble."

Zoe hesitated, then added, "Sorry about the mess in the room."

She wanted to draw Chantal's attention to the book, hoping she would find the note tucked within the book during her cleaning. But with Johan watching closely, how could she? Even while he talked to Roger, she felt his gaze on her.

"Time to hit the road, *honey*," Johan said with a casual smile.

Taking a deep breath, she picked up the thermos of coffee and the bag of sandwiches. After giving Chantal a tight hug, Zoe climbed into the old truck. Now on Johan's lap, she found herself back in his arms, just like last night when he had kissed her. Yet today, he might be the one to end her life.

The drive back was faster in the daylight. Fields stretched on as far as she could see. They were like oceans of plowed earth, frozen and glowing in the tall sunlight.

The Toyota was right where they'd left it the previous

night. A thin layer of frost on its surface was a stark reminder of their luck in finding Roger.

As he filled the tank, the farmer mentioned how temperatures often dropped below freezing at night. He emptied one gas can, then another. "This'll get you to the station," he said, handing them a map and giving a confident nod.

After a round of hugs and goodbyes, they drove off. Zoe looked back to see Roger waving. As they moved farther away, he looked smaller, merging with the backdrop. She felt she might not see him again.

28

─────

Pierre Valmeur paid the cabby and stepped out. Slipping on his trusty old backpack, he paused for a moment, letting the weight of his decision sink in as he sized up the police station—it had clearly seen better days. Doubt gnawed at him. Part of him wanted to turn on his heel and leave. Perhaps he was in over his head. Maybe he should just let things happen the way they were supposed to. But then, the gravity of what was at stake tugged at his conscience, and he pushed that thought away.

With renewed determination, Pierre made his way toward the entrance. The hustle of the precinct surrounded him. Officers in uniform shuffled people about, and he soon found himself in a queue with about ten others, bracing for a long wait.

"Excuse me," Pierre called out, trying to sound confident as he addressed a nearby officer. "Is there a detective I can speak with?"

She shot him a quick, almost dismissive look. "Join the line if you have something to report."

Pierre hesitated. "It's about that missing woman—the one everyone's talking about. I think I know something."

The atmosphere shifted as a few officers moved closer.

"Repeat that," one of them demanded, eyebrows raised in a mix of suspicion and intrigue.

"My son's missing too," Pierre rushed to explain, his voice cracking. "He's been acting strange, and I fear they're connected somehow."

Pushing through the growing crowd, Inspector Dorsey held up a photo. It was of Marianne Deconti, the nurse who had disappeared. "Is this her?"

Taking a moment, Pierre squinted at the photo. "Can I take a closer look?"

After a slight hesitation, Dorsey handed over the picture. As Pierre's eyes widened, his face draining of color. "It's too late for her," he whispered.

Dorsey's eyes narrowed. "What do you mean?"

"She's no longer with us." Pierre traced the edges of the image, his eyes distant. "But I believe I can take you to her."

29

It's Zoe. Johan's got me.
Not my husband. Captor.
He's armed. Dangerous.
We're headed to the Wolves Forest, Normandy.
If you're reading this now—DON'T step in. He'll kill us all.

30

As the sun rose, the car sped down the highway. Zoe had been watching the clock since leaving the farmhouse, and only fifteen minutes had gone by. She wondered if Chantal had found her note yet, a thought that gave her hope. She imagined the old woman, confused, finding the book in the messy bed. She'd opened it. Curiosity would win, and she'd read the message. Learning the truth about her overnight guests would shock her. Zoe could almost hear her calling out in panic, *"Roger! Oh, hell... Roger!"* She imagined Chantal's voice trembling—a sound Roger had never heard before. *"I knew it! I thought I recognized her,"* she would say, scared. Reading the note over and over, Roger would feel his heart racing, realizing the danger they had been in. He would call the police right away. Soon, their tale would be all over town, on local news, and maybe even national TV. They might even make some money from recounting their ordeal, a slight consolation amidst the turmoil.

Zoe darted a glance at the rearview mirror. The road behind them seemed to melt into the morning mist. Were they being followed? She strained her ears, listening for the distant wail of a police siren or the sight of a roadblock up ahead. Worst-case scenario? A full-on police brigade waiting at the edge of the forest.

"Johan?"

"Yeah?"

"How much longer?"

"Why?"

"Because the sooner we get there, the sooner this hell is over."

He shot her a look, his intense blue eyes sending shivers down her spine.

"By noon."

As he skimmed through the radio stations, she tensed up, half-expecting the airwaves to be saturated with news of her abduction. Instead, a familiar tune cut through the tension, lingering as he ceased the search, letting the music fill the car. Zoe shut her eyes and relaxed into the seat, a spontaneous smile gracing her lips. She loved that song.

"I know what you're up to," he blurted.

A wave of fear washed over Zoe.

"What are you talking about?"

As he drove, Johan reached behind him, pulling something from his pocket.

Zoe's heart sank, feeling as if her last lifeline had been severed. He held a crumpled piece of paper aloft—the note she had hidden in the book. Without thinking, she undid her seatbelt, fingers brushing the door handle, poised for a desperate escape.

The car lurched as he reached out to stop her. "Are you crazy? You could kill yourself!"

Screeching to a halt, Johan pulled the car over, gravel flying.

"If I'm going down," Zoe shot back, "I'm doing it my way!"

She jumped out of the car and took off down the road. She hadn't gotten far when she felt him right on her heels.

"You had this coming!" he snapped, grabbing her arm.

Zoe fought back with all her might. There was no way she was getting back in that trunk. She was done. She would've thrown herself in front of any passing car, but the road was deserted—it was just them.

After what felt like an eternity, he released his grip on her. "Fine, Zoe. We're done here." He sat down hard on the curb. "You can go. You're free."

Was he serious? His eyes darkened, making it hard to read his thoughts.

"I'm not buying it."

He sighed. "It's a long walk to the nearest place. I'll be gone by the time you get there. Disappeared. You will never know who I really am. Hell, maybe I won't either. Or..."

The sharp call of a crow broke the quiet. Zoe shivered, wrapping her arms tightly around herself.

"Or—what?"

He stood up.

"Come with me, take a shot at the truth. Decide, but do it now."

He got back in the car and started it up, the exhaust clouding in the cool morning air.

Zoe couldn't think straight. Save herself or finally get some answers?

The car moved, its tires crunching on the roadside gravel.

"Hold up!"

He hit the brakes so hard the taillights lit up like a predator's eyes.

She yanked open the passenger door and locked eyes with him, her voice steady and resolute. "I'll go with you, but on one condition."

He looked at her with caution. "What do you want?"

"No trunk. No backseat."

A hint of amusement flickered in his eyes. "Sounds like two conditions to me."

She stared him down. "And I'm not tied up."

"That makes three," he shot back with a smirk.

"Your move."

He looked like he might argue, but she wasn't backing down.

"If I'm taking the risk, you are too. I stay free in the car."

His smile widened, and a dimple made a brief appearance. Across his cheeks, the faint shadow of stubble was starting to form.

"Deal."

She blinked in surprise. "Really?"

"For a moment there, I thought you'd ask for your weapon back."

"And if I had?"

He shrugged. "Who knows? Maybe."

She sat back, her trust in him still wavering.

"Don't give me that look. I promise you won't regret it."

Zoe wasn't so sure about that.

31

Marianne Deconti lay sprawled under a plastic tarp in the middle of the barn, her head still on her shoulders—a stark deviation from the Reaper's gruesome signatures. Around her, the scene was rife with clues. The forensic team would be busy for hours.

Pierre Valmeur was standing beside a police car, under the officers' watchful eyes.

"I'm not sure if I should thank you or arrest you," said Inspector Dorsey as he walked up.

"It might be too soon for thanks. As for arresting me, you decide. I've told you everything. It might sound unbelievable, but it's true. Check my story if you need to, but it will hold up."

Anthony was watching from a distance, close enough to hear them. There was something unsettling about this stranger.

"What about your son? Are you sure he's with Zoe?" he asked.

Valmeur's eyes met his. They were deep-set and seemed to draw everything in. Anthony felt he could see his own reflection in them if he'd stare for too long. He tried to shake off his unease with a cough, but Valmeur's gaze didn't waver. It was intense, like a sharpshooter focusing on a target. Even from a distance, Anthony could feel it.

"I'm as sure of it as I am of seeing you before me," Valmeur answered, as if he could read Anthony's mind. "We need to act now, or I'm afraid worse is coming."

32

———

Zoe straightened up, her eyes on the road. It seemed to stretch on forever, but a recent sign showed they were close. Now, tall pines stood where open fields used to be, casting long shadows across the road. Every so often, a car would come around the bend, its headlights cutting through the dim.

The road wound its way through the forest, and Zoe caught sight of a stream. It sparkled, reflecting the sky. She couldn't help but stare; the setting was breathtaking, eerily similar to the other sites the killer had chosen.

"You have arrived at your destination," the car's navigation chimed as they approached an intersection. They veered onto a dirt track. The car jolted, its shocks groaning. Zoe gripped the door handle, her stomach churning. The landscape outside became a blur. As they delved deeper, the forest grew denser. Trees, now seeming more menacing, leaned over their path with branches scratching the car, as if trying to stop them. Mud splashed onto the windshield, which the wipers struggled to clear.

"Look out!" Zoe shouted, spotting a fallen tree blocking their way.

Johan swerved, missing the obstacle but veering off the track. "Damn!"

He tried to reverse, revving the engine, but the wheels spun in place. They were stuck.

Zoe leaned back. "Now what?"

"We walk." Johan reached for the glove box.

"What are you looking for?" she asked.

"A flashlight," he said, sifting through the jumble Marianne Deconti had accumulated over the years.

"It's not in the trunk. I checked."

Johan gave her a sharp look. Their eyes met before Zoe's gaze shifted upward to the looming clouds. It wasn't a flashlight they'd need soon, but an umbrella.

"I should've picked one up at the gas station," he muttered.

Zoe tilted her head his way. "Did you check under the seats?"

His eyebrow rose. "Under the seats?"

"In my car, that's where misplaced items usually end up."

Johan gave up on the glove box and started checking beneath his seat. Meanwhile, Zoe searched under hers.

"Found it!" Zoe held out a big flashlight. It was heavy, filled with lots of AAA batteries.

Johan looked stunned, as if he expected to be hit. But Zoe didn't even think about it. She wasn't scared anymore.

"Here you go," she said, passing it to him.

He took it, turning it over in his hands. When he found the switch and flicked it on, the light was so bright that Zoe had to squint. He clicked the switch off, and the cabin went dark again.

"GPS says half a mile more in this direction."

"And after that?" she asked, as he exited the car.

He stepped out, silent. Zoe grabbed her jacket from the back and caught up. They walked around around the tree's broad trunk and kept going for ten minutes until Johan stopped. "It should be right around here," he murmured.

Looking around, Zoe saw no difference from one direction to the next. It was all dense, unmarked forest. "Are we lost?" she ventured.

Johan appeared preoccupied, his focus elsewhere. Despite the lingering daylight, he flicked on the flashlight, and the trees flanking their path were suddenly etched in stark relief. Branches stirred in the restless wind, twisted like arthritic fingers, each one seeming to beckon or warn. "This way," the gnarled limbs of the left-hand trees appeared to urge, while their counterparts on the right pointed with twig-like fingers, insinuating an opposite course. Johan advanced, the flashlight's beam cutting ahead of him, sweeping across the underbrush. Within moments, he halted, a note of triumph in his voice. "I've found it!"

In the torch's beam, tiny spots appeared to hover at the same height, forming a line that extended deeper into the woods.

"What's that?" Zoe asked.

"I don't know," Johan replied, lowering the torch. As soon as the light moved away from the spots, they vanished from sight. "We need to take a closer look."

Avoiding a dip in the ground, Johan climbed a fern-covered rise. Zoe struggled to follow; her dress shoes offering little traction on the soft ground.

"Here, give me your hand," Johan said, glancing back.

She reached out, and with his help, joined him at the top.

At the forest's edge, Johan flashed the torch ahead. Light glided up a tree trunk, revealing a perfectly round shape. Away from the flashlight's beam, the disk blended with the tree bark. "That's odd," Johan muttered, stepping closer.

"Wait, don't touch it!" Zoe's warning came too late as Johan's fingers already blurred what might have been fingerprints. Her eyes widened with realization. It was clear he'd been here before, using these glowing markers as breadcrumbs to guide his way. But to where?

Peeling off the disk, Johan revealed it was no more than a pin, the kind readily available in the camping aisles of sporting goods stores.

"Can I see it?" She asked, reaching out.

"Of course," he said, placing it in her hand.

She studied it in her palm. "These didn't just appear out of nowhere. Someone placed them here."

"I didn't," Johan insisted.

"Then how did you know what to look for?" Zoe pressed.

"I just... did."

Zoe's eyed him with suspicion. "That's not an answer. You were scouring the forest with your flashlight with too much purpose. It's like you were hunting for something specific."

He sighed, avoiding her gaze. "You got me. I had a hunch that I'd find a sign, something leading me in the right direction."

Shining the flashlight further into the forest, Zoe felt an unease creep over her. The woods were dense, with no discernible path, but he appeared determined to take her deeper. Images of a dug grave flashed in her mind.

"Zoe?" His voice pulled her back. "You can stay in the car if you're uncomfortable," he suggested.

"What makes you think I won't report you immediately?"

He shrugged. "By the time anyone figures out where I've gone, I'll have discovered who I am. That's all that matters to me. The consequences are secondary."

Zoe hesitated. "Give me back my gun, and I'll come with you."

He shook his head. "You'll get it back when it's time."

"Why not now? Are you scared?"

He feigned contemplation. "Of being shot in the back by a pretty woman before I even figure out who I am? Sure."

"I wouldn't shoot you without a good reason."

"Fear is a good enough reason, and you're definitely still scared of me."

She flinched when he reached out, tucking a stray strand of her hair behind her ear.

"It's a risk I can't afford right now," he conceded. "I've already explained why." He took a deep breath. "I'm sure the answers lie ahead."

The flashlight's beam caught multiple glinting specks, their glow resembling the watchful eyes of unseen predators in the dark.

33

The leaves crunched beneath their feet, remnants of the past fall. Each step snapped the brittle twigs underneath.

"Are we there yet?" Zoe asked, her breath visible in the chilly air.

The temperature had dropped since they veered off the main path, and the fog, weaving its way through the naked tree branches, had grown denser.

"It's hard to see," she observed.

"Just stay close, okay?" Johan replied.

Picking up her pace, she tried to keep up. Soon, however, Johan's silhouette became fainter, almost swallowed by the mist.

"Johan?"

Her voice sounded muffled, as if smothered by a pillow. With her vision compromised, she focused on her other senses: the musty scent of wet soil and the elusive noises of the forest.

"Johan?" she called out again.

His warm, strong hand gripped hers. He pulled her

closer, and for a fleeting moment, she felt a reassuring sense of safety.

"Told you to stay close," he muttered.

She was ready to snap back, but he silenced her with a gesture. His head turned slowly, scanning their surroundings.

"Do you hear that?" he whispered.

She strained her ears but heard nothing.

"Look," he gestured.

Zoe squinted, trying to see what he was pointing at. She took a step closer for a better view, but a twig beneath her foot snapped. The creature, a deer, turned its head in their direction. Their eyes locked. Having grown up in the city, she'd never been this close to wildlife. It filled her with a sense of wonder, akin to encountering a unicorn. However, as quickly as it had appeared, the deer darted away.

"Let's follow it!" Johan urged, gripping her hand.

Her heart pounded as he led her forward. They were veering off the main trail, onto a narrower path devoid of the reassuring glow-in-the-dark markers. Johan moved briskly, and with each step, Zoe found it harder to keep up. Exhausted and battered, she felt her strength fading.

"I can't keep going!" she gasped, on the verge of collapsing.

Johan halted—not because of her. Just a few feet away, the deer stood frozen, two arrows protruding from its hindquarters, its fur stained with dark rivulets of blood.

"Stay put," Johan instructed.

Zoe backed up against a tree. As if she had the energy to run off! She was more likely to collapse or freeze before finding her way back. Her attention was solely on the injured creature, its chest heaving, eyes wide with fear. If it had the strength, she knew it would have bolted.

Sensing its defenselessness, the deer threw its head back, emitting a haunting cry that sent shivers down Zoe's spine.

"Don't hurt it," she wanted to shout, but her words were trapped in her throat. But Johan approached it with gentleness, guiding it to the ground as he wrapped his arm around its neck. In moments, the creature lay still, its eyes shut, its breathing calm and steady. There was a resignation in its posture, a vulnerability in its bared neck. Zoe shuddered.

"What are you going to do with it?" she asked, her voice a whisper.

Johan remained silent, stroking the animal's coat. Could he actually enjoy its suffering? It didn't seem that way. Or perhaps she just wanted to believe he didn't.

Suddenly, a sound startled them all—the injured deer, Johan, and Zoe. Johan motioned for her to be quiet and signaled toward a tree large enough to conceal them. Pressed together, they could observe without being seen. Emerging from the mist, a silhouette took shape: a dog with short brown fur and droopy ears, trailed by a man and a young boy in hunting gear. The boy, no older than twelve, held his bow with proud.

"There it is, Pa! Knew I hit it!" he exclaimed.

The dog wagged its tail excitedly, then approached to sniff the deer's wounds. The father came forward, his expression stern as he shooed the dog away. He then knelt beside the deer, his stance mirroring Johan's from moments earlier. Yet, his intent was starkly different, a distinction clear to Zoe.

He straightened. "Get over here," he commanded the boy.

The boy's smile faded, replaced by guilt. He recognized his father's tone. Walking over, he took the knife his father offered—a foot-long blade, gleaming sharp, with old blood-stains marking its edge.

"Do it. Finish what you started."

The boy's hand shook as he held the knife, his face pale. Shooting from a distance was one thing; up close, feeling the fight and hearing the distressed cries—it was entirely different.

"It's your mess," his father said. "Next time, aim better."

He pressed the knife handle into the boy's hand. The weapon felt much bigger and heavier in the child's grip.

"Come on! We don't have all day!"

The boy crouched beside the deer, their eyes locking. His hand trembled.

"I... I can't," he whispered.

His father snatched the knife back. "Should've brought your sister."

He positioned himself to end the deer's life.

"Hold it!" Johan's voice cut through the fog like a bullet.

"Who's there?" the man demanded, his knife poised.

Zoe realized the fog concealed their exact location.

"Let the deer go!"

"This is our kill. Get your own," the man retorted, knife still at the ready.

"He's injured, not beyond saving," Johan argued. "I can help him. Your shots missed vital areas. He might pull through."

"You think I'll just hand him over? Think again."

"You're breaking the law!" Johan countered.

The man laughed, "Which law?"

"I didn't see any signs indicating a hunt was underway. So, I assume what you're doing isn't permitted."

A scornful smile stretched across the hunter's face. "You're mistaken, my friend. Putting down a wounded animal isn't the same as hunting it. I'm within my rights. Now, step aside, or—"

"You'll shoot me too?"

The man's smirk sharpened. "How about you mind your own business and stick to picking berries?"

Johan persisted. "He's just hurt."

But the man was unyielding. "If it can't escape, it's as good as dead."

"Let me get those arrows out, at least. If it doesn't run, then fine."

The hunter paused, then challenged, "Show me your game warden badge or scram!"

As he returned to his task, a metallic click froze him in his tracks.

Johan stepped forward, the Sig Sauer in his hand. "Drop the knife."

Zoe added her voice, "Do what he says."

Surprised to see her, especially in her urban attire, the hunter stuttered, "Who are you people?"

His son clung to him.

"It's none of your business," Johan responded. "Leave while you still can."

Fear etching into their faces, they turned and fled.

Zoe watched as the man and his son disappeared into the fog, torn between relief and regret, wishing she had followed them.

Johan turned his attention back to the injured deer. "I'm so sorry," he whispered, his grip tightening around one arrow.

With a swift motion, he yanked it out. The deer, shaky yet still able, stood. Johan managed to remove the second arrow before the animal vanished into the mist.

Zoe approached, her eyes brimming with tears. "That was—"

"Stupid?" Johan interjected, his tone filled with self-reproach as he leaned the arrows against a tree trunk. Was he worried that someone might get injured if they stepped on the sharp points?

"That's not the word I was looking for," she replied, her gaze still on him.

"But it was stupid." he persisted. "And reckless. What if that man reports us? He probably recognized you. We need to…"

His voice trailed off, his expression turning distant.

"We need to do—what?" Zoe pressed, her voice filled with urgency.

Johan, staring at his blood-stained hands, seemed lost in thought, his mind evidently somewhere far away from their present worries.

"Johan?" she called out again, her voice softer this time, reaching for his attention.

He finally met her gaze, but his eyes seemed to look right through her. As if entranced, he took a step forward into the thick fog, leaving Zoe standing alone, uncertainty washing over her about what to do next.

34

———————

The mist wrapped him in a shroud-like embrace, yet his mind remained razor sharp. Around him, a winter's chill clung to the air. But despite the bare branches reaching above, his mind's eye painted a dense canopy, draping the forest floor in a cool, dim glow that hinted at a long-gone summer's day.

A young woman, appearing to be in her twenties, walked ahead of him. Her dress, torn up to her thighs, revealed cuts and scrapes from the unruly underbrush. From his vantage point, he could only catch fleeting glimpses of her disheveled blonde hair, now tangled with dirt and leaves. He felt a strange familiarity with her, her name just beyond his grasp. Who was she? The question nagged at him, lingering on the edge of his memory, and he believed that if he just kept following her, the answer would reveal itself.

Her earlier loud sobs had subsided to shaky breaths. Her wrists were bound, and he held the other end of the rope, giving it a jerk if she moved too quickly and a sharp snap to urge her forward. Every so often, he would push her, taking perverse pleasure in watching her stumble. It was their macabre dance.

But soon, in a more secluded spot, he yanked her to a stop.

"It's here," he declared, his voice anchoring him firmly back in the present.

Zoe scanned her surroundings, seeing nothing remarkable, only isolation.

"Nobody would've heard her," Johan said, his voice blending with the rustling trees. "Her screams? Gone, just like that."

"Who are you talking about?"

Johan pointed, and Zoe strained to see what he saw, but her eyes only found a pile of leaves at the base of a tree, marked by a cross—possibly left by another hunter or hiker.

"I really don't wanna know what's under there," he confessed, his voice laced with unease. "But if it's what I think, then you were right." He nervously ran his fingers through his messy hair, his eyes darting around as if expecting something to spring up. "I can't trust myself, Zoe. The thought of hurting you? I can't live with that."

Her shock was palpable when he handed her the gun. He ensured she had a firm grip before taking a step back, nodding for her to aim. And she complied. "This is it," he whispered, his voice laden with defeat.

With a mix of care and reverence, he began to uncover what lay beneath the leaves. But then he froze, his hands revealing a bloated face, half-buried in the mud.

"Who is it?" Zoe whispered, peering over his shoulder.

He couldn't recall her name; it just kept slipping through

his mind. "I don't know yet," he muttered to himself, his focus returning to the meticulous task at hand.

Johan removed the last few inches of earth, a wave of horror washed over him. Before his eyes lay a head—a young woman's head with blond hair. Trembling, he hesitated for a moment before gathering the courage to touch her, his hand resting on her blistered skin. As he did, he murmured, "Leanne."

As Johan continued to stare at the face, his demeanor changed slightly. His eyes clouded over, filled with a tumultuous mix of recognition and confusion. He turned to Zoe, then back to the body, his gaze intense, as though he were seeing both for the very first time. "It's... you?" he uttered, his voice trembling—not just from shock, but from something deeper, something indiscernible that Zoe couldn't quite put her finger on.

He sprang to his feet.

A chill skittered down Zoe's spine. "Stay back!" she commanded as she braced herself, the Sig Sauer aimed at his chest. "Don't move!"

But he did move.

In a split second, a gunshot thundered, its roar echoing through the forest, sending birds bursting into flight from the treetops.

35

—————

Johan's breath caught in his throat as the shot rang out. Glancing down, he half-expected to see a dark stain spreading across his shirt, but there was nothing. The bullet had merely grazed him, burying itself in a tree instead.

"Don't move, or I swear the next one won't miss!" Zoe's voice shook, her gun still aimed directly at him.

Johan slowly raised his hands, trying to appear non-threatening. "Okay, okay. I won't move. Can I talk?"

"What's left to say?" Her eyes, large and dark-brown verging on black, reflected the horror he had instilled in her —or was it a glint of sadness?

He felt a deep, painful pang in his chest, more intense than he had expected when he'd first seen her portrait. "There's a lot to say… if you'd just hear me out."

His voice was earnest, pleading.

Tears shimmered in her eyes, lending them a glistening quality. "I know all I need to know."

"You really don't." Had it not been for the gun pointed at him, Johan would have pulled her into his arms, confessing everything, whispering the incredible story meant only for her ears. "I... There's so much I want to say. I don't even know where to start."

Zoe lifted her chin in defiance. "How about starting with your real name?"

Johan hesitated, grappling with the decision to reveal his true identity. He knew that doing so would open a floodgate of questions. Questions he wasn't prepared to answer. Realizing the need for time, he decided to craft a believable story first. He was aware that honesty in this situation could lead straight to a psychiatric ward. And that was a risk he wasn't willing to take.

"Johan... Dupuis," he finally said, inwardly cringing at his lack of creativity.

Zoe's gaze bored into him, skeptical. "Did you kill Marianne Deconti?" she cut in.

The question stole his breath. "No, I didn't kill her."

"And her?" Zoe gestured toward the grave he had been digging up earlier. "Didn't kill her either, I suppose."

Johan shivered, the image of the unearthed woman flashing in his mind. He shook his head, unable to speak.

"You knew her, didn't you?" Zoe pressed. "Who is she?"

He swallowed hard, his throat tight.

"And my sister? Where is she? Buried in these woods too?"

"Your sister?" Confusion etched his face.

"Answer me!"

"I don't know anything about your sister—"

"You're lying!"

"I swear, I'm not. Look, you're making me nervous. Could you lower the gun? I won't try anything, promise."

"For two days, I've watched you walk in the footsteps of a serial killer. So, excuse me if I don't take your word for it."

"Two days?" Johan frowned, weary of the lies. He yearned to come clean, to unburden himself.

"Okay, I'll come clean. About everything. My real name, my job, who Leanne is, how I found her, how I met Marianne—and her killer—and eventually to you. But you might not believe a word I say."

"Just spit it out."

"The thing is, some of it sounds—crazy."

She furrowed her brow. "Crazy? What do you mean?"

"Have you ever sought out mediums to find your sister?"

Zoe paused, taken aback. "You mean—you're a psychic?"

"No... Well, it's not that simple. I promise to explain everything, but first, I need you to answer my question."

"You're making fun of me?"

"I'm dead serious. There's no shame in it. Many families do it when the police come up empty."

She sighed, visibly frustrated. "It doesn't matter whether I did or not, since you claim you're not a psychic!"

"I said it's complicated."

"Then explain!"

"There are layers to this you wouldn't understand right away."

"Enough!" Zoe steadied her gun, ready to fire. "Answer my questions. Now!"

"Okay, okay." Johan said quickly, but then he turned his head to the left. "Did you hear that?"

"No. Nothing... Trying to distract me?"

Ignoring her, Johan focused on the sounds of the forest. He hadn't imagined it. Someone was approaching. "There, did you hear it?"

This time, Zoe nodded. "Dogs barking."

And there were voices, too, growing louder. Two men, perhaps more, were drawing near.

"I can't be found here…"

"Sounds like a guilty conscience to me."

Johan moved toward her, and Zoe raised her gun again. "Don't make me shoot!"

He stopped. "You have to let me go."

"I swear, if you move, I'll shoot. I mean it."

"I doubt it." Johan could hear the tremor in her voice.

"You don't know me," she said, her hands shaking as she tried to steady the weapon. "You have no idea what I'm capable of."

Now the voices were clear.

"I'm at your mercy," Johan said, his heart pounding. He took a step, then another, until the gun barrel was pressed against his chest. According to the prediction, Zoe would pull the trigger any moment now. "No escaping fate," Johan muttered. "Do what you have to."

Zoe's eyes widened in astonishment as he slowly pushed the gun aside and leaned in.

"I'm not him," he whispered, and then he was gone, disappearing into the forest.

36

———————

"Where the hell did he go?!"

The urgency in the police officer's voice reached Zoe, even through the ringing in her ears. Nearing the point of fainting, she slid to the ground. How had she let him slip away? Sweat clung to her forehead, and her heart pounded, echoing the fear and confusion in her mind. She looked at the gun clutched in her hand.

"Hey! Lucky's found something!"

The voice belonged to the hunter, the same one she and Johan had bumped into earlier in the woods. Zoe turned to see Lucky, the basset hound, scratching at the soil, letting out sharp whines. At first, she assumed Lucky had found the body Johan had discovered earlier. But the dog wasn't digging in the right place. Dirt spewed as he burrowed deeper.

"Damn it!" the officer shouted. "Call off your dog! He might destroy the evidence!"

Drawn to the commotion, Zoe joined the two men. A few feet down, a pair of eyes stared back at her, leaving her feeling as if the very earth was pulling her into its depths.

37

"Hey, can you hear me?"

Zoe blinked several times before the figure beside her sharpened into view. A man in his forties, wearing a police uniform, looked at her with concern.

"I'm Detective Florian," he said, as if answering the unspoken question in her eyes.

"Where am I?"

"In an ambulance."

She tried to sit up, but a sharp headache pinned her back to the stretcher.

"You fainted. Don't you remember?"

Zoe had no intention of remembering, yet images flooded her mind, conjured up by her subconscious. "Gabriela... Where is she?"

The officer furrowed his brows. "Gabriela?"

"My sister. She was in the woods."

He handed her a tissue. "Are you referring to the second victim?"

Nodding, Zoe wiped the tears off her face, took a deep

breath, and tried to compose herself. "Where is she?" she asked. "Where did you take her?"

The officer shook his head. "A Europol team is en route. The area's been secured for now."

Zoe tried to sit up again, gripping the sides of the stretcher. "You left her there!"

He gently pushed her back down. Exhausted, she didn't resist and closed her eyes for a brief moment.

"Why do you think it's your sister?"

"Because she disappeared, just like those other women."

"When was this?"

"Last year."

Surprise flickered across the officer's face.

"What?" she pressed.

"Well, the victims you found have been dead for only two or three months at most. I'm no coroner, but..."

"I know what I saw!"

"What you saw was a decomposed body," he countered. "I don't think you could've recognized your sister, or anyone for that matter, in that state."

Zoe turned away, shivering at the memory of the barely recognizable, worm-eaten face peeking through the soil.

"You were in shock," he continued, "and you still are."

Torn, Zoe looked away. After spending so long trying to find her sister, she thought she'd be ready to face the truth. She had no doubt Gabriela was dead, had given up hope of finding her alive. But now, faced with this reality, she felt unprepared and vulnerable. Families of the missing often say they'd rather know the truth, even if it meant learning their loved one had suffered. Zoe used to think she felt the same way. Now, she dreaded confronting that reality.

"But you're right," he added after a moment of silence,

"we can't rule anything out. We'll know more in a few hours."

Zoe continued to face away as she heard him stand and shuffle around at the back of the vehicle.

"Here, the paramedics prepared this for you," he said, sitting back down beside her.

In his large hand was a cup of water and a small white pill.

"What is it?"

"It'll help you relax while we take you to the hospital."

She took the cup and drained it, but didn't take the pill. It reminded her of the night at the farm, when Johan had given her a sleeping pill, pretending it was a painkiller. Why did everyone want to drug her? "I need to stay alert," she said, handing back the empty cup. "And I don't need to go to a hospital. I'm fine. Johan didn't hurt me."

"Johan? Is that what you called him?"

His gaze bore into hers, making her shift in discomfort.

"Yes... no... I mean, it doesn't matter. I doubt that's his real name, anyway."

"Hmm."

"What?"

"You spent forty-eight hours alone with this man..."

"What's your point?"

He pressed on. "Well, sometimes in situations like that, emotional bonds can form between the hostage and their captor."

She bristled. Would he say the same if she were a man? She doubted it. "Are you suggesting I fell in love with him?"

"Love is a strong word. I was thinking more along the lines of sympathy, maybe even empathy."

He was referring to Stockholm Syndrome, of course. Why hadn't she thought of that?

"There's no shame in it. It's a normal reaction, probably what kept you alive."

She looked away, unable to meet his eyes. What would he think if he knew she was protecting a monster? A man destined to spend the rest of his days in a cell, since he couldn't be sentenced to death? Yet, that's exactly what she had done. She let him escape. And the worst part? She wasn't sure she'd do anything differently if given the chance again.

As soon as Zoe walked in, the precinct buzzed with attention. Everyone, from uniformed cops to those in plain clothes, turned to stare.

Detective Florian and another cop were at her side, escorting her across the room. Her steps left faint traces of dirt on the shiny floor.

They entered an office, pervaded by the potent smells of sweat, cheap aftershave, and old tobacco.

"Make yourself comfortable," the detective instructed, lingering in the doorway. "I'll be right back."

Unsure of what 'comfortable' meant in this situation, Zoe decided to sit. Standing felt too exhausting. She settled into the only available chair beneath a window. Though it let in daylight, it did little to brighten the gloomy office. A lone calendar hung on the wall, serving as the room's only decoration. When Detective Florian returned, Zoe had to summon all her strength not to ask him to leave the door open.

"Sorry to keep you waiting," he said, moving past her to sit behind the desk. He booted up a computer, its screen hidden from Zoe's view. After a moment of typing, he seemed satisfied and turned his full attention to her. "Would you like something to drink?"

Zoe shook her head.

"Are you sure?"

She nodded.

Mistaking her silence for discomfort, the officer tried to put her at ease. "You've been through quite an ordeal. But you're safe now, and that's what matters."

"An ordeal," Zoe echoed.

She felt the officer pat her hand, like one might do to console a child.

"You look pale. You should eat something." He stood and fetched a plastic container from a small fridge across the room, offering it to her. "Here," he said, "My wife made it."

Zoe stared at the sandwich wrapped in plastic. "Thank you, but I'm not hungry."

He unwrapped it nonetheless . "You're missing out. It's delicious." He tore off a piece of bread and ate it, sighing with satisfaction.

Zoe's stomach tightened, but not from hunger. Memories of Johan flooded her mind, appearing at the oddest times. She recalled another sandwich, one he'd made for her in the basement where she'd been held captive. He'd broken it into pieces, feeding her like one might feed a newborn. She could still taste the bread, feel his fingers brushing against her lips, and see the intensity in his eyes as he assured her he wasn't the monster the European police were after. His sincerity seemed unmistakable. *"You need to trust me,"* he had told her. If only...

"What's on your mind?" the officer inquired, noticing her expression.

She wiped her lips, trying to erase the feeling of Johan's touch, but it was in vain. "It's nothing... I was just..."

"What is it?" he prodded, seeing her hesitation. "I'm a good listener. I understand if you don't want to talk, but trust me, the sooner you share what happened, the quicker you can get back to your life."

Zoe wiped her sweaty palms on her jeans. "What do you want to know?"

"Just tell me what happened, in your own words."

Lifting her eyes, she searched for inspiration on the ceiling. She then began to recount the events, making an effort to stick to the facts, deliberately omitting details of the unique bond she had formed with her captor and how he had won her trust.

She started her story with their initial encounter in Marianne Deconti's basement, a time when Johan had no recollection of his past.

Then she went on to describe the grim discovery of the nurse's body. She moved to the evening they spent at Chantal and Roger Pasteur's farm and from there, detailed their trek to the forest and the finding of another victim. Throughout her narration, she maintained a detached tone, treating the events as if recounting a story that belonged to someone else.

She avoided mentioning how Johan had looked after her, providing warmth, food, and a sense of safety. She skipped over their shared kisses in the car and at the farm. She also left out the times he had given her the choice to leave and the moment he saved the deer.

Zoe's side of the story didn't match what was being said on the news. What really happened was different from the scary picture the media had painted. Catching a serial killer could be a huge win for Detective Florian's career. She could see that even though he acted friendly, he might overlook things that didn't support his own ideas. Johan was in his sights, and he didn't seem interested in sharing the case with Europol.

"Did he give you any clues about who he is? Maybe his job or where he's from?" Florian pressed.

Zoe shook her head. "He didn't remember anything," she reminded.

"Hmm. You bought that?"

Zoe felt a wave of anxiety. "Can I use your bathroom?" she asked, seeking a momentary escape.

"Sure thing. Here, let me give you a hand."

Once she was on her feet, the room seemed to spin. The detective extended his arm to steady her, but she waved it off.

"I'm okay," she said firmly.

He leaned closer, his voice low. "You're safe now. He won't be able to harm you anymore."

His confidence struck her oddly, as if he was privy to something she wasn't. A realization dawned on her, one she was reluctant to accept.

"You killed him..."

The detective flashed a grin, his teeth a perfect row, his eyes glinting with the thrill of the chase. "Kill him? No, that's not it. We captured him. My team found him on the road."

"He's... he's here?" Her words barely made it past the lump in her throat.

"Yes, but don't worry. He's in good hands now."

39

———————

"Breathe in through your nose... Now out through your mouth," came the instruction, echoing in the cold cell. Johan did as told, a shiver coursing through him each time the cold stethoscope touched his skin. "Breathing's clear," announced the man with the medical kit to those present.

A cop, leaning against the door, watched in silence, clad in a light-blue uniform. Johan couldn't make out any badges or stripes that might suggest his rank.

"Okay," the medic said, stepping in front of Johan with a serious look as he started the next part of the check-up. "Let me know if you feel any pain." A wince escaped Johan as probing hands pressed firmly on his torso, finding the tender spots of discoloration.

"Well?" The impatience was clear in the officer's voice, anxious to know if the detainee was in any condition for questioning to proceed.

Peeling off his gloves, the medic gave his verdict. "Two fractured ribs, some minor bruising. He'll survive without a hospital visit."

Johan did up his shirt, the reality of his unbroken bones

contradicting the harsh treatment he'd endured. The fear in the officers' eyes came back to him—not anger, but fear. Lost in the forest, he'd been misidentified as a perilous felon. His protests of innocence had fallen on deaf ears.

They had encircled him, a predatory circle with batons poised to deliver justice as they saw it. To them, he was not a man in the wrong place at the wrong time; he was the menace they had been trained to subdue. Their conviction of his wrongdoing deafened them to his desperate explanations.

The chaos erupted in a blur. He sidestepped the initial assault, only to be overwhelmed by the ensuing flurry of blows.

The medic handed Johan some pills. "For the pain," he said simply.

Johan accepted them, his mind elsewhere. "And the woman from the forest, her condition?"

"Which woman?"

"The one I was with. Is she alright?"

The officer's posture stiffened noticeably at the query. "You mean your alleged hostage?" he interjected with a skeptical tone.

"No, that can't be," Johan countered, his voice tight with worry. "I have to see her."

The skepticism in the officer's gaze sharpened. "What for?"

Johan closed his eyes, struggling with the gaps in his memory. "I can't remember what happened."

The officer sneered, his disbelief clear as he scoffed, "Yeah, sure! Playing the amnesia card again, are we?"

The medic looked from Johan to the officer, his brow furrowed in thought. "What do you mean?"

"That's the story he fed to Zoe Rossi. Claimed he didn't know who he was, all that nonsense."

Turning back to Johan, the medic asked, "Is this true?"

With a sigh, Johan admitted, "I don't know what I might've said or done before..."

"Before what?"

Images of Marianne Deconti flashed through Johan's mind—her raspy voice, desperate cries for help, and the last glimpse of her face disappearing beneath a plastic sheet.

The officer's face tightened with impatience. "Start talking, dammit!" He took a step toward Johan, his intentions clear. But before their eyes could meet, the door opened. Another officer, one Johan remembered from his arrest, stood there. Unlike the others during that chaotic night, he had just watched. He motioned for his colleague to step outside. The two talked, their voices low. Johan strained to catch their words, but could only make out fragments: "...claims he remembers nothing...not him...you believe that?...we know who he is... Europol analyst confirmed... you're joking, right? A psychic... his name is Pierre Valmeur."

Johan's heart skipped a beat. "What did you say?"

The only response he received was the echoing slam of the cell door as it closed shut.

40

———

Zoe had hoped for a moment of solitude, but as the office door swung open, that hope dissipated. A dozen uniformed men packed the narrow hallway.

"The restroom is down there—third door on your right," Detective Florian instructed, noting her hesitation. "Make some space, guys!"

The men shuffled around, clearing a path for her. Zoe made her way through, keenly aware of their penetrating stares, until she found refuge in the restroom. It was a meager sanctuary, but she needed a moment away from prying eyes. Finally alone, Zoe ignored the mirror and went straight to the sink to splash her face with cold water.

Even in his absence, Zoe could feel Johan's presence seeping through the walls as if he were right there with her.

Water dripped from her chin as she closed her eyes, tuning into the distant murmur of male voices. The sounds were muffled, reminiscent of being underwater, with voices filtering down to her from above. For a fleeting moment, she thought she heard his voice. *"Let go, Zoe."* The mere memory sent chills down her spine. She splashed her face again, urging herself to pull it together. She was about to do it once more when another voice, very real and present, interrupted her.

"Zoe? You okay?"

Looking up, she caught her brother-in-law's eyes in the mirror reflection as he stood at the door.

"Anthony? What are you doing here?"

"You're joking, right? I thought I'd never see you again. Thought you were..."

They were a mere twenty inches apart. As he stepped closer, Zoe's instincts kicked in, prompting her to retreat a step.

Anthony stopped, a flicker of annoyance—or was it fear? —crossing his face.

"What's wrong?" he asked, his voice softer now.

"I'm just... surprised to see you here."

A flash of pain crossed Anthony's face. "And where else would I be?"

The moment she felt his hands on her shoulders, Zoe tensed up. Memories of their fight the night before her kidnapping came flooding back. Anthony had overpowered her, pushing her onto the couch with his body pressing down, trying to undo the buttons of her blouse, all while his alcohol-laden breath invaded her space as he forced a kiss on her. Now, there wasn't a single sign of the hit she'd landed on his temple. It was as if she was reliving a nightmare.

Somehow, she knew Johan would never have done such a thing. Even though he had threatened her with his gun, he had never been harsh with her. Zoe could tell it was all an act; his trembling hand had given him away. She now realized he would never have pulled the trigger. Beyond the unusual circumstances, he had treated her with more kindness than any other man she had ever met, and she found that more disturbing than she wanted to admit.

"You okay?" Anthony asked, attempting to make eye contact. "Sorry... stupid question. I'll wait outside."

"No, stay!" Zoe's voice came out more desperate than she intended, disoriented by Anthony's unexpected presence and the memories it stirred up.

"In the woods..." she began, her voice trailing off.

"Yes? What about the woods?"

"There were two bodies."

"I know."

Tears welled in her eyes as she looked up at him. "I'm scared one of them is Gabriela."

A sad smile crossed Anthony's face. "It's not her. They've been identified. Two young women from Belgium."

"Two Belgians," she repeated, taking in the information.

"They vanished last summer at a rest stop somewhere in Italy."

She looked puzzled. "But how did they identify them so fast?"

"Dental records," Anthony replied. "Let's go. They'll fill us in on all the details."

Leanne and Sonya were best friends. Both had plans to join the Royal Academy of Fine Arts in Brussels. Before that adventure began, they chose to explore Italy's southern regions. Their journey, shared on Instagram, was a hit with their followers. Their last picture? A modern art museum in Venice, the Punta della Dogana. But after Venice, they vanished. Their next stop was supposed to be Florence, a city renowned for its art like Michelangelo's "David" and Botticelli's "Birth of Venus." But they never made it.

The investigation took a grim turn when the police discovered only the victims' heads. No creepy packages had arrived for the families this time. But everyone knew what usually came next—postcards leading to the rest of the bodies.

Zoe's attention wavered, caught between the Europol investigator's report and the unwanted presence of Anthony.

In an attempt to escape his gaze, her eyes landed on an older man standing apart from the others. He didn't look like a cop. His clothes were outdated and worn, but there was something oddly familiar about him.

"Let me introduce Pierre Valmeur" Inspector Dorsey's voice cut through her thoughts. "He's played a crucial role in our efforts to locate you."

Valmeur approached, and Zoe found herself captivated by the deep lines etched into his face, reminiscent of dry riverbeds.

"Hello, Miss," he greeted, his voice gentle as he took her hand.

She couldn't help but recoil slightly at the roughness of his palm.

"Are you a detective?"

He shook his head, his intense gaze making Zoe self-consciously wonder if she had something on her face.

"Why are you staring at me like that?"

"It's always startling—and thrilling—to see my visions come to life," Valmeur confessed, winking.

"Mr. Valmeur is a medium hired by Leanne Jalmet's family," Dorsey clarified.

Zoe's brow furrowed. "So, you mean you've had visions about me?"

"About you, and my son," he added with a smile.

Recognition clicked into place, and her heart sank.

That's why he looked familiar; he had the same unsettling, magnetic eyes as Johan.

"Johan is your son," she whispered, a sense of dread filling her.

"Indeed, Miss. He crossed the length of France with a singular purpose—to save your life."

41

———

"Save me?" Zoe couldn't believe it. She glanced around, finding the room now empty except for Inspector Dorsey and Johan's dad, Pierre Valmeur.

"He would never have harmed you," Pierre shot back, his conviction piercing through his sharp tone.

Zoe felt a whirlwind of bewilderment engulfing her, her mind racing to piece together the chaotic puzzle. "Save me..." she whispered, more to herself than to the others, a flicker of doubt crossing her face.

Pierre's lips curled into a slight smile. "He set you free," he said, his voice tinged with a hint of triumph, daring her to see things differently.

Yet Zoe found herself grappling for words, the weight of the truth in his statement bearing down on her. Johan's intervention had indeed thwarted a darker fate at the hands of the man who had abducted her on that secluded road through the Landes forest. Johan's timely arrival had ensured she didn't meet the same fate as Marianne.

Determination flared in Zoe's eyes. She pivoted to Inspector Dorsey. "I need to talk to him. He's here, right?"

"I wouldn't advise—" Dorsey started, but Zoe was having none of it.

"Is he a suspect?" she demanded, her eyes locking onto the inspector's with fierce intensity.

He shook his head, his expression somber. "He didn't kill them," he said. "But he did take you and hold you against your will."

"What if I told you that's not what happened?" Zoe challenged, her tone unwavering.

Dorsey held her gaze, his voice steady. "I'd say you're too involved to see things clearly."

But Zoe stood her ground. "I want to talk to him. Then I'll decide whether to press charges."

Inspector Dorsey exchanged a brief, uncertain glance with Pierre Valmeur before turning back to her. "Before you see him, you should know—he's lost his memory of the past forty-eight hours. He doesn't remember you."

42

———

Johan's eyes widened as the office door opened. The woman from the forest stood there. She was the same as in the portrait. Beside her was a man in regular clothes, likely a detective.

"I'm Inspector Dorsey," the newcomer announced, his tone blunt and authoritative. "Miss Rossi here needs to ask you a few questions. Just a heads up, whatever you say could be used in court. Got it?"

Johan's rights were being read, but his mind wandered. He glanced at the young woman by the door, standing as if ready to flee.

"Did you get all that?" Dorsey pressed.

Johan managed a nod, though he sensed the cop was awaiting a response to some unasked question. "Are you sure you don't want a lawyer?"

"No, I'm good," he murmured, unable to tear his gaze away from the young woman.

She gave a slight start at his comment, and Johan couldn't help but wonder if Dorsey had picked up on it. But

Dorsey didn't say anything. He just moved back to the corner, letting them talk without others listening in.

Johan's focus returned to Zoe Rossi, their gazes locking in a quiet standoff, a palpable tension hanging in the air. Which one of them was the prey, and which was the predator?

"Did you come here by your own choice, or were you asked to?" he asked, breaking the silence.

"Does it matter?" she asked, her voice not giving anything away.

Her words hung in the air, the first she'd spoken to him since their encounter in the forest.

"To me, it does," he admitted, maintaining eye contact.

"I came on my own," she said after a moment.

Johan nodded, allowing himself a small grin despite the pain it caused his split lip. It was a foolish reaction, but he couldn't contain his relief.

"Am I amusing you somehow?"

"I'm just glad to see you again. I wasn't sure you'd want to after... everything."

He wanted her to come closer, but she didn't. She looked away. Was she scared of him or of the man watching her so closely? Johan took a deep breath. "Can we talk in private?" he asked.

Zoe turned to Dorsey, her eyes filled with silent pleading. She looked like a teenager trying to negotiate a later curfew, hopeful yet anxious. Dorsey, however, was unmoved. He shook his head, firm in his decision, prompting a frown to cross her face. Clearly, she, too, desired a moment of privacy.

Johan had a lot to say, things that were just for her. He saw her lean over, whispering to the officer. The words were inaudible, yet his clenched jaw showed he wasn't happy.

"Fine." Dorsey grumbled. As he walked closer, his face was a mix of worry and irritation.

Johan cringed when the handcuffs snapped tight around his wrists.

"That's enough," Zoe interjected, stepping forward as though to shield him.

Dorsey, now with his phone in hand, started a recording. "Don't stop it," he instructed, laying it on the table.

Zoe nodded in understanding. "You can go, now."

"I'll be right outside if you need anything," Dorsey replied, his voice laden with reluctance as he left the room, the door closing behind him.

As soon as they were alone, Zoe reached for the phone and paused the recording.

"I'm sorry for what they did to you," she said, settling into a seat across from him. Her eyes flickered with a mix of empathy and anger, making it clear she was referring to the harsh treatment by the police.

Johan shrugged, wincing at the pain it brought. "They mistook me for the Reaper. I can't really blame them."

She leaned in, her eyes tracing the tapestry of bruises and cuts marring his face. "Does it hurt?"

"Not much," he lied through gritted teeth.

His body was a canvas of pain, every inch throbbing, each breath a stark reminder of his cracked ribs. Yet, none of that seemed to matter now. The only thing of importance was her. "And you?" he asked.

"Me?" she echoed, her voice a whisper.

"Yes, Zoe, you. How are you holding up?"

For the first time since she'd entered the room, she met his gaze. "Uh... I'm okay, I guess."

He could tell she wasn't being truthful. "Did I... Did I hurt you?" he asked, his voice cracking slightly.

"No."

"You don't trust me, though."

"I want to. But I need to know more."

He nodded, understanding her need for clarity. "What do you want to know?"

"Everything. I want you to tell me everything."

A subtle smile tugged at his lips, even as he used his tongue to wipe away a bead of blood from the split in his mouth. The coppery taste served as a stark reminder of painful memories long buried. "The problem is, I don't know where to start."

"Start with the vision."

Johan blinked, taken aback. "What did you say?" he asked.

"I met your dad," she revealed.

"Oh, he mentioned the portrait, then?"

"What portrait?"

"You mentioned a portrait of me, but I thought it was all just a story. Does it actually exist?"

"Sort of... Look, I'll spill everything, but first, I need some answers, too. My old man, what did he say to you exactly?"

"He said he had a vision of the two of us. Said you crossed France to save me."

"That so? Did I save you?"

"Well, I'm here, aren't I?"

Silence fell, punctuated only by the intensity of their locked gaze.

"I've got to say, it's all fuzzy," he confessed. "Our first meeting, everything that followed—I can't quite parse out what's real and what's not."

She nodded, though whether she was disappointed or relieved, he couldn't quite tell.

"You were disoriented when we met," she gently

reminded him, her voice bringing him back to that moment. "You had no recollection of your identity or your past."

"I see... Maybe my memory loss was triggered by an intense emotional upheaval."

"Emotional upheaval?"

"Yes, a trauma so severe that a person—myself included—might detach from reality to cope."

She leaned forward, her eyes searching his. "What sort of trauma could lead to that?"

He paused, feeling the heavy burden of things left unsaid pressing on his chest. "The type where terror grips you, because your own life, or the life of someone you hold dear, hangs by a thread. Maybe facing both at once."

As he spoke, Johan recognized an odd detachment in his words, as if he narrated someone else's horror story rather than his own. A wistful part of him longed for that to be true—to be merely a bystander instead of the protagonist in this grim tale.

"Does any of this tie back to Marianne Deconti?"

At the mention of the nurse, Johan tensed, memories flooding back unbidden. *"I need your help,"* Mari had whispered, desperation in her eyes. But he'd been powerless to do anything.

"You knew her?" Zoe pressed.

"Somewhat."

Rolling her eyes, she snapped, "'Somewhat'? I'm tiring of your evasive answers..."

"I'm sorry. Let's start over."

"I just need to understand how you got tangled up in all this. You find me in Marianne Deconti's basement, lead me to her dead body, then through the woods to find not one, but two more victims. So, if you're not the Reaper, who are you?"

"I'll explain, but brace yourself."

Her eyes, large and brown, flickered with a mix of excitement and apprehension.

"I won't lie. Some of what I'm about to say might sound... irrational."

She leaned back, contemplating his words.

"Given that your dad's a medium, I'd expect nothing less. So, what is it? Can you time travel? Read minds? Talk to the dead?"

"Not the dead. The dying."

Silence enveloped the room once again. He let it stretch, ensuring he had her undivided attention before spilling his truths. It was thrilling and terrifying in equal measure: the thrill of unveiling secrets kept locked away, the fear of her reaction. Realizing he'd been holding his breath, he exhaled, feeling his body relax ever so slightly. Here goes nothing...

"My name is Johan Valmeur. I work as a neurosurgeon at Salpêtrière Hospital in Paris. And... I killed someone."

PART II

The Fallen Angel

"Every surgeon carries within himself a small cemetery,
where from time to time he goes to pray."
— René LERICHE, French surgeon

43

———————

Salpêtrière Hospital, Paris,
   Medical Imaging Department

I stared at the ghostly mass on the MRI screen—a tumor with a two-inch diameter, hidden deep within the brain. It was so perilous that no surgeon had dared to attempt its removal. They had all told Camille Langevin's family it was "too risky."

At 19, Camille had her whole life ahead of her. She'd just gotten into a top architecture school and had big dreams. But then a surprise seizure led to a scary discovery: a tumor in her brain called a Grade 2 glioma.

Right now, it wasn't cancer. But tumors like this can change. Some doctors thought it might turn into cancer later on. The tricky part? No one knew when that might happen. Right now, the tumor wasn't causing her any problems. But it was still a threat.

There was a possible fix: surgery. But the procedure was risky. The tumor was in a challenging spot. Taking it out might cause serious problems for Camille, like affecting her speech or causing paralysis. It was a tough choice: face the risks of surgery now or worry about the tumor becoming cancerous later on.

While I understood the reservations of my colleagues, a deep-seated conviction told me we should take the risk, potentially offering Camille many more years.

Looking up, I saw Camille through the glass window separating me from the MRI room. With a ticking time bomb in her head, she managed to smile back at me. I was her last hope, and I hadn't even committed to performing the surgery yet.

Fifteen minutes later, I entered her hospital room. She sat on the bed, legs crossed, surrounded by her parents and boyfriend. The room fell silent as I walked in.

"Well, young lady," I began, adopting a tone of regret, "it seems like you're going to have to shave your head."

Camille's mother, Evelyne Langevin, stifled a joyous sob.

"You'll do it?" her father asked, needing confirmation of what he hoped he had just heard.

"Tomorrow morning, at eight," I replied.

Evelyne and Thomas Langevin enveloped me in a tight hug.

"You're an angel," they whispered, their voices full of gratitude.

44

———————

An angel—that's what people started calling me after I gave them a second shot at life. The press jumped on the band-wagon, coining the moniker "The Angel with the Golden Scalpel" after a high-profile surgery involving a secretary of state.

Each time I heard it, a smirk would play on my lips. Yet, when I looked in the mirror, the reflection staring back bore a closer resemblance to a boxer than to an angel, with a scar arcing over my right eyebrow and a nose that hadn't set right after a break. Absent those, one might have said my features were almost too refined, verging on delicate.

An angel... That's not exactly the word they whispered behind my back in the hospital corridors. There were many other descriptors, though I suspect few were spoken to my face. My rugged appearance was likely enough to deter even the boldest. While some labeled me ambitious and skilled, others branded me arrogant or even clueless—and those were the gentler terms.

At 33, my rapid rise raised eyebrows. I trained at a top university hospital in France and continued my advanced studies at Cornell Medical School in New York. Soon, I was part of a renowned medical team in Paris. In just three years, my name became known not just in France, but worldwide. Patients from different corners of the globe sought my advice. But for Camille Langevin, she only had to travel a short distance from her home just outside Paris.

"I need your signature here," I instructed, bending over her hospital bed.

"Give me the pen," she responded, her eagerness palpable.

"This isn't just some routine paperwork. It's a promise between you and me. Got it?"

I took the time to explain the procedure in detail. "You'll be unconscious for the craniotomy, but after that part, we'll wake you up. Don't worry, your brain itself won't feel pain. You'll be asked to move your arm, look at pictures, and help me steer clear of important areas in your brain. Lise, our neurologist, will be there to support and guide you through the entire process. As soon as that part is complete, you'll go back to sleep while we finish up."

"I already know all that," Camille said impatiently, having exhausted the subject on the Internet.

"But are you aware of the risks?" I pressed.

"Are you trying to scare me now?"

"I just want to ensure you're fully informed."

"We are," her father, Stephane, interjected. "What about afterward?"

"That might lead to some short-term problems with speaking or moving," I explained.

"But it's just for a short time, right?" Stephane asked, looking for clarity.

"Usually, it is," I responded. "But she'll still need routine check-ups to ensure everything is okay."

"What does that entail?" her mother asked, speaking up for the first time.

"An MRI every six months initially. If everything looks good, we can decrease the frequency. Any issues? You reach out to me immediately."

Camille nodded, indicating she had no further questions, save for one: "What about my hair?"

I reassured her, "It will grow back over the scar."

A few moments later, I stepped out of the room, the signed consent form in hand. I'd given Camille my word that I'd only shave as much as necessary. I'd also guaranteed her that the horseshoe-shaped scar on the left side of her head would be out of sight, especially once her hair fully grew back.

I passed the consent form to my secretary and then shut myself in my office.

Before any surgery, it was my routine to double-check the patient's medical file. However, before I could delve into that, my attention was drawn to a shiny envelope lying on my desk. It had been left there by my secretary a couple of weeks ago. Adorned with a pearl ribbon and a heart-shaped rhinestone clasp, it exuded elegance. My name was written on the front in what I recognized as Maud's handwriting. I scrutinized each letter, searching for any sign of hesitation that might betray her feelings, but found none. Then again, she was a surgeon as well—we weren't exactly known for unsteady hands.

The thought of seeing Maud's name alongside that of my best friend, Cedric, in golden print inside that envelope was more than I could bear. For a fleeting moment, I contemplated discarding it straight into the nearby trash bin. Instead, I suppressed the surge of jealousy and stowed the invitation away in my desk drawer. So, they were really going through with it. Maud and Cedric were getting married.

Setting aside my personal feelings, I powered up my computer and pulled up Camille Langevin's medical records, ready to focus on the task at hand.

The next day, with Camille prepped, and the team poised for action, I readied myself for surgery. Spotting Cedric behind his mask, I listened as he updated me on Camille's condition.

"RSVP'd for the wedding yet?" he threw in casually.

"For the wedding?" I echoed, doing my best to appear nonchalant.

"You in or out?"

"Maybe in. But you know, emergencies..."

"I was hoping you'd be my best man," Cedric said, his eyes revealing a hint of disappointment.

I smirked. "I'd probably misplace the rings."

His eyes crinkled in response, signaling a smile concealed by his mask. "Remember when you lost your house keys?"

"Yeah. Good thing Maud had hers," I blurted out, wishing I could take back my words.

An uncomfortable silence settled.

Cedric blinked, his gaze shifting to the monitor that displayed Camille's vital signs in a flurry of multicolored graphs.

I pushed thoughts of Maud to the back of my mind. Like a boxer gearing up for a fight, I readied myself, taking my position behind Camille. Everything was set for the battle against the disease.

"Let's rock and roll," I declared, my tone filled with determination.

The whirring of the drill, much like that of a power tool, took over from the scalpel. Three holes that I'd soon connect with a surgical saw. Inside this protective case were the thoughts of a nineteen-year-old: her dreams, her fears, and the deep love she had for her family.

Gently, I lifted the piece of bone. Camille's brain shimmered beneath the bright surgical light, pulsating in time with her heartbeat. Soon, my own heart raced in tandem, creating an intangible bond between us.

Holding the scalpel between my thumb and forefinger, I made the initial incision. The meninges parted like the layers of a delicate curtain, exposing a previously hidden reality. The sheer force of what I'd tapped into made me reel. A vision flashed before my eyes: mourners surrounding an open grave, umbrellas snapping open, rainwater pooling on the ground, marking the end of Camille's funeral. Snapshots of a future I was hell-bent on altering.

Fueled by a renewed sense of purpose, I declared, "It's time to wake her up."

Hours later, the tumor lay exposed before us.

"This is a horse. This is a chair. This is…" Camille's voice, steady and clear, filled the room as she named the images presented to her.

"Keep it up, Camille," I encouraged, infusing my voice with reassurance.

Pausing for a moment, I checked in with my team.

"Everything looking good? I haven't hit any functional areas, have I?"

"No motor deficits," Lise, our neurologist, confirmed.

I took a deep breath, closed my eyes for a moment, and braced myself. The most critical phase of the surgery was upon us.

Looking through the microscope, the tumor appeared as a grim, lifeless mass.

"Camille?" I called out.

"Yes..." Her voice, though strong, wavered.

"I'm about to remove the tumor."

"Okay..."

With precision, I excised the first section. As I did, a fleeting vision of Camille waking up post-surgery filled my mind. But the present quickly pulled me back as I heard her voice in the operating room: "This is a rhinoceros. This is a duck..."

With each fragment I removed, a new vision of her life unfolded before my eyes. I saw her leaving the hospital, starting architecture school, getting married, and holding her newborn baby. My resolve only grew stronger.

"What time is it?" I asked, my focus unyielding.

"Twelve forty-five," came the reply.

"We're nearly there, Camille. Most of the tumor's out."

"How much of it?" she pressed, her voice tinged with fatigue.

"About eighty percent, give or take. We'll double-check with an MRI afterward."

"Thank... you," her voice faded, but the gratitude was palpable.

I paused, assessing the situation.

"Should we put her under?" Cedric asked, ready to proceed.

I looked at him, hesitated, then shook my head. Circling the operating table, I positioned myself to face Camille. She was nearly concealed by the sterile drapes, and I bent down, determined to meet her gaze.

"You up for more, Camille? Or are you done?"

"No..."

"You want me to stop?"

"No... keep... going."

That was the answer I was hoping for.

"Hang tight. We're on the home stretch," I said, smiling to convey confidence.

Back at it, my determination was unwavering. Each cut felt like a promise of more life for Camille. Yet, I wanted more for her—I wanted to see her grow old.

Cedric's voice broke through, urgent and alarmed. "Her BP's dropping."

"I'm almost there," I assured him, making one last cut with the scalpel.

Instant regret.

A sudden, loud pop, followed by a rush of red. The hopeful visions of Camille's future were instantly replaced by that haunting graveside scene. An artery had burst.

"I'm not ready," a soft voice whispered, its resonance filling my mind with a haunting clarity. It was Camille, her spirit somehow detached and lingering beside me, observing her own brain.

"Me neither," I whispered back, my voice breaking.

I had never lost a patient on my table, and I wasn't about to let Camille be the first. But as I scrambled to find the source of the bleed, all I could see was red.

Hands reached out to pull me away. Someone else tried to take control, but it was too late. Camille had already slipped away into a never-ending sleep.

45

The operating room was akin to a battlefield. Bloodied gauze littered the tiles, surgical tools lay scattered across stainless steel tables, and sheets were crumpled in a corner. With my back against the wall, I sat on the floor, taking in the chaos. A custodian was already hard at work, preparing the room for the next surgical team.

"I gotta tell my parents."

Camille, standing barefoot and draped in a thin, paper-like disposable gown, appeared like a solemn figure in a tragic play. Rising to my feet, I followed her.

Her family was waiting in a room designed for delivering hard news—a space filled with warm, comforting hues and plush sofas. It was meant to offer solace, yet it was loathed for the heartbreak it witnessed. Breaking bad news was never my strong suit, and this was uncharted territory for me—a patient had never died on my table before.

My hand reached for the doorknob, but I paused, overhearing the murmurs of Camille's parents inside. What could I say? Confess that my arrogance had dramatically shortened their daughter's life? That she had mere hours instead of years left due to the surgery? I couldn't face them. Not yet.

A whisper brushed against my ear.

"I don't have long. They should know."

"I... I don't know what to say."

"Just tell them the truth."

Whether it was Camille or I who opened the door, I couldn't be sure. The Langevin family, whose faces had become all too familiar, all turned toward me: Evelyne, the mother; Stephane, the father; Leo, the younger brother; and then there was the boyfriend, whose name still escaped me. They were all there on the couch, huddled together. Camille joined them, and I shut the door behind her. Standing there, I felt like a dead man walking, about to face a firing squad. They listened intently as I recounted the events.

"I'm really sorry," I concluded, falling back on technical jargon that likely went over the heads of everyone else in the room.

"Can we see her?"

Camille had been moved to a private room, now appearing serene and asleep beneath the sheets. Wrapped in bandages from head to toe, she was a far cry from the lively girl she once was.

"She looks like she'll wake up any moment," Evelyne whispered, taking her daughter's hand. "Sweetie, can you hear me?"

"Don't cry, Mom," the young woman said, sitting beside her physical body, laying frail on the bed.

A shiver seemed to run through Mrs. Langevin.

"Is there anything else that can be done?" Stephan implored.

I could only shake my head.

"She's in a deep coma. It's unlikely she'll make it through the night," I admitted, foregoing the complex medical language. They deserved the unvarnished truth.

"Can we stay with her?"

"Of course. I'll have a nurse bring in some blankets. If needed, we can also set up a cot."

As Evelyne tightened her grip on her daughter's hand, Camille, unseen by her family, did the same. She then turned to me.

"You can go now."

I nodded, forgetting that I was the only one who could hear her.

"I'll check in later," I promised, stepping out.

Through the door, I could hear the suppressed sobs of the Langevin family. There were no angry words, no threats —just acceptance, which somehow made it all the more heart-wrenching. I deserved their anger, their outrage. I stood there, absorbing the sounds of their grief as penance.

When I looked up, I saw Anais, the young nurse who usually blushed in my presence, staring at me, her face pale. Following her gaze, I realized why. I had faced the Langevins, not realizing I was still clad in clothes stained with their daughter's blood.

46

How had I been so insensitive? I swung open the door to the staff locker room, not bothering to grab my toiletries before shedding my surgeon's gear. It fell to the floor, discarded like the shed skin of a snake.

Without hesitation, I stepped into the shower, letting the cold water hit me. I shivered but didn't retreat, my hand resting against the tiled wall.

As soon as my eyes closed, a red wave engulfed me—Camille's blood, spurting from the hole I had drilled into her brain, undoing all my attempts to save her. The scene kept replaying, and part of me didn't want it to stop. I didn't want to open my eyes; I wanted to drown in that moment.

"Stop torturing yourself," a voice muttered from behind the partition.

Surprised, I slid the panel open, half-expecting to see a vision of Camille. Instead, I was met with Cedric's intense gaze.

"You okay?" he inquired, his voice laced with concern.

Shivering, I stuttered, "Towel... please."

I couldn't gauge how long I'd stood under the frigid

water, but it hadn't been long enough. My body was numb, save for the guilt that prickled, alive and insistent.

"Here." Cedric handed me a towel.

Silence stretched between us as he likely searched for comforting words I had no desire to hear.

"Listen," he began, but I interrupted him.

"Don't say it wasn't my fault."

"That wasn't my intention. I have two more surgeries to get through, but maybe we could grab a drink afterward?"

"I don't need cheering up."

His gaze shifted, causing me to avert my eyes. "Maybe I do," he admitted, a hint of hurt in his voice. "You weren't the only one in that OR. We're all shaken. The world doesn't revolve around you, Johan! We all lost her today." And with that, he spun on his heel and left.

Barefoot, with a towel wrapped around my waist, I made my way to the lockers, picking up my dirty clothes along the way and tossing them into the designated cart. The looping thoughts in my head were relentless, drowning out the whispers of my colleagues and the sound of a camera shutter clicking behind me. A grinning intern flaunted his phone screen at me as if he'd won a prize. In no time at all, the tattoos I'd managed to keep hidden were plastered all over Snapchat, Instagram, and Facebook. They were in for a surprise. No pin-up girls or tribal designs like the rumors suggested, but rather a unique take on the caduceus. A nod to the medical profession: two snakes winding around each of my arms and wings spread across my shoulder blades. I covered them up with the coarse fabric of a fresh surgical gown, which smelled of industrial disinfectant.

I had been on my feet since dawn. Typically, after surgery, I'd head home and maybe join the team for drinks later, honoring our longstanding tradition. But today was far from typical; my patients didn't usually die. Yet, the thought of solitude in my apartment, a mere two subway stops from the hospital, was intolerable. I needed a diversion, something to pry my thoughts away from Camille. There were other patients, other lives hanging in the balance, waiting for me. They represented a second chance, my redemption—or so I told myself as I push open the door to my office.

A man with salt-and-pepper hair—Professor Jacques Derosier, my nemesis—stood scrutinizing the wall plastered with my awards and recognitions, his back to me. I paused in the doorway, my fists clenched. Derosier and I had been at odds for years; he had been trying to undermine me ever since I'd risen to prominence in the surgical team. Though I'd mostly managed to sidestep his petty maneuvers, today felt different.

"Hey, what's your game?" I sliced through the silence with my voice.

He turned, all smiling. "You know, you're quite the looker in these photos. 'The Angel with the Golden Scalpel'—journalists sure do have a way with words, huh?"

Rolling my eyes, I responded, "Here for an autograph, Jacques?"

Ignoring my sarcasm, he placed the frame back. "No, just thought I'd be the first to welcome you."

I felt a chill. "Welcome me?"

"Welcome to mortality, dear *angel*."

I clicked my steps toward him. "Getting a kick out of this, aren't you? Been dreaming of my downfall?"

His smile flickered away. "No joy in it. Camille was my patient first. If you hadn't barged in, she might've had a peaceful few months left. But now, thanks to you, she's ticking down her last hours."

That stung, but I kept my composure. "Said your piece. Now, get out of my office."

He moved toward the door but threw one more barb before exiting. "Oh, and Lukas Boylan's file makes for an interesting read. My friendly advice? Step back from this one. Might be time to learn from past missteps."

I held the door, muscles tense, forcing a polite smile. "Appreciated, Jacques. I'll give it some thought."

The door clicked shut and a female voice chirped from behind. "Always thought he was a jerk."

I turned to see Camille idly twirling a strand of hair around her finger on the couch. She had every reason to dislike Derosier—he'd been the bearer of her hopeless prognosis, after all.

"Maybe, but he's not entirely wrong," I admitted, the words bitter in my mouth.

She stood, wandering to a shelf cluttered with scattered papers. "Maybe not. But still a jerk."

As she peered at the mess, she chuckled. "Man, if your patients saw this chaos, they'd run for the hills, thinking you'd scramble their brains or something."

I plopped down at my desk, glancing out at the dense city fog before refocusing on Lukas Boylan's open file. The college football player, just 21, was faced with a ticking time bomb—an aneurysm that could rupture with any spike in blood pressure. Nobody wanted to touch it. Nobody but me. Lukas was next in line.

"You're not gonna bail because of me, right?" Camille's voice whispered softly right by my ear.

Just a moment ago, she had been across the room. Now, suddenly and without a sound, she was right there, reading the file over my shoulder.

"Not bad," she commented, as my eyes lingered on a

photo of Lukas Boylan. His parents had tucked it into the file, a reminder that their son was more than just a case study for the doctor in me.

My watch read one o'clock.

"That's five a.m. in Missoula," Camille remarked, as if she had peeked into my mind. "You can't call them now, not unless you've got good news. And that's not what we have, is it?"

She waited, expecting an answer.

"Why aren't you with your parents?" I snapped, annoyed by her moralizing.

"No thanks. Being around them is gloomy enough. I'd rather be here with you."

Resigned, I closed the file, returning it to its stack.

"I'm not much better company," I noted, my voice tinged with weariness.

She nudged me. "Come on, don't make that face. I'm trying to lift your spirits a bit. Looks like you could use it."

I raised an eyebrow. "And you're not mad? At me?"

She waved a dismissive hand. "Why talk about it?"

I shook my head, baffled. "I don't get it. You should be furious with me."

"Would it change anything if I were?"

I sighed, cradling my head in my hands, fighting back tears.

"Your phone's about to buzz," she blurted.

"Huh?"

I straightened up, alarmed by the certainty in her voice. But she'd disappeared. At the same moment, my phone jittered in my lab coat pocket, set to vibrate.

"Johan?" The voice belonged to Albert Grandini, our neighbor and my dad's best friend. "Your dad had a bad turn and fainted. Can you get here?"

47

———

The motorcycle sped down the county road. I scarcely noticed the tachometer needle dancing or the speed-limit signs blurring past.

The landscape transformed—from the gray hues of Paris and its suburbs to the blue skies and lush green hills of Normandy—yet it passed me by, unobserved. In fields dotted with apple trees, horses shook their coats, while cows and sheeps, mid-munch on hay, lifted their heads to watch me race by.

Soon, the village clock tower appeared, standing sentinel atop a hill. I slowed my pace—not out of a newfound respect for traffic laws, but due to an unforeseen obstacle in my path: a truck laden with cider apples. Lacking a clear sightline for a safe pass, I had no choice but to be patient.

After a tedious five minutes, I turned onto a road so narrow it would barely accommodate two cars passing side by side. The trees on either side intertwined, creating a canopy of foliage. Through this verdant tunnel, the building at the end came into view. A 12th-century leprosarium, it once provided sanctuary for lepers and plague victims in the Middle Ages. Over the centuries, it morphed first into an inn, then into a makeshift hospital when the German army commandeered it during the Battle of Normandy. Now restored, it remained off the beaten tourist paths, yet it attracted dozens of visitors daily. People traveled from all corners of France, and even from abroad, to seek the aid of the man residing there—the man renowned for his healing touch. A blend of physician and mystic, my father was regarded with a mix of reverence and wonder. His address wasn't found in any phone book or online; yet, whether they called him a bone-setter, a healer, or a seer, those in need always found their way to him.

I had just dismounted and was still fumbling with my helmet when Albert Grandini appeared. A retired cop and longtime friend of my father, he moved briskly toward me, undisturbed by the mud that splattered his shoes. I scrutinized his lined face for any hint of my father's condition.

Camille leaned closer, her voice a whisper as she sought to reassure me, "He's okay."

"Don't fret," Albert assured me, clapping a hand on my shoulder. "He's resting."

Inside, I kicked off my shoes, just as I used to do after school, and followed him. My eyes flicked toward the staircase. "What happened?"

"We were working on a case. Then he had one of his visions."

"A case?"

"A missing person."

I nodded. Albert and my father had first joined forces to investigate a cattle theft, and they had collaborated on cases ever since. Even now, retired and making ends meet through painting, Albert remained my father's steadfast ally.

"He was dictating his vision for my sketch when he just collapsed," Albert continued. "I've never seen him like this. I thought he was having a heart attack. I called an ambulance, then I called you."

I needed to sit. "What did the paramedics say?"

Albert shrugged. "They asked about his medications, checked him over. He woke up, seemed fine, but they wanted him in the hospital."

"And he said no."

"To put it lightly. You know how he is."

I glanced upwards, my heart swelling with sympathy for the paramedics, who were likely on the receiving end of my father's verbal jabs—he's never been one to hold his tongue. Albert, noticing my worried expression, offered to stay. I chose to decline, walking him to the door instead.

"Are you sure? It's not like I have anyone waiting at home."

"I know," I said, touched by his concern and aware of his loneliness. Under different circumstances, we would have shared a drink and traded stories until the night fell. "Go home, Albert. It's still light out. I've got it from here."

48

———

I nudged the door open and stepped inside, calling out, "Dad?"

Startled from his nap, my father mumbled something into his beard before turning away. His snores resumed, filling the room and making the walls shake slightly. I walked over and watched him sleep.

"You guys could be twins," Camille observed, breaking the silence.

I chuckled. "I hear that a lot."

Checking his pulse, I found it steady as ever. I'd give him a more thorough once-over in the morning, but for now, I just tucked him in and left the room.

Outside, the night was pitch-dark. How had time flown by so fast? I realized I wasn't even hungry, despite having missed dinner. I headed straight to the living room. What had once served as a quarantine room now functioned as my dad's meeting space. The fire in the hearth was nearly out.

"Is this your sister?" Camille asked, her attention caught by a row of framed pictures.

I picked up the one she was pointing to, a photo of my mom holding hands with my sister and me. It was taken just before... before that day.

"We lost them when I was thirteen," I said, my voice steady as I wiped off some dust.

"Was it a car crash?"

I traced the scar just above my right eye with my fingertips, memories flooding back. "It was pouring that day. We were on our way back from the equestrian center. A car tried to overtake a tractor and didn't manage to pull it off. Instead of hitting the brakes, the driver floored it."

I set the photo back on the mantel. "My sister didn't make it. When I came to, my mom was there, pulling me out before the car went up in flames. There was a woman on the grass nearby, and the tractor driver tried to block my view. I thought she was the one driving the other car, but I was wrong..."

"Your mom?"

I nodded. "She didn't last a week."

"Is that why you became a neurosurgeon?"

I looked at Camille, caught off guard by her insight. "Might be."

I threw another log onto the dying embers.

"And your dad? Must have been hard for him."

"He never talks about it."

"You're worried about him?"

"He's not as young as he used to be, and he always puts others before himself."

I couldn't quite believe what I was saying. My dad had always been a pillar of strength, never falling ill, not even a sniffle. Maybe his healing touch worked on himself, keeping him healthy, or maybe it was just in his DNA. But he wouldn't be around forever, and one day, I'd be on my own. The thought sent a shiver down my spine.

Turning my attention back to the room, I threw another log on the fire, watching as the flames danced. I walked over to the large oak table, cluttered with papers—the things my dad had been looking at when he fainted.

As I tried to sort through the pile, a handwritten letter caught my eye. It was from the parents of Leanne Jalmet, a young Belgian girl who had gone missing in Italy during her summer break. I found myself reading without even thinking. The Italian police seemed too quick to rule out kidnapping. The last time anyone saw Leanne, she was hitchhiking at a rest stop, trying to make her way to Florence with a friend. Months had passed without any word from her. Her parents had even hired a private detective, but all leads pointed back to that same rest stop.

"She's my age," Camille noted, peering at a picture of Leanne over my shoulder.

I quickly flipped through the pages until another sketch caught my eye—a woman reminiscent of a Botticelli painting. Even in black and white, I couldn't picture her with the blonde hair Botticelli favored. For some reason, I imagined her with brown hair and hazel eyes—maybe because that's more my type.

"Do you know her?" Camille asked, her curiosity piqued.

"I don't think so," I replied.

Yet, the longer I stared at the sketch, the more a strange feeling crept in. It was as if I knew her... maybe even loved her. But that was impossible. We had never crossed paths.

49

A crow—or was it a cry?—jolted me awake. The rooster's call and the faint light of dawn slowly anchored me back to reality.

"Morning," Camille said, her voice pulling my attention.

She was perched on the armrest of the sofa where I had crashed last night, eyes fixed on me. A sudden urge to check my messages washed over me, and my heart skipped a beat at a missed call. Keeping my gaze on Camille, I listened to the voicemail left yesterday. It was from Nelly, my secretary, expressing her hopes that my father and I were well, then asking if she should cancel my appointments. There was no mention of Camille.

Ending the call, I decided it was too early to call back; Nelly wouldn't be in until nine. I'd wait to see my father first before making any decisions.

Still half-asleep, I shuffled to the kitchen and started the coffee maker. Amid its humming and gurgling, I thought I detected the distant sound of an engine. Curious, I peeked through the curtain facing the road. Fog swathed the house, obscuring my view past the gate. Despite the thick mist, the unmistakable sound of a car door slamming cut through the silence. Moments later, a knock echoed, signaling a visitor at the door.

Yannick Boilevin, the local baker, stood tense at the doorstep, a ribbon-tied box in his hands, offered like a tribute.

"Pastries. Fresh," he said. "Is your father up?"

"He's still asleep."

The baker's gaze flickered up the staircase. I hoped he'd just leave, but whatever was eating at him seemed to hold him there. Camille appeared beside him.

"Why don't you help him?" she prodded.

I tried to brush off her tone.

"What brings you here?" I asked, stepping aside to let him enter. "You look like you're in pain."

"My damn lower back is killing me. Tylenol's no use."

"I could prescribe something stronger."

He hesitated, his eyes darting toward the stairs at the sound of creaking. My father was awake.

"I'm coming down!" my dad's voice floated through the house.

"Dad, stay in bed!" I called back.

I ushered Yannick into the patient room. My father joined us shortly after, and our eyes met, laden with unspoken questions. Those would have to wait.

"So, Yannick, trying to impress the new apprentice again?" my father teased.

Caught, Yannick admitted to wrenching his back while hauling a hefty bag of flour.

"Let me see." With the practiced ease of a healer, my father's hands moved over Yannick's sore spot. He paused, eyes closed, concentrating.

"You've got a small hernia pressing on a nerve on your right side," he diagnosed, his eyes still closed.

Yannick winced. "My right leg's been killing me."

"All right. Let's get you fixed up," my father said, opening his eyes.

"Will it hurt?" Yannick asked, anxiety written all over his face.

"Not if you do as I say."

I stepped back. When I was a child, I'd spend entire summers tucked away in a corner of our living room, much like I am now mesmerized by my dad's work. Throughout the day, people would stream in: a person with a toothache desperate for relief before their dentist's next availability, another with a persistent cold sore, or someone plagued by a stiff neck. The waiting room was perpetually full. Beneath my dad's skillful touch, muscles relaxed, tendons yielded, and joints popped. With closed eyes, people would marvel at the orchestra of sounds he elicited from their bodies. And then, the moment of relief. Witnessing their taut expressions soften into broad smiles was the highlight for me. Years later, that same euphoria would hit whenever I saved a patient's life. It was an intoxicating high. Until recently, the satisfaction of success was all I had known. Failure? It seemed like a mere notion, a statistic, a speculative "what if". But since yesterday, that abstract number bore a name and a face. I never thought I'd feel so devastated.

50

———————

Yannick Boilevin had slipped away as quickly as a fish. The pastries he'd brought were now sitting in the center of the kitchen table, nestled between the coffee maker and jam jars.

"I need to talk to you," my father declared, adding sweetener to his coffee.

"Me too."

"All right, you go first."

"I think you should get some tests done," I suggested, pouring myself a cup of coffee. "And don't just dismiss this as nonsense. You did faint, after all."

Clearly irritated, my father waved away my concerns with a gesture of his hand. "I'm fine."

"Dad, I'd prefer to hear that from a doctor."

"There's no way I'm going to a hospital. At my age, you know when you check in, but there's no guarantee you'll ever check out."

"Then how about visiting Dr. Aubain?"

"That jackass? I'd rather die."

I'd forgotten the absurd feud between the village GP and my father—the 'frenemies' as the locals dubbed them.

"Dad..."

He reached for a chocolate croissant, trying to change the subject. "Examine me before you leave, if it'll make you feel better. But I assure you, you're barking up the wrong tree. My fainting spell wasn't health-related."

"Is it because of the woman in the sketch? Who is she?"

Surprised, my father looked up. "I should be the one asking you that."

I remained silent. Holding the sketch the previous evening had left me with a strange feeling. My father stood up to retrieve the portrait, laying it on the table right in front of me.

"Well? Do you recognize her?"

I traced the contours of the woman's face with my finger. "A couple of actresses come to mind who look like her," I replied. "Beyond that... I think I'd remember if I had met her."

"Hmm, it'll come to you."

I recognized that look in his eyes. "Are you saying I was in your vision, too?"

"Yes. That's what I wanted to discuss. I saw both of you. Together."

I smiled, not troubled by the revelation. "So, you saw us together. What happened then?"

My father suddenly looked pale. "Are you okay?" I asked.

"No, it's just that... thinking about it..."

"What did you see, Dad? I deserve to know."

"She was holding a gun, pointed at you, and..."

"What? Tell me."

"She shot you."

Everything clicked into place. I knew how vivid his visions could be, even though mine weren't quite as intense.

"So you saw me die, is that it, Dad?"

Taking a deep breath, my father replied, "I'm not certain."

"You can be honest with me."

"I am being honest! I felt sick, and the vision ended abruptly. But now that you're here, I'll try again."

51

Before I could even react, my dad seized my hand. A warmth surged through me, originating at my fingertips, coursing up my arm, and finally settling in my heart. My body seemed to melt away as my mind embarked on a high-speed journey. Scenes flashed before my eyes as if I were on a bullet train: cities, forests, and desolate landscapes. I glimpsed a hospital room, a house, ancient stone ruins, and expansive fields.

Faces began to appear within the landscapes. Some I didn't recognize; they were strangers to me. However, others immediately caught my attention. Tom Boylan was one, the father of my American patient. Then there was Leanne Jalmet, the missing Belgian girl I'd seen on the news. Suddenly, she was there—the woman from the portrait. She looked just as I had imagined her, yet I didn't feel threatened. Instead, a strong, instinctual pull drew me in, sparking a desire to protect her and prevent her from...

"Dying," my dad interjected, releasing my hand.

I clutched at my chest, overwhelmed by the intensity of my emotions and the mysterious connection I felt with a woman I'd never met.

"There's no mistaking it this time. You're meant to save her," he stated firmly.

Just what I needed, one more name on my already crowded list. I almost preferred the version where she was shooting at me.

"And the gun she pointed at me?"

"I can't be certain. There are shadows in the visions, pieces missing. Leanne Jalmet... she could be a part of this puzzle."

"But what's the link?"

"They might not. Sometimes the images blend together, get tangled. It's happened before."

I exhaled heavily and slumped into a chair. "Well, she's in for a tough time if she's relying on me."

"Why do you say that?"

"It's nothing."

He gave me a piercing look. "Is this about that girl who's been following you? Who is she?"

I tensed. Of course, my father could see Camille, too.

"I don't want to talk about it."

As he began to clear the table, a soft voice chimed in, cutting through the noise of clattering cutlery.

"My name is Camille. I'm his patient."

"You're..."

"Dead? Not last time I checked."

He turned back to me, his eyes filled with regret.

"I'm sorry," he whispered.

"Me too. But it is what it is."

His comforting hand rested on my shoulder as he drew nearer.

"You need to move on."

"Why would you say that?"

"You're holding on to guilt, and it's tying her down here."

Tears welled up in my eyes. "I don't know how to let go."

"Then let me try to help her," he suggested, extending his hand toward Camille.

As the door to the living room closed behind them, my phone buzzed. It was Cedric. I took a moment, closed my eyes, and braced myself for the news of the young girl's death.

52

———

The room Camille had occupied was now sterilized, awaiting the next patient.

I stood at the open door, staring at the vacant bed.

"Sir? Visiting hours haven't started. You can't be here."

The nurse's firm tone yanked me back to reality. Turning to face her, I offered an apologetic grin. "I'm sorry..."

Wearing jeans and a biker jacket, I realized she might not have recognized me.

I glanced once more at the bed where, just hours earlier, Camille had taken her last breath. "You're right," I murmured, "I don't belong here." With that, I turned and made my way toward the back stairs. It was the most discreet route to my office, ensuring I wouldn't bump into any colleagues. I wasn't in the mood for consolation or to hear that mistakes were only human.

When I reached the office, I found Nelly, my secretary, engrossed in transcribing surgical reports.

She removed her headphones as I entered. "How's your dad holding up?"

I offered a small smile, appreciating her concern. "He's doing just fine. Thanks for asking," I replied.

"I'm glad to hear that," she responded, her tone shifting as she continued, "I didn't hear back from you last night, so I canceled your morning appointments. Was that all right? Should I reschedule them?"

I held up my motorcycle helmet, signaling for her to pause. "No, leave them be. Did you hear from Lukas Boylan's parents? Weren't they supposed to call this week?"

She nodded. "Yes, they arrived in Paris yesterday."

"Yesterday?" My eyebrow arched in surprise.

"They wanted a few days to acclimatize before the surgery next week. Has something changed?"

I hesitated, my mind racing. "Possibly. I'll keep you posted."

With that, I left her to her work, knowing time was ticking and major decisions loomed ahead.

The file on Lukas Boylan was right where I'd left it yesterday, at the top of the upcoming surgeries stack. The young American was next on the list of patients I'd agreed to operate on.

I took off my jacket and slumped into my chair with a sigh, feeling anxious about the surgery ahead. Deep down, I questioned my real reasons for doing it. I studied Lukas Boylan's brain scans once more. They had been taken by many doctors from various hospitals, all trying to find a fix for his issue: an aneurysm, just about a third of an inch. Tiny but dreadful.

Lukas played football for Montana University. Once, after a hard tackle on the field, he passed out. The scans after the incident showed no injury from the game.

However, they found a small swelling in his brain that most doctors considered it too risky to operate on.

Most brain aneurysms today don't require surgery. Instead of opening the skull, doctors can treat them by threading a small tube through a major artery, from the leg up to the brain. They watch this on a screen and once they reach the aneurysm, they seal it with a tiny device. This simpler method means specialists other than surgeons often handle these cases. But for some people, this approach won't work because of where or how the aneurysm is shaped. Sadly, Lukas Boylan was one of those people.

But was the surgery necessary? Sooner or later, the aneurysm would cause a massive hemorrhage. But when? Sooner? Or later? It was the question no one could answer. All my colleagues had refused to operate. So why had I agreed to? Unable to answer that question, I sifted through the rest of the file, scattering various test results and radiographic reports. My attention was abruptly diverted by a knock. Someone was banging on my door. I got up and opened it. Maud, my ex, stood before me.

"Am I disturbing you?" she asked, as if we hadn't been avoiding each other for months.

I was very tempted to say yes. "No. Come on in."

She scanned my face before stepping inside, her gaze eventually settling on the couch—a poignant reminder of our shared history.

"I heard about your dad," she offered.

"It was a false alarm," I replied, not missing the way her eyes seemed to search mine for something unsaid. "You look like you've been through hell. Rough night?"

She nodded, a weary sigh escaping her. "I was the one who pronounced Camille."

Her name hung heavily in the air between us.

"How are her parents coping?" I asked, my tone softening.

"Devastated, as expected. I tried to console them, but what do you say in moments like these?" Her gaze dropped, a brief flash of sorrow in her eyes. Collecting herself, she looked up again. "They're holding a memorial service later in the chapel, if you're interested."

"Thanks. I might stop by," I lied, and she saw right through it.

"I'll leave you be, then." She turned to leave, hesitating at the doorframe before glancing back. "Look, about the wedding…" She hesitated, her gaze lifting to meet mine once again. "If you decide to skip it, I'd understand. No hard feelings, all right?" She offered a small, sad smile before disappearing down the hallway.

The silence enveloped the room as she left. Alone again, my thoughts raced. I picked up Lukas's photo, questioning my motives for pushing him toward surgery. Was I genuinely acting in his best interest, or was I just feeding my ego by tackling a challenging case? The answer eluded me. Staring back at me was just a young athlete, caught in a tight embrace with his parents. I set the photo down, rummaging through the paperwork for my phone.

"Nelly?" I said once I found it. "Could you call the Boylans back? Now."

"Right now?" she asked, taken aback.

"It can't wait."

"What should I tell them?"

"The surgery's been canceled."

A pause hung in the air.

"Are we rescheduling?"

"No. The procedure's off. For good."

"But..."

I hung up before she could finish. One weighty decision resolved. For the next, all I needed was a piece of paper and a pen.

53

I was in the middle of taking pictures off the wall when Professor Patrick Zajac, Head of the Department of Neurosurgery, waltzed into my office unannounced.

"Moving out?" he commented, his voice laced with a subtle twist of irony as he observed me upending the contents of my desk in a chaotic flurry.

Unfazed, I continued my task without responding.

He wandered over to the window, remarking, "You know, your office has a much better view than mine."

"It's all yours if you want it," I shot back, not missing a beat.

"Does it have anything to do with this? Nelly gave it to me earlier." He dropped a sealed envelope on the only clean corner of my desk.

"You didn't open it?" I asked, surprise and discomfort mingling in my voice.

"No need. The moment Nelly mentioned you called off the aneurysm surgery, not to mention all upcoming procedures, I knew what it was."

I dropped my gaze. "It's a resignation letter," I mumbled, almost to myself.

"I figured as much."

"You're not here to change my mind, are you?" I asked, meeting his gaze once more.

Bending down, he picked up a roll of tape from the ground and handed it to me with a nonchalant shrug. "You wouldn't listen, anyway."

I took the tape from him and sealed another box. If I kept this pace, I'd be packed and gone by evening.

"Don't I deserve an explanation?" he pressed on, a hint of betrayal lacing his words. "After all the hours spent defending you to the board?"

"I apologize for any inconvenience, but I've made up my mind," I replied, holding my ground.

He waited, expecting more. When I remained silent, he pressed, "And?"

I thought back to my father. *"You need to move on... You're holding on to guilt."* He had said to me before taking Camille away.

Swallowing hard, I admitted, "I can't forgive myself."

"Camille's fate was sealed," Professor Zajac began, trying to offer me some comfort. "Now, please, sit down. Your constant pacing is making me anxious."

I stopped, overwhelmed by my emotions. "You don't understand," I murmured, my voice shaking. "I made a terrible mistake."

Without hesitation, he stood and moved to close the door, but I interjected, "Leave it open. Let everyone know. It's all there in the report—I'm responsible for Camille's death. She could've led a full life, married, had children... if only I'd acted differently."

He looked earnestly into my eyes. "There's no way to be certain of that."

I sank onto the couch, weighed down by guilt. That was the problem—I knew. "You can't possibly understand the depth of what I've done."

He sat beside me, his voice soft but insistent. "I know it might sound cliché, but in our line of work, mistakes, even tragic ones, are inevitable. It was a major artery; the bleeding was beyond control. Such things can occur, even to the most skilled among us."

Through my tears, I gave him a wry smile. "Are you going to offer me that 'to err is human' sentiment next?"

He shrugged, nonplussed. "Why not? It's true. You're a skilled surgeon, that much is clear—a virtuoso, even. But, regardless of talent, everyone makes mistakes now and then. I'm not entirely sure if reversing your decision about the young American was the best move. But I am sure of this: people often imagine a surgeon to be this figure with nerves of steel and unwavering hands. They're missing the mark. What's paramount is judgment. Knowing when to operate, when to step back, and when to call it quits. Experience will show you the way. And trust me, from someone who's been around the block, that experience will give you the confidence that seems elusive now."

I glanced at the pending files on my desk, my heart sinking further. "I don't know if I'll ever be able to operate again."

"It's normal to feel that way. But it'll pass."

"And if it doesn't?"

He sighed, choosing his words. "The only way to truly know is to step back in there. Start slow, handle a minor case. Consider it like a top-tier tennis player recovering from an injury. They begin with the basics, regain their confidence, and then aim for the grand slams."

He often resorted to sports analogies, a nod to his history as a tennis aficionado and once a player on the ATP circuit. In different circumstances, his comparisons would have drawn a smile from me, but now, it did little to alleviate the weight pressing on my heart.

He looked at me. "Well? Your thoughts?"

I struggled to find words, realizing the profound change within me. The guilt felt overwhelming, unlike anything I had experienced before. "I'm sorry," was all I could say.

Patrick Zajac picked up the resignation letter, tucking it into his lab coat. "Listen, I have another idea. I was supposed to attend the Annual Congress by the Society of Neurosurgery in Nice. But my wife surprised me with a weekend getaway for my birthday. I'd appreciate it if you could take my place."

"You're asking me to represent you?"

"It's just for three days. A change of scenery might help clear your mind. While you're there, you don't have to commit to every seminar. Take some time to explore the city. Once you're back, we can discuss everything."

"And if I still decide to resign?"

He met my eyes with sincerity. "Then, with a heavy heart, I'll accept it."

54

———

I was drifting off, my earbuds in, when a gentle nudge jolted me awake.

"Sir?"

Opening my eyes, I found my seatmate gesturing toward the flight attendant standing in the aisle, eyeing us. The lead singer of Muse was belting out "Time is Running Out" in my ears, but I could see the attendant's lips moving. I turned down the volume.

"Excuse me?"

"Your seatbelt," he repeated, a bit louder this time. "We're about to land."

I got the message. Yet, he would not leave until he saw me buckle up. So, I complied. My seatmate flashed me a quick smile, which I returned before cranking the volume back up, eager to avoid any further conversation.

Resting my forehead against the window like a child, I watched as the plane banked, appearing to hover in midair for a moment. As the plane began its descent on this sunny day, the shimmering Mediterranean came into view. Below, I could spot people strolling along Nice's iconic Promenade des Anglais. When it leveled out, the wing's shadow stretched toward the pebbly beaches below. Settling back in my seat, I braced myself for the inevitable jolt of the landing gear hitting the tarmac.

Fifteen minutes later, I was joining the flow of passengers making their way off the plane, carry-on in tow, and heading straight for the arrivals area.

A shuttle was ready to take me and the other surgeons to our hotel, but I opted for a cab instead, craving a few moments of solitude.

"Take the coastal road," I instructed the driver.

He shot a glance my way through the rearview mirror. "It's likely to be jammed at this hour, sir."

I shrugged. "Doesn't matter. I'm not in any rush." The conference wouldn't start until tomorrow, and I had no other plans for the day.

Nice was uncharted territory to me. I can't even remember my last vacation. Most of my time was spent working or sleeping. A thought of my ex briefly crossed my mind, but I brushed it off. I wasn't single by choice, but solitude was better than being with the wrong person. I was going to take advantage of these few days to get lost in the city streets. Just to get lost.

For about ten minutes, I watched an old man feeding pigeons from the back seat of a cab, stuck in traffic, motionless, surrounded by dozens of other cars. I might have mistaken it for a congested Parisian street, but instead of Paris's graffiti-covered walls, I was gazing at the sea framed by palm trees.

"Is it a long walk from here?" I asked the driver, catching his sidelong glance. "Don't worry, you'll get your full fare," I added.

He grinned, his teeth stained yellow from nicotine. "Well, it's about a half-hour walk. You picked a good day for it, though. It's been raining all week."

After thanking him, I handed over my credit card, and he swiped it without hesitation. Exiting the cab, I took a moment to orient myself. I avoided a scooter as I navigated the gridlocked traffic, finally reaching the relative safety of the sidewalk. Extending the handle of my rolling suitcase, I set off at a slow pace, breathing in the salty air, feeling the warm sun on my skin, and losing myself in the endless blue expanse stretching out before me.

As I neared downtown, the crowd of pedestrians thickened. My thoughts drifted to the terrorist attacks that had shaken the city back in 2016 during the July 14th celebrations. This very sidewalk had witnessed the loss of numerous lives. My contemplation was interrupted by my ringing phone—it was Cedric. A moment's hesitation, and the call was gone. Knowing he was persistent, I turned off my phone, wishing for a way to also silence the haunting memories of the operating room and Camille's last moments. A gust of sea breeze sent a shiver through me, but I pressed on.

I passed the Negresco, recognizable by its pink dome and white facade embellished with Corinthian columns and gilding. I was scheduled to attend a series of conferences here, at this famous Nice palace, the next morning. My hotel was not far, a pleasant four-star—not quite a palace, but I was soon to find it satisfying.

. . .

At the reception desk, I was informed I'd be staying in a room with a sea view. A bellboy took my suitcase and magnetic key card, guiding me like an urban sherpa. As we ascended in the elevator, he ran off the list of amenities: from a panoramic bar-restaurant, to a gym, to a tranquil hammam spa. I listened with partial attention while we walked down the corridor where our footsteps were hushed by the dense carpet. My room was situated at the far end, and as we arrived, my neighbor from the room on the left made his exit. I recognized him as one of the conference speakers, a neurosurgeon from Rouen University Hospital whose name slipped my mind. If he was surprised to find me there, he didn't let on. We greeted each other, but nothing more. That was promising for what was to come.

Having tipped the bellhop, I gravitated toward the sliding glass doors opening to a quaint balcony. The bellhop had mentioned that on clear days, the Isle of Beauty was visible over a hundred miles away. However, all that met my eyes was the stark contrast between sky and sea, the latter shimmering as if dusted with silver. The hum of traffic from the Promenade des Anglais eventually coaxed me back inside.

A glance at my watch informed me the hotel restaurant was an option, but after freshening up, I hesitated.

Professor What's-his-name, whom I'd met earlier, popped back into my mind. I sensed some unfriendliness hidden under his polite act. This made me reconsider my next move. Walking to the hotel restaurant might cause an awkward encounter with him, or even worse, one of his buddies.

Drained and not in the mood to navigate an unfamiliar city, I settled for room service. Yet, when my meal arrived, my appetite had waned, and I found myself pushing the food around my plate, barely able to take a few bites. The initial excitement had dissolved, leaving me bracing for a restless night.

55

I was already behind schedule when I left the hotel the next morning, missing the first half-hour of the opening speech.

Upon arriving at the elegant Hotel Negresco, I was greeted by two uniformed doormen. Stepping inside, I felt as though I had entered the court of a regent, in a kind of shoddy homage to Louis XIV. The décor was so reminiscent of Versailles that it struck me as a Disneyland-esque imitation. I entered the Salon Royal just as the opening remarks were concluding. The room was round, with Greek-style columns and an impressive domed skylight topped with a dazzling chandelier.

I found an empty seat at the back. A few curious eyes settled on me. Glancing around, I searched for familiar faces. All I could see from my vantage point were the backs of heads—some graying, others baring the telltale signs of age. My entrance had noticeably lowered the room's average age. Unfortunately, the same couldn't be said for the gender ratio, which still skewed heavily male. The speech concluded to robust applause, which I quickly echoed to assimilate.

The head of the French Society of Neurosurgery introduced the first speaker, who turned out to be my roommate. Even though he was well known in his field, he wasn't a brilliant public speaker. Unfortunately, the other talks were just as dull, with boring slides on a big screen, and the audience was losing interest.

The older surgeon sitting next to me was almost asleep. I felt tired too, so I sneaked out when the last morning speaker finished.

Back at my hotel, I swapped my suit for jeans and sneakers, attire far more appropriate for a city exploration.

Old Nice was alive with locals and a few tourists enjoying the warm weather. I wandered the tight streets and ended up in a cozy square surrounded by bars and eateries. Not very hungry, I decided to have a drink at a tapas bar. I tried some local bites like stuffed vegetables with a tasty mix of minced meat, garlic, and herbs. These treats, along with a glass of crisp white wine from Côtes de Provence, made for a perfect light meal.

My wanderings led me to the Museum of Modern Art, where I encountered an array of unusual, and some quite beautiful, artworks.I spotted Niki de Saint Phalle's famous sculptures right away, as the Negresco happened to display one of those whimsical statues in the hall. Her 'Nanas' are easy to recognize with their bright colors and full figures—a fun and lively tribute to women.

The museum's rooftop garden provided breathtaking views of the city, the sea, and the mountains beyond—a sight so captivating it left me feeling a touch melancholic. Thoughts of Camille crept in; she had aspired to be an architect too. I wondered about the heights she might have reached if... A wave of dizziness washed over me, snapping me back to reality. It was time to head back.

I had just lain down in my room, still dressed, when a series of knocks hit my door. My eyes snapped open. Ignoring it in the hope that they would leave, I stayed silent.

"Open the door! I know you're in there!"

The accent was unmistakably American, belonging to Tom Boylan—the father of the young football player whose surgery I had canceled. I opened the door, taken aback. Towering a good four inches above me, his shoulders seemed almost too broad for the doorway. I stood there, awkward and surprised.

"Mr. Boylan? What—"

"We need to talk!" he interrupted, his tone leaving no room for argument.

56

———————

The hotel's panoramic bar was closing in just under twenty minutes. Lukas Boylan's father sat across from me, oblivious to the stunning view of the Bay of Angels. We sat in silence until the bartender served our drinks: a draft beer each.

"Is your son here too?" I asked.

Tom Boylan met my gaze. For a moment, I thought tears might start to fall, but I was mistaken. It was anger, not sorrow, that brought the shine to his eyes.

"He's staying in Paris with his mother," he muttered after a pause.

I observed as he gulped down half of his beer in one go. Mine sat untouched before me; I found myself wishing I had ordered something stronger. This conversation was bound to be tough, and I was in too deep to back out now. *Might as well bite the bullet,* I thought, eyeing Tom Boylan's broad, muscular neck.

The weight of the upcoming conversation about his son's surgery hung heavily in the air. Just as I was about to speak, he interjected.

"Your secretary was the one who told me where to find

you," he said, "right after I got the news that the operation had been canceled."

I exhaled. "Mr. Boylan..."

He silenced me with a raised hand—big and rough, like a bear's paw. "I need to hear it straight from you. Look me in the eye and tell me you won't operate on Lukas. Then give me an explanation."

Our eyes locked, two weary souls poised for a final showdown. My nose, broken in a past soccer match, stood stark against the scar that marked his face, hinting at a confrontation far graver than any sport.

I averted my gaze, speaking in a hushed tone. "Mr. Boylan, it's complicated. I can't go through with the operation on Lukas."

"Then explain yourself!" His voice escalated, filling the room as his hand slammed down onto the table. The few other patrons in the bar couldn't help but turn and stare.

"Look, I never should've agreed to the surgery. It was a grave mistake, and I'm sorry," I confessed, my voice laced with regret.

His face twisted in a mix of rage and despair. "We could've handled rejection. But you, you gave us hope. And now you're backing out. You're just like the rest, yet you couldn't even be upfront with us."

Images of Lukas, along with his brain's angiogram—a complex network of vessels with an aneurysm glaring ominously—flooded my mind. I had once believed I could save him, risks be damned. Now, the very thought churned my stomach.

"I'm sorry," I whispered again.

Under the table, my hands were shaking like a junkie's, except it wasn't withdrawal that made them tremble, but the fear of killing again.

Tom slumped back, his energy spent, defeated. "Backing out on your word... it's just not right."

I felt diminished, insignificant. The Boylans weren't wealthy; they had drained their savings on flights to France, securing an apartment in Paris, hospital charges, and my consultation—all of which had amounted to nothing.

"I'll refund you," I said, standing up.

Tom looked up, his eyes wide with surprise. "What?"

"I'll write you a check," I insisted, my voice steady. "Just tell me how much."

He stood up as well, and before I knew it, I felt a sharp pain on my face, accompanied by a sickening crack. Tom Boylan had just punched me square in the face.

57

I opened my eyes to a young woman in a white coat standing in front of me, stethoscope around her neck, eyes studying my x-rays. She didn't seem to notice I had woken up.

"No fractures," I mumbled, catching her off guard.

She jumped, and I squinted, trying to read the name on her badge, but my vision was too blurred.

"Can you tell me your name?" she asked, flashing a light into my eyes to check my pupillary reflexes.

"Johan Valmeur," I replied, wincing at the bright light. "I'm a neurosurgeon," I added, hoping it might earn me some preferential treatment. She remained unimpressed; perhaps she thought I was lying. "You can check. I work at Salpêtrière Hospital."

"Good for you. What day is it?" she asked.

I paused for a moment, organizing my thoughts before providing the day, month, and year. "Is that right?" I asked, uncertainty tinging my voice.

"Not sure?"

"Uh... yeah, I'm sure."

"Good answer! I would give you a candy, but that girl over there ate them all," she said, pointing at a ten-year-old with a cast on her arm who stuck her tongue out at me. So much for wanting kids, I thought to myself.

"Where am I?"

Frowning, she replied, "You're in Pasteur Hospital's emergency room, in Nice."

When I attempted to sit up, a sharp pain shot through my head, forcing me back down. My cheekbone throbbed, and I could feel a loose tooth.

"You got stitches. Just a scalp wound from when you fell and hit a table corner. Nothing serious," she said, jotting something down on a clipboard.

Reaching up, my fingers grazed the stitches, prompting a stern "Don't touch!" from her. "Now I have to disinfect it again."

"Sorry."

She sighed, making a note in my chart.

"The guy who attacked you is in custody, by the way."

Flashes of memories returned. I remembered the bitterness in Tom Boylan's eyes when I offered him money—my clumsy attempt at a bribe for redemption. *Brilliant, Johan!*

"I don't want to press charges."

"Don't tell *me*. Tell *him*," she said, nodding toward a police officer making small talk with two nurses.

She continued as if reading from a script of routine, "Dr. Palazzi will see you soon. You'll be transferred once a bed opens up."

I tried to protest, but she cut me off. "If you're in pain, let the nurses know."

"I'm fine. I can just go back to my hotel."

"You were out cold when they brought you in. If you really are a neurosurgeon like you said, then you should know better than anyone—we can't just let you leave," she said, and walked away before I could respond.

I swept the room with a single glance. The cop had left, and the two nurses he'd been chatting up were gone, likely huddled over coffee in the staff lounge by now. My eyes landed on a young guy with acne, awkwardly wearing his white lab coat with a stethoscope draped around his neck like a medal he hadn't earned. A rookie med student, no doubt. I caught his attention and motioned for him to lower the side rails confining me to the bed.

He looked around nervously, clearly out of his depth.

"I really need to use the bathroom. It's kind of urgent," I explained.

His head nodded eagerly, keen to assist, and I guided him through the steps.

"No, no, the other lever. There you go. Now you can lower them," I directed.

As I stood, he was right there to steady me, watching as I forced my feet into my shoes. He hesitated, as if considering whether to accompany me.

"Don't worry about it. Stay here; you might stumble into something more thrilling than a bathroom break."

His eyes lit up with relief. With that, I seized the moment and darted down the nearest corridor.

I had to get out of this hospital, and fast.

The thought that they would send someone after me turned every shadow into a pursuer. I avoided Dr. Palazzi at all costs, with my swollen cheek, a loose tooth, and hair in disarray—I was a mess. As two doctors passed by, they barely gave me a second look, which was strange. The whole scene felt eerily familiar. The hospital, the staff—I had seen it all before, in a vision at my father's house. Was the woman from that vision here somewhere? Was this meeting fated? My pulse raced with a mix of anticipation and bewilderment as it dawned on me that I had no idea where I was headed.

58

Eyes scanning, I searched for any sign to help me understand where I was and how to escape this labyrinth. Yet, there was nothing. Despite this, a compelling force urged me to continue down the hallway. Trusting my instincts—or perhaps fragments of a vision—I moved without overthinking. Pushing through a fire door, crossing another corridor, I jumped into an elevator, pressing buttons at random. When the doors slid open, a little girl stared up at me, clutching a stuffed animal in one hand while pulling an IV stand with the other. She tightened her grip on her toy as I stepped closer.

"Hello," I offered, smiling, but it seemed to startle her even more. I vowed never to have kids and figured I should make myself scarce before her tears drew attention.

"Hey! You there!" A nurse's voice echoed from the opposite end of the hallway.

I retreated, picking up my pace. But she pursued.

"Wait!" she called out.

Increasing my speed, I scanned my surroundings for an exit. The hallway took a sharp turn, obstructing her view.

Seizing the opportunity, I burst through the first door I found, finding myself in a tiny room.

"I need your help."

Startled, I spun around to find the nurse I'd been evading right behind me. Now I was cornered.

"You've got the wrong person," I replied. "I don't work here."

I tried to sidestep her, but she blocked me again.

"Listen, it's urgent."

"Why me? Don't you have coworkers?"

She lowered her head, her shoulders drooping. A whisper slipped from her lips. "I've tried reaching out. No one's responding. You're my last resort."

I sighed, glancing at the clock. Time was slipping away, and because of my actions, Tom Boylan was in custody. I needed to slip away unnoticed.

"All right, I'll help. But only if—"

"I'll help you sneak out?" she finished for me.

I paused, stunned. Had I been so transparent?

"I know this place inside and out," she assured me. "My car's parked in the basement. Once we're done here, I'll show you to the exit."

"Fine... What do you need?"

"Just down the hall to the right is a supply room. I need several items moved to my car."

A cold realization washed over me. "You want me to steal?"

"It won't set the hospital back much. Trust me, it's necessary."

I hesitated.

"Are you in or out?" she pressed.

The supply room was nearby, its shelves reaching to the ceiling, laden with an array of medical supplies.

"We have to hurry," she urged, rattling off the items and their locations: syringes, gauze, a resuscitation bag, suture and IV kits, saline bags. "Oh, I'm Marianne. Marianne Deconti. But please, call me Mari."

"Well, Mari, I can't say this is a pleasure."

"Take my word for it. I wish I hadn't been involved either. And you? What's your name?"

"Johan."

"Johan who?"

"Valmeur."

Recognition flashed in her eyes.

"Wait, were you on the cover of TIME last month?"

I remained silent as she sized me up.

"That is you! I expected you to be taller," she mused aloud.

I wanted to tell her that the man on the magazine cover was long gone, that the celebrated surgeon with the golden touch couldn't save a soul now.

"Hey, you forgot the adrenaline," she pointed out.

Sighing, I grabbed the vials and stuffed them into the bag. "Anything else?"

"And a portable defibrillator, too. Right behind you, on the left shelf."

"You should be calling an ambulance!"

"A medevac would be more accurate, but I can't provide coordinates. At this rate, a coroner would be more suitable. So, could you please hurry?"

I stared at her, ensuring she wasn't joking.

"You're serious," I concluded.

"As a heart attack."

"Who's dying?"

"Me."

59

———

"My car's right over there," the nurse pointed out, her voice steady but urgent. "The gray one."

I located the Toyota Yaris, a hybrid model that looked like it hadn't seen a wash in months. As I approached, she added, "The door's unlocked. We need to be quick; time is of the essence."

I tossed the bag filled with resuscitation equipment onto the back seat, then slid into the driver's seat with haste. "Keys?" I asked, scanning the interior.

"At your feet," she responded.

Glancing down, I found the set of keys resting on the floor mat near the brake pedal. "What's—"

"No time," she cut me off. "Start the car. And it's automatic," she added, noticing my momentary confusion. "Just put it in 'drive'—that's 'D'."

I couldn't help but feel like I was back in driver's education as I followed her instructions. "Sorry."

"It's fine. Now take a right out of here," she directed.

I merged into the flow of traffic, trying to keep my composure. "Where are we headed?"

"Up to the mountains. That's where he took me."

"Who?" I questioned, throwing a surreptitious glance at my unique passenger.

"The man who kidnapped me," she explained, her voice taking on a darker tone. "He ambushed me in the parking lot that night."

"When was this?"

"Wednesday, after my shift. I was exhausted and just wanted to get home. I was getting into my car when someone grabbed me from behind. A hand clamped over my mouth—I couldn't scream or breathe. Then everything went black. I woke up at home."

"He... he dropped you at your place?" I asked, disbelief coloring my voice.

She nodded. "I live alone. He must have figured that out; he must have been watching me. He took me to the basement, tied me up, and left me there for hours. When he returned, I got the sense that he wasn't alone. I'm pretty sure there was another woman there with me."

"Another captive?" My voice was tight, and I could feel my grip on the steering wheel tightening.

"That's what it seemed like. And then—"

"And then?" I prompted, my heart racing.

"He threw me back into the car and locked me in the trunk."

"Did you get a good look at him? Would you be able to identify him?"

"Yes."

My resolve hardened. "Should I call the police?"

"Do you have a phone on you?"

I patted down my jeans, a sinking feeling in my stomach as I realized that my cell, along with my wallet and ID, were all back in my hotel room. "Damn it!"

"Forget it," she dismissed.

But I couldn't just let it go. "Tell me where the nearest police station is."

"There's no time for that, and don't even think about turning this car around. I'm barely holding on as it is. What would you even tell them?"

I opened my mouth to respond, but nothing came out. She had a point.

"Just... take a left here," she instructed, her voice softer now.

I let her lead the way.

"Keep going straight," she added as we approached an intersection. A sign marked the entrance to the Paillon expressway, a quick path to the hinterlands of Nice.

"We're leaving Nice?"

She gave a single nod of confirmation.

"Is it far? What if we don't make it in time?"

A truck's horn blared behind us, causing me to startle, though it seemed to go unnoticed by Marianne.

"I don't know," she admitted, her voice low. "Just drive. I'll tell you what to do."

I pressed the gas pedal further, putting more distance between us and the trailing traffic until the truck was just a distant speck in the rearview mirror, and the city of Nice was merging into the horizon.

"Thank you," Marianne whispered after a moment, her tone sincere. "I'm not sure I'll get another chance to say it."

60

———————

The mountains seemed to part as we drove through. Foot on the gas, I tried not to lose control of the car as the road wound. The landscape, both majestic and monotonous, gave me the feeling of standing still. We had left Nice fifty minutes ago, delving deeper into the countryside.

"Are we there yet?"

Marianne's response was absent; she had succumbed to silence quite a while ago.

"Marianne?"

I slowed down to turn toward my passenger. The nurse wasn't moving. The white of her uniform seemed to blend into the air, making her appear almost translucent.

"I feel... strange."

Her voice, a faint whisper, barely reached my ears. I extended my hand, intending to offer comfort, but instead, my fingers brushed against the coarse fabric of the seat.

"No, Mari, not now. Please."

The car swayed as my attention wavered. By the time I regained control, Marianne had vanished.

"Can you hear me? Where should I go? How can I find you if you don't guide me?"

"*On the left... by the barn...*"

The voice, now emanating from the back seat, was soft yet clear. I glanced in the rearview mirror, catching a glimpse of a faint silhouette casting a subtle shadow. Without hesitation, I slammed the brakes, shifting into reverse. A hidden trail, obscured by dense foliage, led up to the top of a hill. Shifting gears, I pressed on the gas, propelling the car forward. A cloud of dust enveloped the vehicle as it jostled and protested against the rough terrain. The Toyota, ill-equipped with its front-wheel drive, struggled fiercely. Resigned, I realized I had to proceed on foot. Parking the car, a sudden chill breeze caressed my neck.

"*It's too late...*"

Her form reappeared beside me, now more fragile and ethereal, as if she might disintegrate upon the slightest contact.

"No! Hang on! You can't leave me now, do you understand? Tell me where you are! I can bring you back! Can you hear me, Mari?"

Her translucent form fractured, with bright lines spreading across like cracks on thin ice.

"*It's a shame... We were almost there.*"

Marianne Deconti's voice reverberated through the air, like an echo trapped inside the car. I slammed on the brakes and jumped out. Shielding my eyes with my hands, I tried to spot the barn she had mentioned. If Marianne was up there, there wasn't a second to waste. With the resuscitation equipment bag slung over my shoulder, I started up the hill, but the sound of an engine halted me in my tracks. A SUV, suited for the rugged terrain, was heading straight for me. I barely had time to jump out of the way. It sped past without slowing down, as if I didn't even matter.

"*It's him,*" whispered a voice at my side, chilling my blood. "*He's the one who killed me!*"

A dirt path, just a bit ahead, sliced through the thick vegetation.

"Mari!"

My call dissipated into the wind, leaving me alone with an expansive meadow before me. And in its midst, the remains of an old stone building.

61

Marianne lay sprawled on the dusty floor, her face shrouded beneath several layers of plastic wrap. Without hesitation, I attacked the plastic, ripping it away until her nose and mouth were free. She wasn't breathing. I applied the respirator mask to her face and squeezed the bag, watching as her chest rose—once, twice. Setting the bag aside, I powered up the portable defibrillator. As soon as it beeped, I grabbed the paddles and placed them firmly on her chest. Marianne's body convulsed, then fell back to the ground, showing no signs of life on the monitor. Without a moment's pause, I began chest compressions, pressing down on her sternum, aware that I was risking broken ribs. One, two, three, four... nineteen, twenty. I didn't make it to thirty before a guttural sound, almost a scream, made me jump.

"Mari?"

I tried to stabilize her as she began to panic.

"Mari, it's me. Calm down. I'm here to help, remember?"

She quieted, focusing on my voice. The plastic wrap acted as a blindfold. I wanted to remove it, but the moment I touched her, she started thrashing again—hitting, scratching, screaming in terror as I struggled to restrain her.

"Damn it, Mari! Stop!"

Left with no other option, I pressed down on her with all my weight, pinning her wrists and stretching her arms above her head.

"I'm not going to hurt you. Do you understand?"

Marianne swallowed hard.

"Who the hell are you?"

"It's Johan. I'm a surgeon. Look, I'll explain everything later. Can you walk?"

She swallowed again, nodding slightly.

"I think so, yeah."

"Okay. I'm going to let you go now."

As I eased my grip, Marianne tried to pull the plastic wrap off herself, but her trembling fingers betrayed her.

"Wait, let me help."

I caught the edge of the plastic, lifting it over her forehead. Marianne opened her eyes, and I offered her a comforting smile. For a fleeting moment, her expression softened.

"You're going to be all right. I'm here with you. Everything will be okay."

Behind me, the defibrillator emitted a long, shrill beep, signaling it was charged and ready for another shock.

62

Johan stopped talking.

"What's wrong? Why'd you stop?" Zoe inquired.

"You're hurting me."

Surprise registered in Zoe's eyes.

"My fingers," Johan winced. "You're gripping them too hard."

Only then did she realize her tight hold on his hand. How long had she been holding it that way? Perhaps since he mentioned being a neurosurgeon at Salpêtrière, which had stirred something inside her. Dr. Valmeur... Could he be the one she was meant to meet?

"Zoe?"

She let go of his hand. "I apologize. I got engrossed in your story."

"It's all true, Zoe. You believe me, right?"

She hesitated, biting her lip. The sensible thing would be to distance herself from him. Yet, she couldn't ignore the feelings she had developed, whether born of Stockholm Syndrome or genuine attraction.

"I believe you," she murmured.

"But there is a 'but,' isn't there?"

She paused. "My sister's gone. Abducted, maybe even killed, just like Marianne."

Johan's face fell. "I'm so sorry."

She observed him. It was unsettling, seeing that he had no memory of their previous conversation on this topic.

"You were there, Johan. You must've seen his face."

Johan paled, and Zoe regretted pressing him. She suggested a break, but he refused. "Would you like some water?"

"No," he said, locking eyes with her. "But would you hold my hand again?"

She grinned. "Aren't you worried I'll hurt you again?"

"That's the least of my worries."

Their hands joined once more. "Go on," she urged.

"Mari... I couldn't save her. I saw him kill her, the man in the SUV. After I revived her, he came back for her. And he..."

She tightened her grip on his hand gently. "Can you describe him?"

"No. I only saw him from the back, and the few times I glimpsed his face, it was shadowed. The only thing I recall is an overwhelming sense of dread, like facing a wild predator."

Before she could ask another question, he added, "I didn't see his license plate. I was too focused on Mari. But the SUV was white."

"A white SUV doesn't help much," Zoe muttered. "Any distinctive marks?"

"A sticker," he said. "A deer's head with text. It read, 'A picture is worth more than a trophy.'"

"That's odd. I assumed our killer would be a hunter, not an advocate for animal rights."

"Zoe, he's deranged."

"I know…"

"But you don't get it. I think he was there from the beginning. After he drove by, he must've turned back. He watched me try to save her."

Zoe nodded in understanding. "So, he got to kill her twice," she said, locking eyes with Johan.

"I'm sorry I can't tell you more," he added. "If only I could have seen him face-to-face. Unfortunately, the rest is a gigantic black hole."

Zoe furrowed her brows, confused. "Why didn't he kill you?"

"I think he believed he had."

"What do you mean?"

Johan began to unbutton his shirt, revealing more of his story. "Gel is applied to the defibrillator's paddles to increase conductivity and minimize burns," he explained. "But I doubt he bothered. If he had shocked me, as I suspect he did, there should be burn marks where the electrodes made contact."

Struggling with the last few buttons, Johan found it difficult to open his shirt with just one hand.

Zoe stepped forward. "Here, let me help."

She unbuttoned his shirt, parting the soiled, blood-streaked fabric to reveal his bare chest. Memories flooded back as she saw the tattoos; she remembered the first time she had seen them at Chantal and Roger's farmhouse.

"Well? Do you see anything?"

Zoe leaned in closer, spotting a faint red mark. "Right here," she said, touching his skin.

Johan flinched.

"Did that hurt?"

He shook his head. "No, your hands are just cold," he noted, managing a weak smile. Johan twisted, trying to see the mark, and winced, reminded of his broken ribs. "My heart must've stopped—long enough for him to think I was dead."

"And then what happened?"

He paused, reflecting on that moment. "I can't remember. I must've regained consciousness. I probably took Mari's car, mistaking it for mine."

Zoe thought about this for a moment. "That's what you were trying to explain when we first met," she mused, nodding. "The GPS led you to her house—a house you thought was yours until you found me in the basement."

Their eyes locked before Zoe broke the silence. "What do you remember after that?"

Johan swallowed hard, his throat constricting. "The woods. Leanne, her face smeared with dirt—or what was left of it. My father had pinpointed a location on a map. I glimpsed that map the night I returned to our home in Normandy."

Zoe shivered, recalling his words. Johan had told her repeatedly, *"I'm searching for something. Once I find it, I'll know who I am."* Throughout his journey, even in confusion, he sought Leanne Jalmet, much like his father before him.

"And yes, I remember you. The terror etched on your face, the gun in your hands, aimed directly at me. You shot at me."

"Just like in your father's vision," she murmured, lost in thought.

"Not exactly. You missed. You can't imagine my shock, seeing you there, in person."

"Your father said the same thing when he saw me."

In that moment, Johan took her hand, mirroring her gesture from earlier. "Speak to him. If anyone can lead you to your sister, it's my father."

63

Inspector Dorsey looked on as Zoe recounted her statement once more, firmly asserting, amidst a web of deceit, that she had willingly followed Johan.

"Are you certain about this?" he probed.

"Yes," she said, signing at the bottom of the page.

Dorsey shook his head, observing as her pen glided across the paper.

"Have you discussed this with your brother-in-law? Does he know what you're up to?"

"Anthony has no say over me. I make my own decisions."

He sighed, clearly not convinced.

"And what about you, Inspector? What are your plans moving forward?"

"I'm sorry?"

"Regarding my sister."

"Your sister..."

"Why didn't you ever respond?" she interjected. "I reached out to Europol multiple times, and I was told each time that you'd get back to me, but you never did."

His brow furrowed in confusion. "I never received your

messages. It seems the information must have gotten lost somewhere along the chain of command."

Zoe leaned back in her chair, feeling deflated. "How convenient," she muttered under her breath.

"Miss Rossi, please, just hear me out. Your sister—she's on the Reaper's list now. Europol's stepping in. We're taking over the investigation. This is serious."

Zoe was left stunned. She had invested so much effort in trying to persuade them.

"I... I don't know what to say."

He moved to sit on the edge of the desk, placing a comforting hand on her shoulder—a gesture that felt paternal or perhaps like that of a professor encouraging a top student.

"Just promise me you'll stay out of harm's way. Let us handle your sister's case, okay?"

Zoe thought back to her recent interaction with Johan and her impending request to his father. "Okay," she lied.

"Do you promise?"

She had already woven a tangled web of deceit; one more lie wouldn't matter. She promised him.

"We need you to stay off social media for a while. Don't post anything or interact. We're monitoring your accounts to see if he tries to contact you there. That said, it's unlikely. He must have realized by now that you're under protection."

"Protection?"

"Your brother-in-law graciously volunteered to be your bodyguard."

Zoe decided to ignore his light-hearted jab. The last thing she wanted was Anthony smothering her.

"I don't know what happened between you two, but I think you might change your opinion of him if you saw just how concerned he is for your safety."

Choosing to end the conversation, Zoe stood up. "I'm exhausted. Is there a place where I can shower and change?"

"Of course. We've arranged a hotel room for you. Your brother-in-law will escort you there."

Anthony was waiting for her in the hallway, eager to get going. She knew he wouldn't leave her side, even if she asked, so she brought him into her plan.

"You can't be serious!" he exclaimed in disbelief.

She gestured for him to lower his voice. "I'm not forcing you to do anything, Anthony. But I've made up my mind about this. It's up to you if you want to be a part of it or not."

PART III

The Angel's touch

Life and death are one thread,
the same line viewed from different sides.
— Lao Tzu

64

———

Like a brown bear at an apple tree, Pierre Valmeur stood before the vending machine, shaking it and muttering curses.

"Need a hand?" Zoe offered.

He stepped back, allowing her access.

Zoe pressed the coin return. "You're twenty cents short," she observed, counting the change.

Pierre Valmeur searched his pockets and produced the coins. "Machines and I have never gotten along," he admitted, watching as she slid a coin into the slot.

A cup dropped, filling with steaming coffee.

"Here," he said, offering her a bill. "Get one for yourself. And one for your brother-in-law," he added, nodding at Anthony.

Anthony was leaned against the wall, arms crossed, a blank expression on his face.

"No caffeine for him. He's wired enough as it is," Zoe quipped.

Pierre Valmeur settled into one of the plastic chairs, waiting for Zoe to join him.

"Your son will be released soon," she informed him, taking a seat beside him.

He nodded.

"He told me everything," she continued, locking eyes with him.

For a moment, Pierre Valmeur's gaze was so intense that time seemed to stand still, as if the world had shrunk to just the two of them.

"Would you like to see it? Your portrait. I have it here," he offered.

Zoe's eyes darted to the backpack by his feet. Her heart raced as she gave a hesitant nod.

With a smile, he set his coffee aside and rummaged through his bag. The well-worn, kraft envelope he handed her was slightly crumpled.

"It's the original," he pointed out.

Carefully, Zoe pulled out the drawing. Puzzling and thrilling—that's how he had described it. As she looked at it, she was struck by the same sentiment. It was undoubtedly her, but there was something else, something intangible captured in the pencil strokes.

"Your friend is incredibly talented," she remarked.

Pierre Valmeur beamed. "And this sketch doesn't even capture half of what he can do with paint. Albert was the best in the police force. But now they've switched to software for composite sketches, which, if you ask me, lack the human touch."

Zoe slid the portrait back into the envelope. "There's something I can't wrap my head around," she began. "Why didn't you sketch the killer from your visions?"

He shook his head. "What I experienced was through his eyes. I can tell you about his emotions, his nature, but I can't describe his face."

She cast a fleeting glance at Anthony. She could sense his disapproval, even if she didn't grasp its reason. "Johan told me you could help me find my sister," she said.

Pierre Valmeur repacked the portrait into the bag.

"She disappeared under the same circumstances as the other victims," she continued, her eyes dropping to her cup.

"Do you have a photo?"

Zoe almost spilled her coffee.

"You'll help me?"

"Of course. Why wouldn't I?"

Zoe gestured for Anthony to come over, but he seemed uninterested in leaving his vantage point.

"Stubborn," she muttered as she stood. In a few strides, she was in front of him. "I need your phone," she stated.

"For what?"

"I need a picture of Gabriela for... you know why. Oh, just damn it!"

She reached directly into the right pocket of his jacket, where she had seen him store his cell phone countless times. But as she grabbed the device, Anthony's hand closed around her wrist.

He glared at her for a few moments, his eyes dark.

"Let me go," she whispered.

He loosened his grip. "Stop," he said, using the same tone. "It's no use. I don't have any pictures of Gabriela."

Zoe shook her head in disbelief. "None?"

He sighed, looking to the ceiling. "I deleted them all. It was... it's just easier that way."

Zoe took a moment to absorb the information.

He trailed off, searching for words. "You understand, right? Zoe..."

But she was already on her feet, phone in hand, her brother-in-law's emotions pushed to the back of her mind.

She needed to find a photograph of Gabriela, and fast. So, instead of handing back the phone, she took it with her.

"Is everything okay?" Pierre Valmeur asked when she returned to her seat beside him.

Zoe nodded, her attention elsewhere, as she didn't notice Anthony approaching.

With her eyes fixed on the smartphone, she opened the internet browser. Carefully tapping on the virtual keyboard, she brought up the website for an association assisting families of missing persons. The disappearance notices were categorized by year, and Gabriela's was still online.

"This is my sister," she announced, her heart tightening.

Pierre Valmeur accepted the phone she handed over, the device seeming to shrink in his large, commanding hands.

"She's your elder," he noted, fixated on the static portrait illuminated on the screen.

Zoe turned away, unable to bear the sight of her sister's joyful smile any longer. Soon after, she felt a gentle hand envelop hers. Anthony was seated beside her, looking pale. Zoe couldn't remember seeing him like this, except perhaps on the day he had informed her that Gabriela hadn't returned home.

Pierre Valmeur continued to scrutinize the screen for several moments before returning the phone to Zoe.

"Well?" she probed, his prolonged silence weighing heavily.

"I'm sorry," he whispered.

Zoe swallowed, feeling Anthony's hand tighten around hers.

"I feel nothing," Pierre Valmeur added.

"What does that even mean?"

"It means your sister has passed away."

Zoe nodded, as though he'd merely confirmed a truth she'd always known.

"I can't tell you where she is," he added, interpreting the question in her tear-laden eyes before she could ask.

"But you did for that Belgian girl, so why is it different for my sister?"

Pierre Valmeur shook his head. "I don't know. Sometimes, it just happens that way."

His gaze remained on the photograph as Zoe struck upon a new idea.

"What about this?" she said, pulling something from her jeans pocket. "It's my sister's wedding ring. She was wearing it when she vanished. The killer sent it back to us."

Pierre Valmeur accepted the ring, gently cradling it in his hand. He closed his eyes, gripping the delicate band between his thumb and forefinger, as Zoe sensed a palpable tension radiating from him.

"What is it?" she asked.

He shook his head. "Nothing."

"You're lying. What did you see?"

"I'm not sure..."

"Mr. Valmeur!" called out another voice, breaking the tension. "Over here, please!"

Inspector Dorsey, stationed at the opposite end of the hallway, was gesturing for the elderly man to approach. Zoe watched as Pierre Valmeur began gathering his belongings. As he stooped to hoist his backpack, she seized his wrist.

"Wait," she implored. "What were you going to tell me?"

"Mr. Valmeur?" the officer called again, more insistently this time.

Pierre Valmeur gestured to indicate he was on his way.

"I really have to go, or he might just arrest me too," he said, a flicker of a smile crossing his face.

Zoe, however, was not in the mood for humor. "I'll wait for you here!"

Anthony began to voice his objection, but the old man silenced him with a wave of his hand.

"No," he said, his voice a blend of calm and resolve. "You'll go back to the hotel and rest. I promise I'll reach out as soon as I'm done here."

65

"Your son's in quite a mess," Inspector Dorsey announced as he closed the office door behind him.

Pierre Valmeur's brow furrowed tightly. "I don't understand. Miss Rossi assured me she hadn't pressed charges."

Dorsey waved Pierre's words away. "We've got to wait for the prosecutor to review the case. Just because Zoe Rossi didn't file charges doesn't mean your son won't face prosecution. I'd get him a good lawyer if I were you."

"My son is not a criminal."

"Well, the witnesses currently being interviewed might see things differently."

"Witnesses?"

"A couple of farmers where your son and Zoe Rossi stayed the night recognized her from her photo in the paper." He paused, watching the older man's reaction before continuing in a lighter tone, almost as if sharing an inside joke. "Everything depends on what they say. Did they see any violence between your son and Miss Rossi? Hear any threats? That sort of thing. You want some coffee?" Without waiting for an answer, he headed toward the coffeemaker.

Pierre shook his head, but Dorsey poured the steaming liquid into a navy mug anyway. Returning to his desk with his cup in hand, he continued. "But if there's nothing to back up a kidnapping theory, he'll be out in seventy-two hours."

Relief washed over Pierre, loosening the tension in his shoulders. Despite an intuitive sense that his son would be all right, worry gnawed at him, as it would any father. "Can I see him?"

Dorsey's face twisted into a grimace before he set his mug down. "You'll see him. But first, I need something from you."

"I've already told you everything."

"I know, and I appreciate it. But now I want to know about the killer."

Pierre, sensing the turn in the conversation, reiterated his previous statement to Zoe—he couldn't provide the description Dorsey was after. "But there might be something else I can help with."

The inspector's eyes lit up a bit. "Oh? And what's that?"

"It's complicated. I need to see Leanne…"

A shadow seemed to cross Dorsey's features. "We only found part of her…"

"Which part?"

"Her head."

Pierre closed his eyes, his expression tranquil, almost serene, as if he had already been aware of this gruesome detail. "That will work," he whispered. "Take me to her."

"I can't do that. How about a photo instead? Isn't that what you psychics usually need?"

"I use different things. A child's left-behind toy, clothes from a husband who never came back, jewelry from a missing sister or wife. And yes, photos. Families send them so I can help find their loved ones. But with Leanne, I need physical contact to find the rest of her body and maybe identify her killer."

"That's not happening. It's against protocol."

"I thought you didn't always play by the rules."

Dorsey winced. "That might come back to bite me. My bosses don't know you're involved yet. I don't have enough to convince them."

"I'll give you what you need."

"How?"

"You said you could get a morgue photo of Leanne?"

"I can do that."

"What if I asked for something else?"

Dorsey's eyebrow arched. "Like what?"

Pierre listed a couple of items, their descriptions sounding like they belonged in a spellbook.

66

Dorsey hopped from foot to foot, clutching his jacket. The icy wind from the hospital parking lot was biting. However, it was Pierre Valmeur's daunting task that truly sent chills down his spine.

Just a few yards away stood the morgue, within which a refrigerated compartment—usually reserved for preserving the deceased—now held two heads discovered in the woods, awaiting transfer for a detailed forensic examination.

Dorsey turned toward the car and caught Pierre Valmeur's piercing gaze from the passenger seat. "This guy's nuts, but I must be even crazier," he muttered under his breath as he entered the building.

Moments later, he was flashing his ID at the desk sergeant, who noted down his name and rank in a ledger. A morgue attendant led him to the cold room, and with a twist of a stainless-steel handle, he slid out the drawer containing the remains of Leanne Jalmet.

Dorsey met the attendant's gaze. "I need to do this alone," he said with a firmness that brooked no argument.

"It's part of an investigation that I'm not at liberty to discuss. Understand?"

The attendant looked taken aback, but nodded. "Very well. Call me when you're finished. I'll be in the office down the hall."

Dorsey kept his gaze on him until he was out of sight, then strained his ears for the sound of the office door closing. It never came; the door had been left slightly ajar. He realized he would need to proceed with utmost caution, as his imminent actions bordered on the desecration of a corpse.

Slipping on a pair of latex gloves, he scanned the room for scissors, a syringe, or any other suitable cutting tool. The morgue was so quiet that every movement he made seemed to echo off the walls. Dorsey's nerves were stretched thin, fueled not only by the fear of being discovered but also by the eerie ambiance of the room. The near-freezing temperature was the only reason he wasn't breaking into a sweat.

Surprising himself with his own efficiency, Dorsey quickly completed the next step. After gathering the samples as Valmeur had instructed, he sealed them inside a fresh pair of latex gloves and stowed them in his jacket pocket.

"I'm done!" he called down the corridor, his voice steadier than he felt.

67

─────────

Anthony eased off the gas pedal upon spotting the glowing sign of the hotel. The nearly empty parking lot allowed him to pick a spot close to the entrance.

Zoe took in the sight of the building, its silhouette stark against the starlit night sky. The unlit windows gave her the impression that they might be the hotel's sole guests—an unsettling thought after what had transpired in Bordeaux. Thankfully, they wouldn't have to share a room this time.

"You coming or what? You planning to camp out here all night?" Anthony called out, waiting at the entrance with a suitcase in his hand—*her* suitcase—the one she had left behind before their unexpected meeting in the Landes Forest. Seeing her belongings again brought a fleeting smile to Zoe's face, reminiscent of a child reunited with cherished toys after a long separation.

The reception desk was empty until Anthony rang the service bell, at which point a door creaked open and a young man in sweatpants and a crinkled t-shirt with the words *The Truth is Out There* printed on it, came rushing out.

He slumped into a chair, powered up the computer, and greeted them with a face marked by sleep lines.

"One room or two?" he asked, stifling a yawn.

"Two," Zoe responded, finding herself yawning as well.

He looked at her through heavy eyelids, and for a fleeting moment, Zoe thought she saw a flicker of recognition in his eyes before Anthony's voice brought him back to the task at hand.

"The reservation is under Lavera and Rossi."

"Got it," the clerk muttered, turning back to the computer. "Rooms 202 and 301. Can I see some ID, please?"

"Wait, we're not on the same floor?" Anthony asked, sounding annoyed.

"She's on the second floor. You're on the third. Is that all right?"

Zoe tried to intervene, "It's okay—"

"It's not," Anthony insisted. "Get us adjacent rooms on the same floor. And don't tell me it's impossible. The parking lot's empty."

"We're expecting a tour bus later. Rooms are reserved," the clerk explained, almost in tandem with Zoe's attempt to soothe Anthony once again.

Clearly irked, he shot back, "Then move some reservations around. Make it work."

The clerk's irritation was clear, but after a moment, he relented. "I can put you in rooms across the hall from each other."

"Fine."

"Do you have a preference for a view of the forest or the parking lot?"

"Parking lot," Zoe interjected, having no desire to be anywhere near a forest again anytime soon.

With the payment processed, Anthony took their key

cards and they headed down the dimly lit corridor, the questionable cleanliness of the carpet muffling their footsteps. When they reached their rooms, Anthony paused. Instead of handing Zoe her key, he placed her suitcase aside and unlocked her door. Then, with a swift yet careful motion, he drew his service weapon and began to search the room. Zoe found this precaution absurd. The man who had contacted her on Facebook couldn't possibly have known in advance that she would be occupying this very room, in this hotel and not another. Yet she said nothing, just watched as he checked behind the door, the bathroom, the windows, and even lifted the curtains. After a moment's hesitation, he pulled back the bedcovers, his face flushed from the effort.

"So, find any Boogeyman?" Zoe attempted to lighten the mood, but her joke fell flat; Anthony did not respond.

"It's clear," he said, holstering his weapon. "You can come in."

Zoe eyed the gun. "Can I hold it?" She felt a wave of instant relief as the weight of the firearm settled into her palm; she planned to keep it close while she slept.

"I'll be back with some food. Get cleaned up."

With that, Anthony left, leaving Zoe alone to take in the room and its outdated decor. Her gaze lingered on the wallpaper, an odd mix of ancient and modern, before her thoughts inevitably drifted back to Chantal and Roger's farm and memories she wished she could forget.

"Damn it," she muttered to herself, realizing she needed to stop the flood of memories before they overwhelmed her. With a sense of urgency, she locked herself in the bathroom, stripped down, and stepped into the shower, letting the water wash over her as she allowed herself to cry.

68

———

Didier Dorsey felt like a bona fide criminal as he gave the doorman a nod and hustled back to his vehicle. "I got what you wanted," he muttered, sliding into the driver's seat. Eager to rid himself of the objects in his pocket, he reached in to pull them out.

"Hold on," Pierre Valmeur interrupted. "Not here."

Dorsey froze. "Then where? The police station's out of the question."

"I'm aware," Pierre replied, his voice cool and deliberate. "Drive us to the forest."

The Wolves Forest was a brief, twenty-minute drive from the hospital. Upon arrival, Pierre instructed him to park the car in a small clearing strewn with gravel, a spot favored by hikers and hunters when the sun was up.

"The relics," Pierre demanded in a low voice.

With a sigh of resignation, Dorsey reached into his jacket pocket. He pulled out the samples he'd taken from Leanne Jalmet: a strand of blonde hair and a syringe filled with blood. He handed them to Pierre, who received them with an almost unsettling reverence.

"Time to get started."

A shiver coursed through Dorsey's spine. He might not have been a regular at Sunday Mass, but the remnants of his Catholic upbringing echoed with warnings of severe retribution for his actions—and for the ominous ritual he was on the verge of witnessing.

"Uh, do I need to... help with something?" Dorsey asked, anxiety coloring his voice.

After a moment of contemplation, Pierre extended the syringe toward him. "Pour the blood into my hand."

Dorsey hesitated, making the sign of the cross. He then took the syringe from Pierre's hand and began to press down on the plunger.

"Careful," Pierre cautioned, as he started to transfer the blood.

"And after this?" Dorsey asked, uncertainty flickering in his eyes.

Holding the lock of blonde hair in his other hand, Pierre whispered, "Now, be quiet."

Pierre leaned forward, examining the thick liquid in his hand. Corpse blood doesn't clot. He swirled it gently, handling it with the reverence reserved for a fine Bordeaux. As he stilled his hand, the blood's surface became sleek and reflective. Instead of his own face, Pierre saw Leanne Jalmet's. She stood in front of a rest stop bathroom mirror, wiping away mascara streaked by tears—tears resulting from a betrayal discovered on social media.

She reached for her makeup to touch up when her phone interrupted. Taking a deep breath, she answered, releasing a torrent of French expletives directed at her unfaithful boyfriend. To the women in line, her words were indecipherable. With a definitive click, she ended the call.

Pierre watched her, their faces almost meeting, separated only by the thin, reflective veil of blood. He wished he could warn her about the lurking danger outside, but the past was set in stone. Only the future was malleable.

When Leanne left the restroom, the blood in Pierre's hand wavered and shifted. Moments later, she was back, sitting in the back of a car, sharing a smile with her fellow traveler bound for Florence.

"Hitchhiking is illegal in Italy," the man behind the wheel informed them, eyes glued to the road. *"You're facing the possibility of arrest by the police, and there's a substantial fine to be paid if you're aiming to steer clear of a jail sentence."*

"What a cheapskate," Pierre whispered, his attention riveted to the shimmering surface capturing the young Belgian woman's last moments.

"Can you see his face?" Dorsey asked.

"Not yet."

Things escalated. Leanne's eyes flicked nervously between the rearview mirror and her best friend Sonya. Why had they left the main road? He had promised to take them to Florence, so where was he leading them now? And why was he blatantly ignoring their questions? Catching her reflection in the mirror, Leanne realized he had been observing her the entire time. The doors were locked. They were ensnared, at the mercy of this man, and his true intentions were about to be revealed.

Pierre Valmeur adjusted his hand, the blood on it wrinkling like stretched plastic before smoothing out again. Now the man loomed over Leanne, a hunting knife glinting in his grip. The blade caught the light, reflecting her anguish. Leanne had lost consciousness several times under his brutal treatment. He had removed her gag, allowing her screams to echo through the dense woods; he reveled in her agony. Her fear fueled him, made him feel more commanding, more dominant.

Then he withdrew and leaned against a tree. His shirt was unbuttoned, revealing a hairless, lean chest, and his pants were undone. He appeared exhausted and, worse, disinterested. Leanne watched as he succumbed to sleep.

Closing her eyes, she surrendered to the depths of despair. She had abandoned all hope of rescue. All she desired now was for everything to come to an end.

And then, her wish was granted.

The Reaper stirred, eyes wild, and leaned in. "Look at me!" he shouted, driving the knife into her.

But Leanne had already slipped away, her tears glistening in the fading daylight.

69

Fifteen minutes later, Zoe emerged from the bathroom, now dressed in her preferred simple outfit of jeans and a black sweater.

Anthony was sitting on the edge of the bed, which was spread with multicolored packages of candy and other sweets, resembling a Halloween haul. He looked up as she entered, a hopeful smile playing on his lips. "Feeling any better?"

Zoe nodded, though her eyes were still red from crying.

"Thought you could use some comfort," he said, his smile transforming into a half-grin.

But Zoe was in no mood for jokes, and she felt an irritation bubble up inside her at the sight of him. His mere presence seemed to shrink the room, stealing her space, her air. She felt suffocated and wondered if Gabriela had ever felt the same way.

"Got you some mini-madeleines. You love those, right?"

Upon hearing the name of the famous pastry, a wave of sadness washed over Zoe. A brief memory surfaced, taking her back to the days of sharing a room with Gabriela at their parents' home. Gabriela had a profound sweet tooth, and she spent all her allowance on cakes and candies. She would stash them away in their bedroom, creating a secret hoard of sweets like a squirrel gearing up for winter. Their 'winter' came in the form of their father's unpredictable outbursts. These episodes often led to severe punishments, like going without food for two days straight. During those hard times, Zoe could always count on finding a candy bar or a packet of sweets under her pillow. It was Gabriela's way of offering comfort. As Zoe savored the treats, Gabriela would gently brush her hair, finding her own solace in sucking her thumb.

"Oh, damn it! I'm so sorry," Anthony blurted, standing quickly to wrap his arms around her shoulders.

Zoe wiped her tears with her sleeve, subtly pulling away from his embrace. "It was Gabriela who loved them," she said, her voice strained as she fought to keep it steady. "How could you forget? And how could you delete all her photos?"

He released her abruptly, taken aback, and she scrutinized his face for any hint of reaction. Anthony was not one to wear his emotions on his sleeve, unlike Johan, whose vulnerability was something she had come to adore. There were few men with that kind of strength.

"Zoe?"

Jolted from her thoughts, a wave of shame washed over her, as if thinking of Johan was a forbidden, almost sinful act. But she couldn't help it; her mind kept drifting back to him, to the last forty-eight hours they had shared.

Anthony maintained eye contact as he pointed out, "You're clearly exhausted. You need to get some rest." He started cleaning up the candy-strewn mess, pulling back the covers and patting the pillow, inviting her to bed. "Come on."

She hesitated, her gaze flitting between the bed, now tidy and inviting, and Anthony, whose presence filled the room with a palpable tension.

"Europol's taking over Gabriela's case," she finally said.

He nodded slowly, as if needing a moment to process the news and its implications. "That's good," he replied after a pause. "You won't have to play detective anymore."

"That's pretty much what Inspector Dorsey said."

A tense silence hung in the air, as if words had been exhausted.

"Well, goodnight," she said, a finality in her tone.

Instead of leaving, Anthony circled the bed and settled into the room's lone chair, positioned between the window and the radiator. He draped a blanket around himself, seemingly preparing to stay the night. She watched him, disbelief evident in her eyes, the words caught in her throat. *Just tell him*, she urged herself. *Tell him to go!*

Yet as she stood there, indecisive, a chilling realization crept in: if Johan wasn't her would-be abductor, then the real threat was still lurking in the shadows.

"Could you turn off the lights?" Anthony asked, seemingly oblivious to her distress.

She almost did as he asked, but then hesitated. "No." Her voice quivered.

"What?"

She inhaled deeply, meeting his gaze. "I said 'no'. You shouldn't stay. It's not right."

His gaze briefly darted to the door. Then, he slouched further into the chair, spreading his legs and burying his face in his hands. "Is this about the other night?"

Their argument right before her kidnapping flashed in her memory, causing Zoe to stiffen. "I don't want to talk about it," she stated.

Undeterred by her resistance, he continued, "I need to apologize."

"You were drunk, you didn't know what you were doing," she responded, her words coming out quicker than she intended.

"That's not an excuse."

She exhaled in exasperation. "Anthony, I can't deal with this now. Either leave or I will."

Before she could approach the door, he was up, standing in her way.

"Zoe," he implored, seizing her arm.

"Let go of me!"

But he held on. "I need to say it. I deeply regret what I did. If I hadn't acted so thoughtlessly, you wouldn't have been abducted. I should've been with you."

"Anthony..."

"No, hear me out. I can't rewrite the past, but I promise I won't ever let it happen again. You're not just my sister-in-law, you're my confidant. I care about you deeply. I never intended to cause you pain. You understand that, don't you?"

His expression was earnest, almost childlike.

"You were the only one I truly trusted," she murmured, her voice trembling.

He lowered his head. "I know. I'm so sorry. Being around you... I see so much of her in you."

Zoe's body tensed, this perspective having never occurred to her before.

"I miss her," he whispered.

He wrapped her in a gentle hug, and she found herself unable to resist his embrace.

"I'm so sorry, Zoe."

In the distance, she imagined Johan's voice echoing the

same sentiment. How she wished he was with her. The thought of him behind bars tore at her heart, and she realized how deeply she yearned for him. As her mind wandered to him, she didn't even realize she had sunk down onto the bed, lost in her yearning.

Then, the soft click of the door latch brought her abruptly back to reality. Anthony had left the room, gently closing the door behind him..

70

———

Pierre Valmeur was hunched over, his hand pressed against his stomach as if he were the one who had been stabbed. The blood from Leanne Jalmet oozed through his fingers, soaking his shirt and forming a dark crimson halo.

Dorsey stood by, witnessing the uncanny display, as Pierre embodied the victim's agony.

"It's okay," Pierre gasped out, although his ashen face and blood-soaked shirt said otherwise.

The inspector leaned in closer, examining the gruesome scene. "Doesn't look okay to me," he observed, his voice laced with concern.

"Just drive, please," Pierre implored, lifting his head to lock eyes with Dorsey.

"Drive? Where to? Back to town? The hospital?"

"No. Just drive. Get us away from here. I can't stand to hear the screams any longer."

"Leanne Jalmet? You can hear her?" Dorsey's voice rose in disbelief.

Pierre nodded, his eyes filled with torment. "Her, and the

others. They're all throughout the woods. We need to leave. Now."

Dorsey placed a gentle hand on his arm, wishing he could tell him he understood what he was going through. However, he had the feeling that his own experiences with crime scenes were worlds apart from what Pierre Valmeur had just endured. His suspicions were confirmed when Pierre shared more details a little later. It was as if he had personally experienced the young woman's horrifying ordeal, which had stretched out over several hours. Pierre had managed to gather a remarkable amount of information during his journey through time and space—details about how the killer approached his victim, the car he drove, his clothing, his scent, the sound of his voice, even the type of knife he used to decapitate the young woman. Yet, he still hadn't shared the most crucial detail.

"And his face?" Dorsey asked, his voice anxious.

"I'm sorry. I didn't see it. But I know this is where he buried the heads of the other victims," Pierre responded, avoiding eye contact.

Dorsey felt a lump form in his throat. "How many?"

"Dozens, from the sounds of it."

"My God. And you can hear them?"

"Their screams, yes."

"Can you tell where they are?"

Pierre turned to look at the trees blurring past the car window. "I can try."

Dorsey took his eyes off the road for a moment, sensing he wasn't finished. "There's more, isn't there?"

Pierre nodded once again, his expression grave. "I saw a hand."

"A hand?"

"Leanne's. Find it, and you'll find your killer."

Dorsey's mind raced as he tried to process Pierre's words. "What are you saying? Is Leanne's body out there in the woods?"

"Yes."

"But where?"

"Everywhere. He..."

"He dismembered her?"

"Yes. He was in a rage. I couldn't see why. But he didn't plan to send a postcard to her parents like he did with the others."

Dorsey's heart sank. "Why not?"

"I don't know. Maybe he was just furious. Or maybe he realized he made a mistake."

"A mistake?"

"He was careless with her. He left a trace."

Dorsey's mind clicked. Up until now, the bodies they had found—thanks to the macabre postcards sent to the victims' families—had offered no leads. But this was different. Leanne had fought back.

"Leanne pulled some of his hair out. Find her right hand, and you'll have his DNA."

71

The glow from the news broadcast lit up the dim room. He reached into the cardboard bucket, his fingers finding a sticky cluster of popcorn, a delicious yet messy mixture of butter and sugar. In his mind, the twisted game of hot and cold continued, and at this moment, they were neither close nor too far away.

As he brought the popcorn to his mouth, he muttered, "Lukewarm… Lukewarm," while his eyes followed a police officer who was separating from the group, moving toward a pond.

He held his breath, thinking 'hot,' but not daring to voice it this time. The officer paused at the pond's edge, peering down and parting the tall grass with a stick. After a moment, he moved on, shaking his head—likely signaling to a colleague that he hadn't found anything.

"Cold!" he exclaimed, delight in his voice as he shoveled another handful of popcorn into his mouth.

He reveled in watching the police scramble. Their efforts were almost pitiful to him. With so many resources poured into searching for remains, they could barely differentiate from animal bones. All that overtime—on the taxpayer's dime. He should have been irritated, considering he, too was a taxpayer. But the flattery he felt overshadowed any hint of resentment. The number of women he'd killed had grown so vast, even he had lost track.

Fooling the police was almost child's play. The trick was simple: think differently. Obscure the links between victims so no pattern could be discerned. No one could pin down his methodology because he didn't fit their predefined categories. His victims spanned all age groups. Some lived solitary lives, while others had families. A teenager who ventured a bit too far from her campsite. A middle-aged jogger trying to fend off the weight of age. A woman loading groceries into her car. However, he made it a rule to avoid prostitutes. They were all too easy a target, and sadly, law enforcement tended to invest less effort into cases involving street workers. No, he relished the thrill, the surge of adrenaline from abducting a woman in plain sight, unseen by anyone. His methods varied with every crime. But one element remained constant: he always looked them in the eye as he took their life.

Back on the screen, the search in the woods continued, desperation etched on every face. But even if they found the heads, what could they possibly learn from them? It all seemed so futile.

As these thoughts raced through his mind, the reporter, microphone in hand, seemed to address him through the camera.

"A mysterious witness has come forward, assuring the police that the killer made a critical error, leaving behind a crucial piece of evidence on the body of Leanne Jalmet—the young Belgian tourist who vanished last June."

Choking on his popcorn, he coughed a piece onto the carpet.

The screen flashed Leanne Jalmet's portrait. He remembered the rage he'd felt when the girl he'd picked up at a rest area had stopped breathing, literally suffocated by her own fear. She'd died too soon, slipping out of his grasp and control. He hated losing control. He needed everything to unfold as planned; any deviation sent him into a fury. Her premature death had ruined everything. Maybe that's why he'd dismembered her body. She didn't deserve an intact return to her family like the others. But even in mutilation, he'd found no satisfaction. He'd left the woods where he'd abandoned her, exhausted and frustrated.

72

―――――

"Wake up!"

Zoe's eyes fluttered open, her sister's voice vivid in her mind, almost tangible. It was surprising, therefore, not to find her in the room. But then she recognized the sound of knocking at her bedroom door—a muted thudding, as if the person in the hallway was trying to be discreet. Knowing it couldn't be Anthony—he was anything but subtle—she grabbed the gun and, emulating action movie heroines, approached the door. Her bare feet sank into the thick carpet. Holding her breath, her heart pounding in anxious constraint, she leaned in to peer through the peephole. Pierre Valmeur's face, slightly distorted by the lens, came into view. She unlocked the door slowly, cracked it open, and before he could speak, she put a finger to her lips, nodding toward the door behind him. Understanding, Pierre stepped inside.

"The kid at the front desk gave me your room number," he said, after she had closed the door. "Told him I was your dad. Hope you're not upset."

"No, you did what you had to." Zoe had grown fond of

the old man, feeling as if she'd known him her entire life—a stark contrast to her distant relationship with her biological father. "Thank you for coming," she continued. "My brother-in-law is right across the hall and—"

"You don't want him to know."

"It's just that he can be a bit—"

"Overbearing?"

Zoe glanced toward the door. "Overprotective, actually."

Pierre raised a skeptical eyebrow. "Well, it's good he's not here," he said. "Saves me having to ask him to leave."

A pang of guilt hit her. "But Gabriela was his wife."

"This isn't about your sister," he said, handing back the wedding ring she had given him earlier.

"I don't get it. I thought you were going to help me find her. That's what you promised."

"I know what I promised. And in a way, that's why I'm here. I've had another vision."

Zoe eased onto the edge of the bed, swallowing hard. "About me?"

He nodded. "You need to head back into the forest. Go to where Johan regained his memory. You need to leave right now, and you must go alone. That's the only way to find out what happened to your sister."

"Why can't you just tell me where she is? Wouldn't that be easier?"

"No, my dear. I wish I could shield you from all this, but my hands are tied."

Zoe squinted, stood up, and looked around, deciding what to take. She pulled on a thick wool sweater, followed by her parka.

"Don't forget the gun."

She froze for a split second, then relief flickered in her eyes as she secured Anthony's Sig Sauer, grateful he had let her keep it overnight. Then it hit her. "Anthony... he has the car keys!"

Pierre dug into his jacket pocket. "Here, take mine." Gripping her arm, as if hesitant to let go, he added, "Remember, no matter what transpires in the next few hours, just because some dreams fall apart, doesn't mean you should stop dreaming."

"What does that mean? What dream are you talking about?"

Pierre shook his head. "I apologize, I'm rambling. It's something we old folks do sometimes. Now go."

73

"You're free, Doc!"

Johan's attention snapped to the door as it creaked open. The hallway's harsh light spilled into the dim cell, making him squint. Seated on the edge of his bunk, he shielded his eyes, trying to make out the figure of Inspector Dorsey, who stood in the doorway, straddling the line between confinement and freedom.

Suppressing a groan, Johan struggled to his feet. The effects of last night's painkillers were waning. He felt much like one of his own patients, like the rugby player he had once operated on after a rough match.

"Let's move, Doc," Dorsey murmured. "Just some paperwork now."

Johan followed him to the makeshift police office. Photos of Leanne Jalmet and Sonya Nbaké, the two young victims he'd found in the forest, covered the wall.

"Coffee?" the officer offered.

With a nod, Johan accepted the mug. Its warmth was comforting to his hands, and the rich aroma promised to soothe his parched throat from a night spent in the dry, stale air of the cell. After a tentative sip, he managed a clearer tone. "Where's my father?"

"Back home, I'd imagine. He couldn't wait to get away after yesterday's fiasco."

"What fiasco?" Johan asked, his voice edged with confusion after being in solitary confinement for the last few hours.

Dorsey succinctly recounted the fruitless leads that had stemmed from Johan's father's recent vision. "In short, he thought it best to make a swift exit. He assumed you'd understand why."

Johan nodded. Knowing how much his father disliked traveling, it was telling that he had made the journey to search for him.

"Sign here," Dorsey said.

Johan scribbled his signature, sliding the form back toward the cop as he stood. A sudden thought halted his steps; he needed to ask about Zoe.

"Is Zoe—?" Johan began, but the rest of his question was lost to the cacophony erupting outside the door. Dorsey held up a hand, motioning for patience, and stepped out of the office, leaving Johan with a knot of concern in his gut.

The voices in the hallway escalated, the words almost intelligible. "I want to talk to Valmeur!" The demand was sharp and anxious.

"Lavera, calm down!" Dorsey's attempt at peace was nearly drowned out by the commotion.

Peering through the doorway left ajar, Johan's gaze met that of a man he didn't recognize, standing starkly in the corridor. The man stopped abruptly, as if surprised to find Johan watching.

"It's him!" exclaimed the stranger, pointing an accusing

finger at Johan. "He has to know! After all, it's his father who's behind all this!"

All eyes turned to Johan.

"What's happening?" he asked, directing his question to the least hostile-looking person there.

Dorsey exhaled deeply. "Doctor, I'd like you to meet Anthony Lavera. He's Miss Rossi's brother-in-law. It seems your father dropped by her hotel early today, and—"

"She's gone. Took my gun," Anthony cut in, his voice edged.

Johan's heart plummeted. "Are you sure?"

"Your father was there early, around five. They let him in."

Dorsey's face showed deep concern. "Could you call your father? We need to know if she's with him."

Johan snatched up the cell phone handed to him. Relying on memory, he punched in his dad's number and waited.

His dad answered almost instantly, as if he'd been waiting by the phone. Johan wouldn't have been surprised if he had.

"Dad! Is Zoe there with you?"

"You alone?"

Johan dropped his gaze to the floor, aware of every eye on him.

"Her brother-in-law's here, and so is Inspector Dorsey."

"Okay, hand him the phone."

Knowing it'd be futile to press for details, Johan gestured to the officer. "He wants to talk to you."

Dorsey's focus sharpened as he listened. As the conversation went on, his features relaxed. "Good to hear. Yeah, I'll hand it back to him."

Johan reached out for the phone, ready to continue the conversation.

"Listen and don't say a word," his dad started with no preamble.

Johan stiffened, relieved that no one seemed to notice. The attention was on Dorsey, who was sharing a version far different from what his dad was saying. Zoe hadn't gone back to Paris to avoid the media.

"She's headed to the woods."

A shiver ran through Johan.

"You were in my vision, too. You need to find her. Understand?"

"Yes," Johan whispered, hoping his response went unnoticed.

"Pay attention. Go back to where you discovered Leanne. Everything will fall into place once you're there. Go! Now!"

74

"You need to head back into the forest. Go to where Johan regained his memory. That's the only way to find out what happened to your sister."

Those words haunted Zoe. No matter how much she wrestled with the medium's cryptic message, its meaning eluded her. Dawn's early light, filtering through the trees, brought no clarity to her thoughts. What was expected of her? Her eyes swept the area, an instinct suggesting she might have missed something important. Yellow police tape bordered the scene, marking where Leanne Jalmet and her friend's severed heads were found. Could Gabriela have been there too? It seemed unlikely; forensics were usually thorough, and missing another body was improbable. Yet, something didn't feel right to Zoe. With determination, she stepped under the tape and walked to the spot where Johan had stumbled upon the gruesome find, the discovery that had jolted his memory. She knelt down, her hands cautiously combing through the soil. Finding another head was a long shot, but she needed to be sure. Her fingers touched something solid—a piece of a jawbone. She was examining it, turning it over in the light, when a voice from behind caused her to start.

"Hi there!"

The jawbone dropped from her hands.

"Oh! I didn't mean to scare you," said the stranger, Zoe's startled reaction.

A man in camouflage gear stood just beyond the police tape, his eyes flicking from Zoe to the bone in her hand, a mix of curiosity and uncertainty on his face.

"It's just an animal bone," she said quickly, trying to ease his apparent concern.

His brows furrowed with suspicion. "Are you some kind of reporter?"

"Reporter?" Zoe echoed, her voice laced with surprise.

"Yeah, with the digging and all. You don't look like police. But I've seen your face before," he continued, narrowing his eyes in thought. Then it clicked. "You were on TV, right? The woman who was kidnapped?"

He was bubbling with enthusiasm, like a fan who'd just bumped into his favorite movie star. Zoe wouldn't have been surprised if he'd pulled out his phone and asked for a selfie.

"Are you here by yourself?" He glanced around, as if taking stock of the surroundings.

"Not exactly. I'm meeting someone. The police," she added, her heart racing a bit.

He smiled broadly, but it was hard to read whether he believed her. "Oh! Is this some crime scene reconstruction? Like on those TV shows?"

"Uh, yes. Something like that," Zoe replied, eager for him to go away. "I apologize if I disturbed any hunting you were doing."

His expression turned amused. "Hunting?" With a swift gesture, he pulled out a high-end camera from his bag. "I'm a wildlife photographer. I capture images, not prey. Wouldn't dream of harming an animal," he clarified with a genuine smile. "I'm Raphaël," he introduced himself as the first raindrops began to dot the earth.

Zoe felt the chill as the rain began to set in, making her scenario of waiting for the police less convincing by the second.

"Come on, I'll walk you to your car," Raphaël offered, noticing her discomfort.

Zoe was about to decline the offer when she realized she wouldn't be able to find her way back on her own. The idea of wandering around in the rain in the freezing cold wasn't particularly appealing. "Okay," she conceded with a nod, acknowledging her situation. "I parked quite far."

"No problem. My truck's close. We can wait out the rain there."

75

With nothing more than a plastic bag of sparse belongings, Johan stepped out of the police station and into uncertainty.

A sudden realization of his dire situation halted him mid-step in the parking lot. What in the world was his dad thinking? Why did he have to head back home instead of waiting for him right here? And how on earth was he supposed to find Zoe in the vast expanse of the forest, armed with nothing, alone, penniless, and without a car? To make matters worse, he didn't even have a cell phone to call his father back. *Damn it!*

Just as he was about to turn back, Anthony Lavera stepped in front of him, blocking his path.

"What did he tell you?" Zoe's brother-in-law demanded, his voice sharp.

"Excuse me?"

"Your father! You talked to him on the phone. What did he say? And don't feed me some line about Zoe skipping town to avoid the press conference. I know she didn't go back to Paris. If you're hiding something, you'd better spill it. I've already lost my wife—I can't lose her too. Understand?"

Johan sighed and met Anthony's intense gaze. "You're right," he conceded. "She didn't go back."

A flicker of relief softened Anthony's expression, but it was fleeting; his jaw soon set in determination once more. "So, you're meeting up with her, aren't you?" he asked, his voice tinged with a possessive edge.

The clock was ticking, its relentless beat echoing in Johan's mind, urging him to act. He realized he couldn't shake Anthony Lavera; perhaps this encounter was meant to be, their paths intertwined by fate or by his father's mysterious plans. Either way, Zoe's brother-in-law was now caught in the same web.

Anthony nodded toward a car parked at the far end of the lot, motioning for Johan to follow. "So, where to?" he asked as he slid into the driver's seat, his gaze flicking toward Johan.

Securing his seatbelt, Johan responded, "Just hit the road. I'll explain on the way."

76

––––––––––

They had been driving for about half an hour, but to Johan, it felt much longer. As soon as Anthony found out what Johan and his dad had talked about, his frustration soared.

"I knew it! He's been feeding her that 'vision' nonsense!" Lavera burst out, fuming over the outlandish stories the psychic had told Zoe. Each declaration was punctuated with a violent slap against the steering wheel, as though it were an improvised punching bag. "If anything happens to Zoe, I swear..."

Johan cut him off, gesturing out the window. "Look! There's a car over there."

Anthony pulled over, and they got out. The forest loomed before them, the trail to the burial site starting just a few yards away. As they walked, the dense canopy overhead seemed to swallow the sound of their footsteps. The forest had changed since Johan's last visit; what had once been a wild thicket was now a beaten path, the aftermath of the search for the remains of Leanne Jalmet and her friend.

An icy wind swept through, rattling the remaining dead leaves on the branches. Just a few yards away, a fluorescent tape snaked between the tree trunks, encircling the area where two shallow graves lay. Yellow flags, dancing in the wind, marked the spots where potential clues had already been collected by the crime scene technicians.

"Zoeee!" Lavera's voice echoed through the forest as he shouted her name, using his hands to magnify the sound.

A flock of startled birds burst into flight, their wings slicing through the still air. Johan and Lavera listened. Beyond the subtle symphony of rustling leaves, the forest remained silent, devoid of any human response.

"You sure she was supposed to meet you here?" Lavera asked, his eyes scanning their surroundings with a hint of suspicion.

Johan, shivering, realized it was not only the chill in the air that unsettled him. Were he supposed to meet Zoe here? His father's instructions had been vague. "We need to wait."

"I don't get it. She's had a two-hour head start," Lavera pressed, his worry apparent.

Johan felt a seed of anxiety take root in his mind. *"You'll know what to do once you get there,"* his father had said. Trying to shake off Lavera's trepidation, Johan turned his attention back to the forest. That's when he saw her—a silhouette of a woman just a few yards away.

"Zoe?" he whispered.

"Where?" Lavera swung around, searching.

"There!" Johan pointed.

"I can't see a thing. Are you sure it wasn't just an animal or something?"

Johan sighed, his patience wearing thin due to Anthony's negativity. "Stay here if you want," he snapped. Without waiting for a response, he ducked under the fluorescent tape and started moving toward the shadowy figure.

As he neared, the silhouette sharpened. It was her,

unmistakably so; Johan didn't harbor a single doubt. Yet, why wasn't she stopping? Perhaps she hadn't seen him in the distance?

"Zoe!" Johan's voice broke through the silence, urgent, desperate. She glanced back—a fleeting look of recognition. He narrowed the distance between them rapidly, his breaths coming in short, sharp gasps. There she was, suspended in a moment of time, framed by the trees on either side.

"I've been looking for you everywhere," she whispered.

Johan moved closer.

"I'm sorry. My dad was meant to call me earlier. It makes no sense for him to send us both out here."

A sigh escaped Zoe's lips, laden with exhaustion.

"I'm just so tired," she confessed.

"Let's head back," he suggested gently.

But something was off. With each step Johan took forward, the space between them remained unchanged. It was as though Zoe was backing away at the same pace as his advance, except she was completely still—not a step taken. Yet, she was utterly still, not a single step taken. That's when realization dawned on Johan.

"Tell me where you are," he urged, fear tightening his voice.

"It's so dark here," she sighed, her words almost swallowed by the murmurs of the forest.

"I'll find you, Zoe. Don't worry."

"He found me too," she murmured.

"Who?"

"The Reaper."

A chill crept down his spine. "Where is he?"

"Here. With me."

Johan took a step forward, reaching out, but she remained just beyond his touch. "Can you lead me to you?"

Before she could respond, a harsh voice rang out.

"Hey, asshole!"

Johan spun around to see Lavera charging toward him. Too late, he was knocked to the ground. Lavera hovered over him, pinning him down with one hand while his face remained close, filled with accusation.

"Let go!" Johan shouted, trying to push him off.

"What was the plan, huh? Did your father send you here to get rid of me?"

Johan hadn't realized Lavera had followed him. Lost in his urgency to reach Zoe, he had lost track of him. "You don't understand..."

A punch cut him off, the taste of blood filling his mouth. He spat, glaring up at Lavera. "I saw Zoe," he muttered, just as another fist was poised to strike.

Lavera froze. "When?"

"Just now."

His grip loosened, his eyes scanning the surroundings. "I don't see her," Lavera's voice was laced with frustration.

At a loss for words, Johan decided to offer the truth. "I see her but... I don't know where she is."

"You just said..."

Realization hit Lavera. "You had a vision, like your father... So, does that mean she's... dead?"

Johan shivered. "No. But she's hurt. We need to find her, and fast."

"Do you just said you didn't know where she is?"

Johan looked again at where Zoe stood. She gave a faint nod—a silent beckon—and then turned, drifting among the trees like a wisp of mist. He fixed his eyes on her retreating figure, a signal for them to follow.

"She's showing us the way."

77

Zoe vanished. Moments later, she reappeared between two trees, then disappeared once again. Johan had to quicken his pace to keep up. He focused on her elusive form, which seemed to play a whimsical game of hide-and-seek. She was like a sylph, a fairy, or perhaps even an elf.

The men surged forward, weaving through the tree trunks, some of which were as slender as the bars of a prison cell. The ground was covered in leaves, creating a slippery surface. More than once, they nearly lost their balance.

All at once, a haunting sound reverberated throughout the forest. It was reminiscent of a stag's bellow or a distant foghorn.

Anthony had heard it too. He stopped walking almost at the same moment, straining his ears to listen. The noise resonated once again, filling the forest with its ominous tone. "What was that?!" he exclaimed, his hand darting to his right hip before his face darkened with realization. "My gun..."

The haunting sound, like the agonized groan of a

wounded creature, lingered in the air. Johan shot a questioning look at Zoe. She pointed downward. About thirty feet away, a man was dragging himself toward them. Gasping for air, his voice strained with desperation, he croaked, "Help...me."

Dressed in camouflage and face hidden by a hood, the man blended with the forest. But the Sig Sauer clenched in the stranger's hand was unmistakable—it was Anthony's service pistol, the one he had given to Zoe. Eyes flaring with rage, he yanked the man up by the collar, voice seething, "Where is she? Speak!"

Ripping off the man's hood and shaking him, Anthony's patience snapped. The man moaned, blood bubbling from his mouth. His grip slackened, and the pistol dropped onto the damp, leafy ground.

Zoe's voice trembled, but her eyes remained fierce. "I shot him," she gestured to the fallen weapon, "But... he just kept coming."

Johan looked at the young woman, who seemed to be pulled back by an unseen force. Then he saw her—Zoe, very much alive, but bleeding.

78

She leaned against a tree, naked. Her stomach, smeared with blood, bore the marks of desperate fingers that had tried to stem the flow.

Johan rushed toward her, nearly twisting his ankle as he stumbled over a thick root snaking across the damp ground. He wished for Zoe to flinch or show any sign of life as he approached, but she remained motionless. She lay there, eyes open, her back pressed to the trunk, arms and legs stretched out. Neatly folded clothes sat beside her, atop her perfectly arranged shoes—like a well-behaved schoolgirl or someone compelled to bathe in the moonlight on a chilly November night. A shovel was half-buried in the soft soil nearby, its wooden handle marked with bloody fingerprints. Moans pierced the forest's silence, coming from the man who had started to dig Zoe's grave but collapsed from a wound in his abdomen.

Kneeling beside the young woman, Johan felt disoriented, his years of training seemingly forgotten. He extended a trembling hand, hesitating as their skins met. Hers was cold, and he feared his warmth might dissolve her.

His eyes then settled on her stomach, where she'd been stabbed twice. The wounds were nearly obscured beneath the dried blood. Zoe was no longer bleeding.

"Am I dead?"

Johan jerked, startled by the voice behind him. It was her—Zoe's spectral form—standing at a distance, as if hesitant to approach her own motionless body.

Gently, he lifted her arm, resting it on his knee, his fingers quivering as they sought a pulse. "No," he answered with a steady voice, feeling a faint beat against his fingers. "No, you're not dead. I won't let you die. I promise."

Tenderly brushing the hair from her eyes, what he saw next filled him with dread. He realized he might have made a promise he couldn't keep.

"Shit, shit, shit!" Anthony Lavera exclaimed behind him. Over and over, he repeated the words, his voice laced with panic.

The bullet had left a tiny, bloody mark, mere inches above her right eyebrow.

"Damn it!" Anthony yelled again, his voice louder, more frantic. "Shot right in the head! I just can't believe it!"

He couldn't remain still. Johan tried to fight off the panic, but having Lavera there only made it harder. "I need you to call for help," Johan finally managed, his voice steady despite the chaos.

But Anthony stood frozen, as if rooted to the spot, his determination to stay by her side evident. "I don't want to leave her."

"Just do it," Johan ordered, his tone authoritative. "You're no use to us here."

Dazed, Anthony nodded, finally moving away to search for a cell signal with an outstretched arm.

Alone now, Johan focused on the situation at hand. He

supported the young woman with one arm, cautiously tilting her forward. "No visible brain matter," he muttered, speaking aloud without realizing.

The back of her skull remained intact; the bullet was lodged inside her head—a cold comfort. He tried to reassure himself, knowing only a brain scan could reveal the full extent of her injuries. For now, all he could do was wait.

"They're sending a helicopter!" Anthony's voice cut through his thoughts.

"How long?" Johan asked, urgency in his voice.

"Fifteen minutes, maybe less. I gave them our location. They told me to stay on the line for geolocation."

Johan nodded, taking the young woman's hand in his own. "You'll be alright." She looked so delicate, as fragile as a porcelain doll, ready to shatter with the slightest misstep.

"We should get her clothes back on," Anthony suddenly said, his eyes awkwardly averted, as if he had just realized his sister-in-law's state of undress.

"Absolutely not."

"The rescue team will be here any minute, and I won't have strangers seeing her like this!" Anthony's voice rose, anger evident.

"You don't understand. By stripping her, the murderer made a mistake. He let her body succumb to hypothermia."

"But she's freezing! We need to warm her up!"

"Warming her now could be dangerous. The cold's preventing her from bleeding out. Her blood vessels are constricting, narrowing to prevent further heat loss. The same is happening in her brain. It's the body's natural defense mechanism, and it might just save her life. We wait for help without changing a thing."

. . .

Thirteen minutes later, they watched as the helicopter disappeared behind the treetops, touching down.

"I'm going to meet them!" Lavera shouted, gesturing emphatically to ensure his message got across amidst the roaring noise of the rotor.

He sprinted toward the aircraft. Soon after, he came back with two men. Their uniforms with glowing stripes shone in the dark forest.

"I'm a doctor," Johan introduced himself, quickly briefing them on the situation.

The paramedics laid out a stretcher and set down their bags. One began to check Zoe, using a stethoscope on her still chest.

"How long has she been in cardiac arrest?" he asked, completely focused on her while his colleague unpacked resuscitation equipment.

Johan stiffened. "In arrest? No, you're mistaken. She had a pulse when I..." His voice faltered as he came to a terrible realization: the Zoe he' been speaking with, her spirit, had been silent for too long.

"She had a pulse when you found her?" the rescuer prompted gently.

"Yes, yes. And she was breathing. It was weak, but she was breathing. You have to believe me!"

"I believe you. Now, just try to calm down."

But Johan couldn't. He realized he should have noticed sooner. He could have started CPR and—

"Here," said the rescuer, handing him a plastic pouch.

"What's this?"

"A survival blanket."

"What?"

"You're hypothermic, Doc," the second rescuer said. "You need to get warm."

"If you don't, you're going to pass out on us," the first rescuer added more gently. "We've got her covered."

As Johan wrapped himself in the material, which resembled a large sheet of aluminum foil more than a blanket, he felt warmth slowly return to his numb limbs. His mind, however, took longer to catch up. "Wait! You can't lay her down."

The paramedics paused.

"I know it sounds strange," he said, his teeth chattering, "but she needs to stay in this position."

The paramedics looked at each other, confused. They probably thought he was out of it from the cold. Zoe's position looked weird and scary. But for brain doctors, this was normal. A lot of brain operations need the patient to sit up straight. There's a good reason for that.

"Her torso and head have to stay upright," Johan insisted, his voice firming. "It's the only way to prevent cerebral edema. If that happens, it's game over. She'll die."

The paramedics looked at each other again, but Johan couldn't bring himself to consider what their glances might mean. "She's in severe hypothermia," he continued. "Her metabolism has slowed, so she needs less oxygen, protecting her heart and brain. If we move now, we can save her in the ER. But we have to go now!"

Without waiting for a response, Johan began adjusting the stretcher, preparing to transfer Zoe's frozen body onto it.

"Help me lift her!"

One of the rescuers stepped forward, placing a hand on his shoulder. "We've got this, okay?"

A knot formed in Johan's stomach. He recognized that tone—it was compassion, the kind you offer to a family member of the deceased. His fears seemed confirmed when he saw the other rescuer start to pack up the gear, moving deliberately, as if the urgency had dissipated.

"What are you doing?" Johan demanded, his voice shaky.

"What's happening?" Anthony Lavera, who had stepped back to give them space, chimed in.

A groan—or more accurately, a gritty, deep moan—spun them around.

"What was that?" one rescuer asked.

"Probably an animal," Anthony Lavera replied, his gaze locked on Johan, ready for any contradiction.

Another moan sounded, almost pleading to be heard. Leanne Jalmet's killer wasn't going to be ignored. "Help..."

With his torch in hand, one paramedic dashed toward the voice, with Anthony right on his heels.

"Hey, another injured person here!" he shouted, voice tinged with shock and frustration. "An animal, you said? Why was this kept quiet?"

Anthony just shrugged. "So? What's the problem?"

"The problem is, we have to choose. We can't save them both!"

Lavera edged closer, prodding the man with his foot who moaned in response.

"Hey!" the paramedic snapped.

"Let him bleed out!" Anthony shot back. "He's looking at a life sentence anyway. Might as well save the taxpayers some money."

The young paramedic met his gaze with a look of pure disdain. "I'm not here to judge him. And neither are you."

Anthony clenched his fists, unable to watch the man trying to save the one who'd harmed Zoe. He turned away, heading back to where she lay.

Zoe looked almost ethereal, her skin pale, motionless.

No rise and fall of her chest to indicate she was breathing. Still, Johan refused to accept it.

"We can't pronounce her dead in this cold," he argued with vehemence.

The other paramedic seemed to have given up, as if there was nothing more to be done. "She has no pulse, she's not breathing, and—"

"I know all that!" Johan cut in, his face flushed with anger. "For God's sake, haven't you been listening? We're wasting precious time!"

The paramedic's attention had shifted to his partner, who was tending to the injured man.

It became crystal clear to Anthony whom they'd chosen. A resolution formed in his mind. He wouldn't let these naive responders let Zoe die to save a murderer. Checking his gun and ensuring it was loaded, he made the final call.

A gunshot pierced the quiet of the forest, settling the matter once and for all.

79

The helicopter sliced through the air, rising at a steady pace. Anthony Lavera shielded his eyes with a hand, tilting his head back to track the aircraft as it vanished into the cloudy sky. The police would be on his tail soon, eager to nab him for murder. The young medic's promise to testify was clear in his mind.

Venturing a few steps into the woods, Anthony paused, then doubled back to the body that was still radiating warmth. He stripped it of its anorak and put it on. Rummaging through the pockets, he discovered the man's wallet: Raphael Ritter, born in Paris, 1983. A pack of cigarettes was also inside. Without a lighter, he simply tucked one between his lips. Zipping up the anorak, he started making his way toward the distant, flickering lights.

80

The helicopter climbed straight up, making a gentle rotation as it went higher. Johan adjusted his helmet, which was equipped with a microphone, making sure he could communicate with the crew over the steady beat of the blades.

"The University Hospital, they've got a neurosurgery wing," piped up one paramedic.

It was a good sixty miles away.

"Time?" Johan asked.

"About half an hour," responded the pilot.

Johan shook his head, frustration in his voice. "Too long."

"The nearest rural hospital is about twenty miles from here," the other paramedic noted.

A thumbs up from the pilot. "Under ten minutes."

"Their tech isn't top-tier, though," the paramedic interjected.

Johan's gaze shifted from one to another, finally resting on Zoe. Time was of the essence. "Do they have a surgical department?"

"Yeah. They can manage the abdominal wound, but the head injury... Who's going to do it?"

A weighted silence filled the helicopter. Johan took a moment, closing his eyes for a moment. When he spoke, his voice was steady but lacked the confidence he wished to convey. "I am."

81

Ninety percent of people shot in the head didn't make it to the hospital alive. Of those who did, half didn't survive past the emergency room. The odds haunted Johan. He shuddered, pulling himself from his dark thoughts when the pilot's announcement about landing came through his headset. He reached for Zoe's hand, giving it a gentle squeeze as the aircraft started its smooth descent. "Hold on, Zoe," he murmured. "Stay with me."

From the window, he glimpsed the hospital's helipad—a concrete slab that, from this height, looked no larger than a postage stamp. The chopper touched down with a soft thud. Though the rotors still churned the cold air, figures in white coats—hair and fabric whipped by the gusts—rushed toward them.

Standing at a respectful distance, Johan watched the resuscitation team work without wanting to get in their way. The grim statistics he was trying to forget kept creeping back into his mind. Doctors and nurses surrounded the lifeless body, fighting to restart Zoe's heart. They had been at it for half an hour. But it was too soon to give up.

Somewhere, he recalled a record—a team in Pennsylvania who had brought someone back after two harrowing hours.

Johan felt a tightness in his chest, his hands clenched into fists, the skin stretched thin over his knuckles. He sought any sign of defeat or hopelessness in the expressions of the medical team. But there were none. At the thirty-four-minute mark, the room's ECG monitor stirred. Eyes were drawn to the graph as it spiked: once, twice, thrice...

"We have a sinus rhythm," a nurse declared, exhaustion clear on her sweat-streaked face.

No celebratory outbursts followed—just a collective, silent sigh of relief.

But this was only the first of many challenges. Zoe was quickly whisked away to radiology. The resulting images were swift and chilling: the bullet had penetrated only a few inches into her right frontal lobe, halted by the brain tissue. But a wound in her abdomen caused a more immediate alarm. She needed surgery—now.

"Wait," Johan interjected, stepping closer to the radiographic image displayed on the light box.

"We don't have time for this," a surgeon retorted, his voice edged with impatience.

Johan's finger outlined a shadow on the image—a two-inch-wide anomaly.

"It's a tumor," he murmured, voice breaking.

The bullet was lodged within it.

82

———

In the operating room, Zoe lay with a raised belly, similar to an early pregnant woman. This was because of carbon dioxide used for the surgery. Three slight cuts were where they put the surgical tools. A screen showed the inside of her belly, lit up by the surgical camera.

Johan found the images unsettling. Despite wanting to be present for Zoe, seeing her so vulnerable, exposed in this way, made him uneasy. He found himself looking away from the screen, as if there was something indecent about the sight of this bloody flesh.

Stepping away from the surgeons, Johan moved toward the anesthetist. She was a middle-aged woman with crow's feet around her eyes. Even with a mask on, her gaze radiated warmth and assurance. She kept a close attention on Zoe's vitals, jotting notes on a tablet. When she noticed Johan, she gave a comforting nod, letting him know things were on track.

Johan's eyes darted to the monitor. Taking into account Zoe's hypothermia, the doctors found her vitals to be stable. He shifted his gaze from the numbers and graphs to look at her. With eyes closed and a tube protruding from her open mouth, she appeared vulnerable. He longed to reach out, to slide his hand beneath the sterile covering and grasp hers. *Damn!* They were in a predicament. He pondered how he'd muster the courage to operate on her.

The mood in the room shifted when the lead surgeon announced that the bleeding was under control. The tension that had been pervading the space lifted, replaced by a light-hearted comment that drew laughter from everyone in the room—everyone, that is, except Johan. As the surgery neared its end, his internal turmoil heightened. For the first time, he wished to be anywhere else.

"I'll be back," he said, his voice low.

"How long?" the anesthesiologist inquired, understanding the implications for the procedure ahead.

"I don't know."

Everyone in the room shared a puzzled glance, but Johan was already gone, slipping through the swing doors before anyone could question him further. Just as in the hospital in Nice, he navigated the empty corridors, seeking an exit. He was desperate for fresh air.

A nurse directed him to the nearest exit that led to the emergency department on the first floor. As he entered the waiting room, an elderly woman and a man in his thirties stood up, eyeing him. But he moved past, eager for the fresh air beyond the glass doors.

The sharp wind hit him like a slap in the face, halting his frantic exit. Dazed, he stopped in his tracks. To his left, sheltered under an awning, two EMTs stood smoking, their eyes fixed on him. He walked over.

"Can I..."

One man, misinterpreting his request, extended his pack of cigarettes.

"Uh, no thanks. A cell phone. I need to make a private call..."

The man stuffed his pack back into his pocket, while his partner, a cigarette dangling from his lips, unzipped his reflective-striped jacket to retrieve a phone from an inner pocket.

"Thanks," Johan mumbled, accepting the device. "I'll be quick."

He stepped back to ensure privacy for his conversation and dialed the head of neurosurgery at Salpêtrière Hospital.

"Johan here," he announced, a hint of urgency in his voice.

A pause, then, "Professor Zajac isn't here. Who's asking?"

Johan's grip tightened on the phone.

"Valmeur? Is that you?"

Only one person twisted his name with such disdain. Professor Derosier. Johan's pulse quickened. He was seconds away from ending the call when Derosier added, "Where are you? Everyone's been looking for you!"

"At Argentan Hospital in Normandy."

There was a pause. "And why, pray tell?"

Johan sighed. "It's a long story."

"I'm listening."

"I don't know what to do," Johan admitted, his voice tinged with desperation. "There's a woman—a patient. I'm not sure if I should operate."

A pause.

"Are you messing with me? Because if you are, I—"

"No! I wish I was. Look, you accused me of being a rogue, right? I just... Forget it!"

"Wait, you're asking for my advice?"

Johan took a deep breath, his eyes closed. "I need help."

"Go on, then."

Johan continued, laying out the situation as he would to a neurosurgery team.

"I see," Derosier said.

Johan, frustration mounting, pressed on. "So?"

"So, what?"

"What would you do?"

"I'd send her to the university hospital ASAP. They have a top-notch trauma center."

"So, you're saying I shouldn't operate?"

"No, I'm saying I wouldn't. But then again, I'm not you, am I?"

Johan was left pondering the implications of those words.

"Valmeur, you there?"

"Yeah."

"Listen carefully, because I'm only going to say this once, and if you ever repeat it, I'll deny it all. You might be the most reckless surgeon I've ever met, but you're also the sharpest. Honestly, if that were my daughter on the table, I'd beg you to operate. If you can't save her tonight, I doubt anyone can. Got it?"

"Yeah."

"Goodnight, then."

Johan stood there, phone still pressed to his ear, lost in the silence that followed, accompanied only by the dial tone. Was he imagining things, or had Derosier just—

"Doctor!" The voice of one of the OR nurses snapped him back to reality. "They need you in the OR."

Johan's heart raced as alarm bells rang in his mind. "Is something wrong?"

"You need to see for yourself."

83

Zoe lay before him, semi-reclined, her head stabilized by a makeshift metal frame crafted from available orthopedic surgery equipment. A sterile sheet nearly fully obscured her face, and that was for the best. Seeing her now would've stopped him cold.

Wrapped in his sterile surgical gown, tied at the side like a Roman general's toga, Johan examined the damage through the opening in her skull. Zoe's brain, drowning in blood, was beginning to swell. If only the skull were made of something elastic instead of hard, unyielding bone. Time was running out. Soon, Zoe would stop breathing, her heart would stop beating. Johan, vision blurring, stepped back from the operating table. How could he have thought he could save her? He took another step back when he felt an unexpected chill wrap around him—a comforting, familiar presence amidst the cold. He didn't need visual confirmation; he knew her touch, her embrace. It was Zoe, or at least a piece of her essence, bridging the gap between them. She held him tight, and he shivered, feeling her icy breath on his neck. Johan closed his eyes for a moment, succumbing to this final embrace. He tried to hold her in return, but his gloved hands merely brushed the folds of the blood-soaked gown.

"Goodbye."

Zoe's voice exploded in his head, obliterating doubts, banishing them with the might of a gust sweeping dark clouds to reveal a clear sky. He knew what to do. He'd always known.

"Let's dehydrate her brain," he said, not hesitating. He turned to the anesthesiologist, then glanced at the surgical nurse. "I'll need a suction cannula. I'm going to aspirate the cerebrospinal fluid from the ventricles. It'll give the brain more room."

Johan had a backup plan or two, but luckily, he didn't need them. The brain began pulling back into the skull, buying him some precious time. Without missing a beat, he grabbed the scalpel and the forceps. Zoe's tight hold seemed to inject him with a burst of needed courage. The tumor was right there, just a few inches beneath the skull surface. It might as well have been a distant star. Those inches felt so unreachable. He clenched the tools tighter, burrowing into the nervous tissue, shifting and parting until a mass—kind of like a cross between clotted egg white and a marshmallow —showed itself. Johan took a steady breath, guiding the instruments to excise as much tumor as he could.

The first piece came free. The cannula's suction eased, and the nurse's silhouette at his side began to fade. The operating room, with all its occupants, himself included, seemed to fade away...

. . .

Zoe opens her eyes, blinking away the beam of light as an ICU nurse shone it into her pupils.

"Everything's okay. You're in the hospital," the nurse said. *"Squeeze my hand."*

As Johan removed another piece, his mind flickered to visions of a tentative future.

There she is—Zoe, taking those first fragile steps after the surgery. Her movements are careful, shaky. It's like watching a kid trying to walk for the first time. He can almost hear the encouraging whispers of the physical therapist at her side.

Despite the emotional imagery in his head, Johan stayed centered, making sure the bleeding was under control.

Zoe's leaving the hospital, camera flashes sparking around her as she weaves through a sea of journalists, their questions hurling toward her like gunfire. *"How do you feel?" "What was it like, facing a serial killer?" "Are you going to write a book?"*

Now, she's casual in jeans, a silk blouse, and a navy blazer. The man ahead of her is also in navy, but with "Penitentiary Administration" glaring in reflective letters on his back, visible even from a distance. They halt before a door leading into the visitor's room. Anthony Lavera sits there, handcuffs binding his wrists. He raises his head, peers at her, and lets a smile creep across his face. "I'm glad to see you," he says.

Zoe places the cane that aids her walking against the table. She, too, sits. Anthony is imprisoned, awaiting his trial for the murder of Raphael Ritter, the man suspected of kidnapping and murdering eight women, the man who tried to kill her... The Reaper.

Anthony's cheeks are hollow, his eyes rimmed with dark circles. He looks like he's taken a blow, but Zoe won't let herself be moved.

"You know why I'm here," she says.

Anthony's eyes slide shut. When he opens them again, Zoe is met with an expression she hadn't expected. She thinks, maybe it's relief she sees there.

"Ask," he murmurs.

She glances at her cane, extending her hand to feel the handle beneath her palm, to brace herself, to avoid collapsing, for she already knows what he's going to tell her. It was in the letter that Johan had left for her at the rural hospital before she was transferred to Paris.

"What I want to know, Anthony, is why. Why did you kill Gabriela? Was she cheating? Were you jealous?"

Anthony rubs his temple. "It's not what you think. I loved her."

Zoe's gaze sharpens, her fingers clenching the cane. "Then tell me. Why?"

"I just told you. I did it out of love, okay?"

"You killed her, you bastard! How dare you talk of love!"

"Because..." he hesitates, "I didn't want someone else to do it. If it was me, she wouldn't suffer. She was going to expose a dangerous secret."

Zoe leans forward, her eyes searching his. "What secret?"

Anthony swallows hard. "She found about the other cops. The web of corruption. The higher-ups, some of the most respected officers, they had a system."

"What are you talking about? "

"What do you think? Drugs, of course. Or rather, the

money. Lots of money..." He sighs. "Gabriela started suspecting something," Anthony admits, his voice shaky. "She cornered me."

Zoe's eyes widen, disbelief and anger fighting for dominance on her face. "You? She found out you were involved in this mess?"

He nods, his voice steadier now, as if each word is a step toward unburdening himself. "Yes. I was in the thick of it, Zoe. I thought... I thought it would be a one-time thing, a way to give her a better life. But it spiraled. I was trapped in a network of deceit, and when Gabriela uncovered it, she... She wanted me to come clean, to expose the rot. But I... I couldn't. I was in too deep."

Tears prick Zoe's eyes, her voice rising with emotion. "And instead of standing by her, you betrayed her! My sister trusted you, Anthony!"

He meets her gaze, his own eyes brimming with tears. "You don't understand. They would've made her suffer. I couldn't let that happen."

"You're saying you... you protected her?" Zoe chokes out, her eyes moistening.

"She didn't suffer," he concludes. "That's all you need to know."

"You made me believe she was the victim of a serial killer. My God, Anthony! You even sent the ring to yourself!"

Anthony stretches his handcuffed hands toward her. "You needed explanations, reasons. I knew you'd move heaven and earth to find her. I wouldn't have been surprised if you'd uncovered the truth. I couldn't allow that. Do you understand? You were also putting yourself in danger. So, I thought the best way to protect you was to have you chase a decoy."

"You disgust me!" Zoe spat. "Do you really think I'm

going to believe that everything you did was for the good of Gabriela and me?"

"That's the truth."

"Prove it, then."

Anthony nods. "All right. Ask me anything, and I'll do it."

Zoe takes a deliberate breath. "I want you to confess to killing my sister," she declares.

"Okay."

"And rat out the bastards you've been covering for."

Anthony's face drains of color. "They'll kill me before I have the chance to testify against them. But I guess that doesn't matter to you, does it?" he adds, his voice bitter as a sarcastic smile dances on his lips. "If I do it, will you forgive me?"

Zoe had promised herself she wouldn't cry, but the tears flow, regardless. "Nothing you do can ever make up for what you've done. I will never forgive you. Now, tell me where she is."

With a hand trembling with emotion, Zoe writes the address of a storage unit and the identifier of the locker Anthony had rented under a pseudonym. Then she lets her cane clatter to the floor as she stands. Zoe...

Past and future blurred together. The metallic sheen of the bullet materialized. Johan sucked away the pooling blood. It was the bullet, no mistake. He clenched it with his forceps. Metal scraped against metal. He gently eased the tool backward, maintaining a steady pressure around the projectile. He was so close, but the sight of the burgeoning blood made Johan's head spin. His vision fuzzes. He's going to lose Zoe, too. Just like he lost Camille. Zoe was going to die. Zoe...

. . .

Flashes of a possible future flicker before him. Zoe is in a hospital bed. She turns her head, eyes meeting a screen... And she smiles.

Johan, like a captain steadfast at his sinking ship's helm, was the last to exit the operating room. But this time, there was no wreck. Zoe had been moved to intensive care. When she would awaken, he wouldn't be there. Another patient needed him. He opted to call Tom Boylan back, letting him know he wouldn't pursue charges for the hotel incident, and that he would attempt the surgery if his son gave him another shot.

As he walked past, his colleagues looked on. He could sense their tension; there were still so many things that could go wrong. Brain abscess, meningeal hemorrhage, intracranial hypertension—those were just the most lethal possibilities. Yet, for the first time since Camille's death, he felt a sense of serenity. He was certain the operation had been successful. Seeking solitude, he retired to a quiet space, his mind replaying the vivid visions he experienced during the final moments of the surgery—the removal of the projectile. There, away from prying eyes, he borrowed some prescription paper and a pen.

Alone, seated on the staircase, he began to write.

84

Hi Zoe,

I'm writing to you now while you're in the ICU. Once your condition gets more stable, you'll be moved to Salpêtrière in Paris—that's one of the top hospitals in the city, and it's also where I work.

Our paths will cross there, but I won't come to visit you in your room. We won't talk, and I won't be asking how you're holding up. Not just yet, anyway. Because by the time you read this, you'll remember me as the person you can't stand the most in the world. The man who threw your career off its tracks.

I know that when you read this, you'll be back on your feet and making your way in the world on your own. Progress will be made, but deep down, you already know: you'll never dance on the Opera stage again.

I won't say I'm sorry, because I'm not. What matters to me is that you're still alive.

By the time you get to this part of the letter, you'll be thinking of my father and his words. He promised you answers if you went back into the forest. Now, I get what he meant. The answers you're looking for are in Marseille. Your brother-in-law is in jail there, accused of murdering the man you thought was responsible for your sister going missing. I can almost hear your heart racing as you read this. To really understand everything, you're going to need to face him. But I have a feeling you've already figured out the truth. You sensed it when you were in the forest.

When you get to this point, you'll never want to see me again. You might even try to put all of this behind you and start picking up the pieces of your life. But if you ever change your mind, just know that I'll be here. Waiting.

I really hope you decide to come, because there's something else I need to tell you. Something I can't put into words on paper.

Johan

EPILOGUE

Paris, eighteen months later...

The wind was howling, tearing leaves from the trees and playfully tugging at the tourists strolling down the boulevards. It even caught the commuters off guard as they emerged from the metro, forcing them to brace themselves against the sudden chill. Johan was no exception; he tightened his coat around himself, preparing for the icy blast as the escalator carried him up to street level. Daylight was fading fast, and the streetlights were just starting to come alive, casting a warm glow on the city. People flowed in streams along the sidewalk, breaking off into smaller groups as they each headed to their own destinations. Before Johan knew it, he found himself alone, wandering toward the Seine. His phone vibrated in his pocket, probably a reminder from Cedric about the church visit planned for the next morning. He stopped for a moment to shoot back a quick text.

Tomorrow, he'd be cradling his goddaughter, guiding her down the aisle for her baptism.

A warm smile played on Johan's face as he slid his phone into his pocket. The wind gave him a firm push from behind, urging him forward. That's when he saw her. Her hair was longer, but there was no mistaking that it was Zoe. Leaning on a cane, she stood outside the apartment, seemingly waiting for someone. Waiting for him, maybe? Not wanting to call out, he took a few more steps before she turned around. Their eyes met, and he fought the urge to run over and wrap her in his arms. Maybe Zoe didn't feel the same way he did—feelings he'd brought back from the future to the present.

"Hey," she called out.

Johan was at a loss for words, his throat suddenly tight. Her voice was so achingly familiar, and it took him completely by surprise. He hadn't heard it in a whole year.

"Been waiting long?" he finally asked, managing to keep his voice casual, as if they'd seen each other just a few days ago.

She shook her head, a slight smile playing on her lips. "No, I just got here."

Johan noticed the letter—his letter—in her hand, gripped so tightly her knuckles had turned white. "Let's head up. It's freezing out here."

He led the way into the building's lobby, not waiting for her response.

The elevator ride to the top floor was filled with silence.

"Right here," he said, pointing to the single door on the

landing. His nerves got the best of him, making him fumble and drop his keys twice before finding the right one. "Please, come in."

Zoe made her way inside, slowly soaking in the expanse of the loft. The living room boasted grand windows that perfectly showcased the Seine and Bercy Park.

"How do you like it?" Johan called out from the open kitchen, the hum of the coffee machine starting in the background.

Casting a shy glance around, Zoe's eyes swept over the stark white walls, the empty shelves, and the bare concrete floor. "It's spacious. New place?"

Shaking his head, Johan responded, "Been here a year actually."

Zoe couldn't hide her surprise. "Like this the whole time?"

"*Like this?* Is that your nice way of saying it feels cold and uninviting?"

She looked away, a flash of embarrassment in her eyes. "No, it's not that..."

"I'm teasing," he assured her. "But I could use some ideas to warm up the place. What do you think?"

Taking another look around, Zoe suggested, "Maybe start with some rugs? And perhaps a few lamps and some plants?"

"I was thinking about adding some artwork too. What's your take on that?"

He gave her a sidelong glance, hoping she'd catch the hidden meaning. But it seemed to fly right over her head.

"Um... yeah, artwork could be nice."

"You see, I'm just not great with this décor stuff. I figured I'd leave that up to my wife."

Zoe's grip on her cane wavered. "You're married?"

"No, no. I bought this place with the future in mind, though. Spare bedrooms, an office and a gym, a master suite, and maybe a couple of kids' rooms someday."

Once again, he tried to gauge her reaction, but Zoe seemed unaware of his implications.

"You just need to find the wife to fit the picture," she commented, her gaze shifting away.

"I'm working on it," Johan replied, a hint of meaning in his voice.

Zoe's eyes dropped to the floor. "Oh, I see."

No, he thought, frustration bubbling up inside him. She clearly didn't 'see' anything at all.

"Take your coat off. Come on, I'll show you around," he encouraged.

"No, I'm good," she replied, her tone dismissive. "I didn't plan on staying long anyway."

Disappointment flickered across Johan's face. This reunion was turning out to be nothing like he had envisioned. He switched off the coffee machine, taking a few steps toward her. "At least take a seat," he insisted.

She cast a wary glance at the sofa but remained standing. "It's my leg," she explained, patting her thigh gently. "Standing helps with my balance practice."

An uneasy silence settled between them, its presence almost tangible.

"I heard you're working on a show at the Opera Bastille, as a choreographer," Johan ventured, attempting to break the tension.

She looked at him, a flash of surprise crossing her features. "Who told you?"

He slid his hands into his jeans pockets, trying to appear nonchalant. "Your therapist and I lunch sometimes."

"And *sometimes*, chat about me?"

"Sometimes..." he admitted, his voice trailing off.

She let out a sigh. "I see. Isn't that technically a breach of confidentiality?"

"Um... no, not exactly, since you're a patient of both of us. Plus, I was the one who operated on you," he explained, though he could hear the uncertainty in his own voice.

Johan wished he could take back his words as he saw her expression change.

"You could have come to me instead of talking to my physical therapist about me," she pointed out.

"I wasn't sure you'd want to see me," he admitted, his voice low.

"I know. That's what you wrote in your letter." Zoe's eyes flickered to the envelope she'd placed on the coffee table moments earlier. "I assume my PT told you about my sister, then," she said, her voice steady but her eyes revealing a world of pain.

Johan knew all about it; Zoe had buried her sister, Gabriela, months ago. Just like the vision he'd had in the operating room, Anthony had confessed to everything, including where he had hidden the body.

"I'm sorry," he said.

"Why? It's not your fault." She turned away, her eyes drawn to the Simone de Beauvoir footbridge that spanned the Seine. "I've also learned some things about you," she said, her voice low.

"Oh?" Johan was taken aback, not expecting the conversation to turn in this direction.

She nodded. "I heard about the young American you operated on."

"That's true. It was a week after you were transferred to Paris."

"Did you manage to change his future?" she asked, her voice filled with a curious intensity.

He smiled. Johan replayed the glimpses he'd seen of Lukas Boylan's life during the operation. The young man would shine in the professional league until a knee injury cut short his career. Yet, he'd find success off the pitch, becoming a respected college coach. He'd marry, then become a father, and after a divorce, he'd wed again—this time for keeps. The last vision that stayed with Johan was of Lukas Boylan, surrounded by his grandchildren. One grandchild, in particular, would realize the professional soccer dream that his grandfather had once held.

Zoe had edged closer, catching him off guard. He jolted slightly, realizing she was now right in front of him.

"In your letter, you mentioned there was something else you needed to tell me. Is it about my future too?"

"Um... Maybe..."

She gave him a playful nudge in the side before her expression turned serious once more. "Is it so bad that you couldn't put it in writing?"

"No, it's not that."

"So, are you going to tell me what's in store for me?"

Johan's mind flashed back to the last image that had seared itself into his memory. He saw himself once again steadying the claw of the forceps around the bullet, gently coaxing it out. The visions of the future that had flashed before his eyes in that moment had haunted him ever since. He had pushed those thoughts away, refusing to acknowledge them—until today, when he caught sight of her at the foot of his apartment complex.

"Do you like Asian food?"

Zoe looked puzzled, thrown off by the abrupt change of topic.

"Yes, but—"

"Great! My treat. I know an amazing place."

"And will you finally tell me what you saw about my future?"

He rolled his eyes.

"Um... Maybe..."

She nudged him in the ribs again, this time with more insistence.

Zoe, reclined in a hospital bed, turns her head to gaze at the screen while a woman in a white coat maneuvers an ultrasound wand over her swollen belly. She's watching the baby growing inside her—a little girl. Clara. She's five years old now, with brown hair like her mother's, the same profile, and that infectious smile. Zoe wraps her in a tight embrace, kissing her chubby cheek. The scent is unmistakable, and utterly sweet.

"Run to daddy!" she opens her arms wide.

Clara takes off, moving with the effortless grace of a butterfly just discovering its wings. She runs with her hair flowing behind her, laughing, her tutu fluttering around her. A few yards away, Johan crouches, arms outstretched, his eyes full of anticipation, yearning for the moment he can wrap his daughter in his protective embrace. And in his daughter's eyes, he sees it—that peculiar gleam. The one the Valmeurs have passed down through generations.

ALTERNATE ENDING

CLICK OR TAP THE PICTURE BELOW

Looking for a shocking spin?
Dive into the alternate ending!
Click the link, punch it into your browser, or give the QR
code a quick scan.
Discover a new way the story
might have played out!
www.julia-salvador.fr/find-you-alternative-ending

Scan me

NOTES

A QUICK WORD FROM THE AUTHOR

Dear Reader,

Thank you for diving into the twists and turns of this novel. I hope it has been an exciting and entertaining escape for you.

Sharing your thoughts and opinions would be a wonderful way to support the story that has hopefully captivated you. If you enjoyed the journey, please consider leaving a review on the book's page. Your insights not only guide other readers but also greatly enrich the community's experience.

Should you wish to discuss your experience further, offer suggestions, or provide feedback, I would be delighted to hear from you at julia@julia-salvador.fr

Here's to many more adventures in reading, and I look forward to possibly hearing from you soon.

Warm regards,

Julia Salvador

FROM THE SAME AUTHOR

- I Will Watch You
- I Will Save You

coming soon...